I0666458

Book 3

O'Connor Girls

RHONDA BREWER

Dedication

To my husband, Danny.

I might now always say it but it's because of you that I had the courage to finally follow my dreams. I love you with all my heart and no matter what we face, I know we can do it together. You are my support, my rock and my biggest cheerleader

Thank you for always being there.

Acknowledgments

With so many people in my life to thank for making publishing this book possible, I could almost write another book on that alone. However, a simple thank you never seems like enough to convey my gratitude, but I will try to do that the best I can with this acknowledgment.

First, thank you belongs to the many authors who have become both friends and mentors to me. Then there are the amazing ladies who help with editing and errors. A special thank you goes to Michelle Eriksen, Abbie Zanders, and Amabel Daniels for their constant support and keen eye. To my dedicated betas and dear friends, Jackie Dawe Ford, Nancy Arnold-Holloway, and Karie Deegan thank you so much for the support and constant encouragement. To my readers, you are the reason that I can continue to do this.

To my two children Laura and Colin, both of you show me every day how proud you are and how much you love me. To my beautiful granddaughter, Emma. You may not be old enough to read yet, but your smile gives me the inspiration to keep going. I love all of you.

Chapter 1

Cooking oil covered the floor of the kitchen and Isabelle O'Connor wanted to scream. She still had a restaurant full of patrons who needed to be fed, but one side of the white ceramic floor of her normally immaculately clean floor was partially covered in the slick fluid.

She started to think maybe she should have taken *Landell Corp*'s offer to buy her building and give up trying to hold everything together. She didn't know how much longer she could keep her place afloat.

Isabelle shook that thought from her head as quickly as it entered. No matter what had gone wrong over the last several months, *A Taste of Hopedale* was her dream. The one thing that she gave her blood, sweat, and tears to build on her own. She was proud of her fine dining restaurant, and to allow a huge corporation to buy her out went against her morals.

The residents of the small town managed to keep numerous greedy companies from turning the town into a smaller version of St. John's. The capital city of Newfoundland was a nice place, but it didn't have the peaceful feeling of living in Hopedale.

To allow large shopping malls and condos to invade the scenic view of the town would be sinful. It would strip the natural beauty of the place and Isabelle wouldn't contribute to that.

It was also the reason she couldn't allow the umpteenth thing to go wrong in her restaurant to cause her to change her mind. Isabelle had cleaned the fryer herself the night before and she could swear she closed the drain valve. She was meticulous about that sort of thing. So why was there a huge mess in front of her that neither she nor her kitchen staff had time to clean?

"Fuck," Isabelle muttered under her breath.

"Relax, Tiger. We'll get this cleaned up in a jiffy." Her new chef stepped to the other side of the fryer and smiled.

Roman Young was an incredible chef and an extremely diligent worker. The problem was Roman was hot with a capital H. He was tall, in great shape, and sinfully handsome. He was also a huge flirt which was why Isabelle kept him at arm's length. At least she tried to, but he seemed to be around every corner and since he'd become so close to her cousin Nick, Roman was constantly at her large family gatherings.

"Stop calling me Tiger," Isabelle grumbled and stomped back to grab the mop from the supply closet.

When she returned, she honestly wanted to slap Roman with the mop. He smiled and gave her that flirty wink which made her stomach flutter. When he took the mop from her, Isabelle was about to argue, but Roman motioned behind her. One of the waitresses entered the kitchen and looked ready to burst into tears.

"I don't need this right now," Isabelle mumbled under her breath.

"Go deal with tonight's drama, I got this." Roman chucked Isabelle under the chin then he turned away with the mop in hand.

Cindy practically ran into the staff area before Isabelle could stop her. It was almost six in the evening, which meant it was about to get crazy busy and she was already short one waitress.

The previous evening another waitress, Angelina, ended up at the hospital because a broken glass mysteriously appeared in the ice cooler. She needed nine stitches in the palm of her hand and would be off for at least ten days.

"Cindy, are you okay?" Isabelle asked as she stepped into the staff room and closed the door.

"No, this snobby guy just told me I was too slow and I was too damn clumsy. I didn't mean to knock the fork on the floor, and I got him a clean one, but he was a dick." Cindy dabbed her over made-up face with a tissue.

"Cindy, you've got to let that stuff roll off your back. There are always assholes when you work with the public." Isabelle tried to sound empathetic, but it was difficult since Cindy found a reason to cry almost every shift.

"I know but it hurts." Cindy pouted.

Isabelle wanted to shake the girl sometimes, but no matter what the asshole said, Cindy was a good waitress and most customers loved her perky personality. She was a breath of fresh air, when she wasn't complaining.

"Look, we're about to be at full capacity and I've got a situation in the kitchen. Do you think you can pull yourself together quickly and show that ass you're better than him?" Isabelle forced a smile and kind of felt like a bitch for her lack of sympathy.

"Of course. I just need to fix my face, and I'm sorry for being so sensitive." Cindy sniffed and scurried into the bathroom.

Isabelle blew out a breath and headed back to deal with the other mess. When she walked into the kitchen she could literally feel her blood pressure rise. Not only had the oil not been cleaned up, but the floor was covered with what appeared to be flour. She turned slowly and stomped toward Roman. The minute she stepped in front of him, he held up his hands.

"Don't panic. It's baking soda. It will soak up the oil, and the floor won't be slippery. It will give us a chance to get through the rush and I'll personally clean it up after we close. Okay?" Roman grasped her hands in his and squeezed them gently.

It took everything she had to ignore the warm feeling she got when he touched her. Roman was much too charming for Isabelle's own good, which was why she took a step back and let her panic take over.

"Are you freaking kidding me?" Isabelle looked at him as if he were insane.

"Trust me, please, Tiger?" Roman stepped toward her but she backed away again.

"Stop. Calling. Me. Tiger." Isabelle fisted her hands at her sides.

Isabelle tried desperately to be annoyed by the ridiculous nickname but the truth was, she got a warm fuzzy feeling every single time he lowered his tone and almost purred the name.

"Isabelle, trust me." When Roman used that deep sexy voice, it sent shivers of desire through her body.

He seemed to know what to do to help her calm down when she was overwhelmed. Roman was different than most of the men in her family. He always had that relaxed *I've-got-this* attitude and it annoyed the hell out of her.

"If the Department of Health comes in here, they could shut me down for that mess." Isabelle rested her fists on her hips as she kept her eyes averted from his tight ass because he'd picked that exact moment to bend over and pull something out of the oven.

"They won't," Roman assured her as he set the large pan on the counter and turned to the computer screen over the prep table.

Isabelle saw the blinking light that indicated orders had started to come in. Roman didn't give her a chance to respond as he pulled on his gloves and got to work without another word. It was his way, when the orders came in, Roman was a professional.

Isabelle watched him for a moment before she turned her attention to the mess, then the screen. With a huge huff, she double-checked the valve on the fryer again and did what she did the best. Worked her ass off to make sure her customers left happy and satisfied.

By the time the last of the customers walked out of the restaurant, Isabelle forced a smile and thanked them. She quickly locked the door and leaned against it as she let out a huge sigh of relief. Thank God the rest of the night went by without any major catastrophes.

There had been a full house the whole evening, as usual, but every time she walked near the fryer, she wanted to scream. The whole night she questioned herself, but the more she thought about it, the more pissed she got for not having someone else check the valve as well.

After having to replace a cooler behind the bar, fix her huge walk-in freezer, and replace one of her propane tanks on the back of her restaurant, the last thing she needed was to shell out more money to replace a fryer. Business wasn't that good.

Isabelle walked into the dining hall and smiled at Milly as she carried the linens from the tables into the kitchen area. Milly Boland had worked as head waitress since the restaurant opened eleven years earlier. Milly's husband Jake was the head bartender and one of the happiest people she'd ever met.

"I'm gonna toss these in the washer before I head home," Milly called out as she walked into the kitchen.

Isabelle gave her a nod as she headed to do the final check of the dining room to make sure all the tables were prepared for the next day. The staff was the best and were always on top of everything, but Isabelle still had to check.

Isabelle's staff was the heart of *A Taste of Hopedale*. Except for Roman, most of her staff had been with her for years. She respected them and for the most part, they all got along, which didn't always happen with staff.

The restaurant was one of the best in the province and Isabelle had bookings three months in advance. Of course, she did always have a table or two left open in case one of her family members wanted to have a romantic dinner or an important business meeting.

Between her parents, her aunts and uncles, her cousins and her younger sisters, there was always one of them who needed a last-minute table. Isabelle didn't mind because her family was the best.

Isabelle shuffled behind the bar after the last of her staff left. She always made sure to distribute their tips every night and then she'd complete the deposit for the day. Isabelle grabbed a bottle of Newfie Screech from the top shelf and a shot glass. It was her paternal grandfather's drink of choice.

"A shot of screech cures what ails ya," he would say with his Irish lilt.

He and her grandmother were born in a small town called Cape Broyle on the Southern Shore. Like everyone from the Southern Shore, both Granda Jack and Nanny Betty spoke with what most people would think was an Irish accent.

Even though he'd passed away more than a decade ago, Isabelle could still hear him when she really concentrated. It devastated her family to lose him, especially her grandmother, but Nanny Betty was by his side until he took his last breath. Jack O'Connor and Elizabeth Power O'Connor was the start of their strong family foundation.

"You really shouldn't drink alone, Tiger." The rumbly voice startled her, and she almost dropped the bottle.

"Jesus, just shoot me next time. It would be quicker than trying to scare me to death." Isabelle huffed as she managed to keep the bottle from hitting the floor.

"Sorry, I thought you knew I was still here." Roman rested his arms on the bar and tapped the glass she'd placed there.

"Is that your subtle way of saying you want a drink?" Isabelle smirked.

"Yep," He grinned and Isabelle's libido turned up another notch.

He was a huge flirt and that made Isabelle believe he was a playboy. She didn't have the time nor the energy to deal with guys like that. Mostly because she wasn't twenty years old anymore. Although, in the few months he'd worked for her, she couldn't remember him going out with anyone. Her cousin Nick had vouched for Roman, saying her new chef was as far away from a playboy as any guy could get.

Nick O'Connor was the second youngest of seven brothers. John, James, Ian, Keith, Mike, Nick, and Aaron were more like brothers than cousins. Their father, Sean, and Isabelle's father, Kurt, were brothers who lived next door to each other not far from where Isabelle had bought her house.

Her cousins were popular with the ladies through the years, but Mike, Nick, and Aaron used to change girlfriends more often than most people changed their socks. Over the last few years, all the brothers had gotten married and started families, but Isabelle still remembered the stream of women that the three youngest brothers had gone through.

Isabelle didn't want to be another notch on someone's belt, but Roman played havoc with her hormones. That deep voice, his smile, and those deep-brown eyes made it hard to not be stupid.

"Come on, I worked hard today." Roman tapped the bottom of the glass on the bar top.

"Did you really, though?" Isabelle teased.

"Would you like me to show you the sweat rolling down my back?" Roman stood up and grabbed the bottom of his shirt.

"No, I'll take your word for it." Isabelle rolled her eyes.

"Then come on, Tiger, tip that bottle up." Roman wiggled the glass on the counter.

"I don't know if you can handle this stuff." Isabelle grabbed a second shot glass and filled both.

"Tiger, I can handle anything you want to give me." Roman raised one of his perfectly arched eyebrows and reached for the shot glass.

"Stop calling me Tiger." Isabelle narrowed her eyes and quickly threw back the shot.

The liquid burned as it slid down her throat, but she wouldn't dare let Roman see her discomfort as she crossed her arms over her chest. She glanced at his glass then back to his eyes.

"Your turn." Isabelle smirked.

"You're a tough cookie, aren't you, Tiger?" Roman put the glass to his mouth and quickly tipped his head back, emptying the glass.

He grinned as he slammed the glass down on the bar and grabbed the bottle. He filled the glasses again and held his glass out in front of him. Isabelle picked up her glass and rested her elbows on the bar.

"Are you trying to challenge me, Mr. Young?" Isabelle raised an eyebrow.

"I'd never do that. I want to offer a toast." He held up his glass.

"Oh, to what?" Isabelle asked.

"To the most beautiful boss a guy could have." He clinked his glass against hers and then quickly tossed back the shot.

Isabelle stared at him for several seconds. It was getting harder for her to resist his charms. Especially when he said things like that. She emptied her glass and reminded herself that she didn't get involved with employees. Plus, two weeks earlier, she'd gone out to dinner with Roman's best friend, Ethan.

It wasn't actually a date, but that didn't matter. Her number one rule still applied. Employees were off limits, and as sexy as the chocolate-eyed chef was, with his muscled forearms, thick biceps, full lips, and skin that looked like it was lightly tanned, Isabelle had to resist.

Isabelle decided it was time to talk about anything that would distract her. She told Roman about her previous chef and how she'd hated to see him leave, but she understood that Dominic and his wife wanted to go back to their home in Quebec.

Roman told her his last employer had fired him for making a pass at the man's wife. The truth was the woman was the aggressor and when Roman turned her down, she went to her husband. Roman was fired and that was when he realized he'd had enough. He moved back to Newfoundland to be close to his mom, but she passed away a few months after he'd returned

Four shots later, Isabelle laughed so hard that her stomach hurt. Roman did a hilarious impression of one of the chefs he'd worked with in Montreal. Between the flamboyant way he strutted around the bar and mocked the man's French accent, she could hardly breathe.

"Stop, stop." Isabelle laughed and wiped the tears running out of her eyes.

"I swear, that guy was so over the top, it was unbelievable. Then after he reprimands me, he offers to rock my world." Roman plopped down on the bar stool.

"Did he rock it?" Isabelle teased, but there was no doubt Roman was straight.

"Nope, I like women, and I especially like one woman in particular." Roman ran a finger across her hand on top of the bar.

"Roman," She met his eyes as he tugged her around the edge of the bar and pulled her between his legs.

"I like you, Isabelle." His voice dropped to a low rumble.

"I think we both need to go." Isabelle stepped back and slowly pulled her hands from his.

"I'll walk you home." Roman cleared off the bar and grabbed his coat from the bar stool.

"I can get myself home." Isabelle pulled on her coat and almost tripped when Roman stepped in front of her.

"You're not walking home at eleven o'clock at night by yourself." Roman flicked off the light over the bar.

"Excuse me?" Isabelle snorted.

"I wouldn't forgive myself if something happened to you because I wasn't the gentleman I was raised to be." Roman stepped outside the exit as Isabelle set the alarm and locked the door.

"It's out of your way." Isabelle rolled her eyes and started up toward her house.

"It's literally five minutes up this road. It might take an extra two minutes for me to get back to Ethan's place." Roman strolled beside her.

They walked in silence up Beach Street toward her house. Roman seemed relaxed as he shoved his hands into the pockets of his wool military peacoat. He had the collar pulled up around his neck and he wore a navy-blue wool hat on his head. It pissed her off because it was a look she found very sexy.

Isabelle turned onto the path leading to her front door and held her breath as he followed her up the steps. Roman leaned against the house as she reached into her purse to grab her keys.

"You should leave your porch light on when you leave for work." Roman looked up at the light over her front door.

"The bulb needs to be changed but I haven't gotten around to doing it." Isabelle mindlessly dropped her purse on the rail and continued to dig to the bottom of her bag.

"You should also make sure you have your keys in your hand before you leave work." Roman chuckled as Isabelle spun around and unlocked her door.

"When exactly did you become my father?" Isabelle snapped.

“Tiger, the last thing I want to be is your father.” His voice was seductive, and a shiver of desire ran through her body.

Isabelle turned to look up at him and her eyes locked with his. Roman took one step and then another. Isabelle was mesmerized by his intense eyes and couldn’t move. Her tongue instinctively slipped out to moisten her lips as Roman’s gaze dropped to her mouth.

“Tiger,” Roman whispered against her mouth as he cupped the back of her head. “Tell me to stop.”

Isabelle opened her mouth to speak but instead of doing what she should, she stepped closer and fisted the front of Roman’s jacket. He seemed startled, but a second later, his mouth was on hers and any resistance she could have mustered was melted away. The kiss was desperate and carnal as she tugged him against her and swirled her tongue around his.

Roman’s hands were buried in her hair as he angled her head and slipped his tongue into her mouth. She moaned as he backed her through the opened door while he continued to devour her lips, mouth, and tongue.

Isabelle barely heard the click of the door closing or her purse and keys as they dropped to the floor of the foyer. The only thing she wanted was to get out of her jacket and get him out of his. Isabelle needed to get closer to him and their jackets were keeping them too far apart.

“Jesus, Tiger.” Roman groaned as he almost tore off his coat while he placed kisses across her jaw. “Are you sure about this?”

His hot breath against her ear caused goosebumps to rise on her skin and her core throbbed with need. She might be about to break her very own rule, but she’d never been more sure of anything in her life. Isabelle grabbed the front of his dress shirt and ripped it open causing the buttons to fly off in all directions.

“I’m sure,” she growled.

Chapter 2

Roman's dick was painfully hard as Isabelle rubbed her hot body against his. They were still dressed with the exception of his now buttonless shirt hanging open as they kissed, nipped, and tasted each other. Her sweet scent filled his senses and he knew if he didn't regain some control, he'd come in his pants.

From the first day he met her, Roman wanted Isabelle, but she didn't appear interested. Then there was the fact that she was his boss so he tamped down his desire and worked his ass off. He needed her to know she made the right decision when she hired him.

About three months into his employment, he caught her staring at him more and more. He knew desire when he saw it, but the intense attraction he had to Isabelle was something he never experienced before. It was magnetic and intense. It was why he tried to keep things light with her most of the time. She was everything he ever wanted, but so much more. Roman knew with her, it would never be just a fling.

Isabelle was the type of woman he could see himself with long-term. Beautiful, but she didn't know it because she would roll her eyes when anyone paid her a compliment. She was witty, sarcastic, smart, and worked hard everyday. She made sure her staff was happy and from what he'd seen, they all loved her.

"Isabelle, I need to know that you want this. We've both been drinking. I know I'm not drunk and I'm damn sure I want you more than I want to breathe. I just need to know you want this." Roman held her a few inches away from him to regain his composure.

"Yes, I want this. I want you." Isabelle stepped backward as she yanked her white shirt over her head and dropped it to the floor.

He almost went to his knees when he saw the pink lace bra under her shirt. Isabelle's nipples strained against the thin fabric as if they begged him to suck them. He bit his lip as he raised his gaze to meet the bright blue eyes that drew him in from the first minute he looked into them.

"Fuck." Roman shrugged out of his shirt.

"That's what I'm hoping for." Isabelle smirked as she slipped her black slacks down her legs and kicked them to the side.

Roman popped the button on his pants as he drank in her beautiful peach skin with his eyes. Isabelle was perfectly proportioned with full breasts, wide hips and slim waist. The black boy shorts she wore hugged her curves flawlessly, and all Roman wanted to do was rip them off and plunge his cock deep inside her.

Isabelle's eyes bore into his as she slowly feathered her hands down over his bare chest. Her touch caused goosebumps to rise all over his body and he shivered. He couldn't pull his gaze away from hers as she lowered the zipper of his trousers. It wouldn't be hard for her to see how much he wanted her because his cock bulged against his boxer briefs and he could feel the wetness of the tip against his stomach.

She slipped her fingers inside his black pants and dragged them down his legs, Isabelle's eyes never left his. Her desire was evident in her blue eyes and he found it hard to slow his heartbeat as he stepped quickly out of his shoes, socks, and pants, leaving him standing in just his boxers right there in the middle of the foyer.

"Are we going to stay here, Tiger? I think your bed would be more comfortable." Roman's words were strained because she was crouched in front of him with her lips pressed against his stomach above the band of his underwear.

"You're very impatient," she cooed and kissed her way up to his chest.

Isabelle pressed her body against his. The lace of her bra brushed his skin as she continued to kiss and nip her way to his neck. When she gently bit his earlobe, Roman growled because he couldn't take anymore. He swung her into his arms and kicked their clothes to the side.

"Where's your room, Tiger?" Roman strained to get out the words as she licked behind his ear.

Isabelle giggled and pointed to the bottom of the stairs. He'd figure out where her room was when they got to the second floor of the house. It was difficult to make it there because she had him ready to take her in the middle of the stairs.

By the time they made it to the bedroom, he could feel her wetness against his stomach through her underwear. He lowered her until her feet touched the floor and he stepped back to gaze into her eyes.

After months of flirting with the woman, he never thought he'd ever get close enough to touch her so intimately. Roman had dreamed and fantasized about this moment more often than he cared to admit. He'd taken more cold showers in the last few months than he'd ever taken in his teenage years, but nothing dulled the ache he had for her.

Now he was about to fulfill his dream of being with the smart, beautiful, sexy Isabelle O'Connor. He must have done something in a previous life to be so damn lucky. Roman cupped her face between his hands and gazed into her eyes. It was at that moment he saw the doubt.

"Tiger, are you sure you want this?" He needed to know she hadn't changed her mind.

"Are you?" She lowered her eyes as she rolled her lips inward.

Isabelle had a tendency to do that when she was nervous, and it was the cutest thing he'd ever seen. Isabelle might show she was the boss at the restaurant, but she also had an insecurity that she tried hard to hide from everyone. Roman had seen it more since things started going wrong at work.

Roman placed his finger under her chin and lifted it until she had to look into his eyes. He needed her to see there was no doubt in his mind what he wanted.

"Isabelle, I've never been more sure in my life." Roman held her face between his hands and ran his thumbs across her jaw.

For a moment she didn't move or speak. Roman held his breath as he waited for her decision. After a minute passed and she didn't reply, he stepped away from her. He was about to leave until she reached behind and unhooked her bra.

"Me too," she whispered as she slipped the bra off her shoulders and let it drop to the floor.

Roman drank in the sight of her naked breasts for several seconds. Her dark nipples were hard and ready for him to savor the taste. He held on to his restraint long enough for her to slip out of her underwear. When she was beautifully naked in front of him, Roman pulled her against him and crushed his mouth against hers. There was no going back once they stepped over that boundary, and he was never so thankful in his life.

He lay her on the bed and brought one of her legs up and over his hip. The scent of her arousal filled his senses and it only made his cock throb more to be inside her. The problem was he hadn't planned ahead and realized he didn't have any protection. He quickly pulled back and groaned.

"Don't stop." Isabelle growled and tried to tug him back down on top of her.

"Fuck, tell me you have condoms," Roman said through gritted teeth.

"If I say yes, are you going to think badly of me?" Isabelle smiled.

"No, I'll think you're a fucking genius." Roman moaned as she rolled him onto his back and reached for the nightstand.

When she straddled his hips with the foil package between her teeth, Roman couldn't remember ever seeing anyone look so damn sexy.

Chapter 3

Isabelle opened her eyes and turned her head slowly to gaze at the man on the other side of her bed softly snoring. She squeezed her eyes shut and resisted the urge to curse as she opened them again. It wasn't a dream this time. Roman rocked her world. Isabelle had the best sex of her life with a man she should never have slept with in the first place.

"Shit," she whispered to herself as she glanced through her open drapes to see it was still dark.

Isabelle slipped from the bed, trying hard not to wake Roman. She really needed to talk the situation out with someone besides the sexy man who made her lose all common sense. Isabelle grabbed her phone off the dresser and she thanked Roman silently for going downstairs earlier to retrieve their clothes and phones. That was, of course, after they'd had sex a second time.

He'd teased her about how she always needed her phone next to her at the restaurant and he figured she'd be like that at home as well. Then he proceeded to make her scream with ecstasy for the third time.

She pulled up her contact list and prayed her sister was still awake. Jess worked as a police officer from noon to midnight and she was the type of person who wasn't able to go right to sleep after working for twelve hours. Like Isabelle, Jess would need to wind down and probably wouldn't go to sleep until about two in the morning. That worked out great because it was a little before that time.

Isabelle needed to talk to one of her sisters and it probably wouldn't be a good idea to call Kristy, the youngest of the three of them. When Isabelle had seen Kristy that morning, she'd told Isabelle she wasn't feeling well.

Plus, Kristy was married with a little boy who was almost a year old. Jess was still single, and Isabelle didn't have to worry about her needing to get up with a crying baby. She typed the one word to her sister that would get a response if Jess saw the message.

Isabelle: HELP

Seconds later, her phone vibrated in her hand and she tapped it frantically, hoping the buzz wouldn't disturb Roman. She glanced at him as she put her phone to her ear and stepped as far away from the bed as she could get and still be inside her room.

"Oh my, God," Isabelle whispered.

"What's wrong?" Jess' concern was evident in her voice.

"Jess, I did something really, really, really, bad. I mean colossally stupid." Isabelle's tried to keep her voice low as she tugged a T-shirt over her head.

"Okay, first, why are you whispering, and second, what the hell did you do?" Jess asked.

Isabelle tiptoed to the bedroom door and tried to open it as quietly as possible. When it made a soft squeak, she cringed and turned back to see Roman still sound asleep with one arm over his head and the other across his stomach.

"I'm whispering because I don't want the person that's here to hear me," Isabelle whispered.

"Who's there?" Jess sounded tired.

"Hold on a second," Isabelle grumbled as she pulled the bedroom door closed.

Isabelle quietly tiptoed down the stairs and made her way into the living room. At least she'd be able to speak a little louder on the main floor of her house. She let out a long breath and plopped down on the couch when she heard her sister's irritated voice.

"Isabelle, what's going on?" Jess asked.

"Okay, so I've been really stressed at the restaurant because some weird shit happened. Mostly stuff that's just annoying, and nobody seems to know what's going on," Isabelle explained.

She didn't want to go into the other issue of the *Landell Corp* trying to convince her to sell her building. That not only would piss Jess off but it would probably end up with her whole family involved and that was the last thing she needed.

"Go on," Jess urged.

"Anyway, tonight, one of the fryers mysteriously started to leak out through the drain. The only way that would happen is if someone didn't close the valve all the way, but I know for a fact that I closed it tight. I always double check after I clean them." Isabelle tried to tell her everything and knew she was probably rambling.

"Isabelle, get to the point," Jess grumbled.

"I slept with Roman," Isabelle spat out.

"Your chef? Ethan's best friend?" Isabelle knew Jess was trying not to laugh by the crack in her voice.

It took Isabelle almost a year to make the decision to hire Roman. Mostly because of her control issues and the fact that she didn't think she'd ever find anyone that she could work with as well as she had Dominic and Petra. Then when she met him, she was uneasy about the instant attraction, but between Nick and Lora's constant urging, she interviewed him and hired him on the spot.

Lora and her brother grew up with Roman, and when Isabelle mentioned she needed to hire a new chef, Lora suggested her brother's friend. He'd moved back to Newfoundland and was looking for a position with a reputable restaurant as a chef. Roman had trained with some of the best chefs in the country and had gone to one of the top schools. She couldn't afford not to hire him.

"Yes, that Roman," Isabelle snapped.

"Didn't you go out on a date with Ethan a little while ago? I didn't know you and Roman were seeing each other." Jess was pissing her off mostly because Isabelle could hear the amusement in her voice.

"That wasn't a date with Ethan. It was a… dinner, and I'm not dating Roman. It's just that we were the only two left after everything was cleaned up, and I was so damn pissed I had a shot or two of Newfie Screech. Okay, maybe six, and he did too, and then he walked me back to my house, and well, he's really hot, and it's been way too long, and…" Isabelle's voice trailed off.

"And you like him," Jess finished.

"Yes. No. Yes. Shit. I don't do one-night stands, and I don't do my employees." Isabelle swallowed hard because she didn't want her reputation ruined if Roman decided to brag about banging the boss.

"Isabelle, calm down. First of all, maybe this won't be a one-night stand, and you actually did do an employee." Jess snickered.

"Not. Helping." Isabelle groaned.

"I know. I'm sorry, but if you like him, what's wrong with you two going out?" Jess asked.

"Because he's a big flirt. He reminds me of A.J. and Nick before they got married. He keeps calling me Tiger, and I have no idea why," Isabelle continued.

"Does he flirt with all the women at the restaurant or just

you?" Jess asked.

"I don't know. I just know he does it with me. A lot." Isabelle sighed.

"Is he still there?" Jess asked.

"Yes, that's why I had to leave the bedroom," Isabelle explained.

"Look, you have a hot man in your bed, and I'm assuming the sex wasn't awful." Jess laughed.

"So not awful. Amazing. Incredible. Freaking mind-blowing." Isabelle sighed.

"Then don't complain. Just go with it," Jess said.

"What if people find out?" Isabelle whispered.

"Isabelle, you're a thirty-seven-year-old adult woman. Who the hell cares if people find out?" Jess asked.

Growing up in a small Newfoundland community, it was hard to keep secrets. There were people in Hopedale who made a life of starting gossip, and before all her cousins got married, the biggest gossip about the O'Connor family was that the boys were all playboys. Of course, that was only partly true. John, James, Ian, and Keith dated but not often. Mike, Nick, and Aaron were the ones who caused the rumor to spread.

Cora's daughter, Pam, did have a bit of a rumor spread when she moved to Ontario right after high school. It was stopped when

Cora told everyone about the great job her daughter had with a huge clothing company. Pam returned home five years earlier but nobody knew why she left her job. Isabelle had a feeling it had something to do with a man, especially when Damon Blackwood appeared in Hopedale.

Isabelle and her sisters managed to avoid the gossip through the years. Isabelle didn't want to start the rumor mill because of all this. It could not only ruin her own reputation, but her restaurant's as well.

"I don't need it getting out that I slept with one of my employees." Isabelle glanced up when she saw the light come on in the hallway and gasped.

Roman stood propped against the archway into the living room and seemed amused with the way she stared at him. In his usual sexy way, Roman pushed up straight and slowly sauntered toward her with his pants still unfastened. He chuckled and she knew he'd seen her gaze drop to his crotch. The dark hair pointed down to what she knew she'd never get enough of.

Roman wasn't hard muscle, but he had the hint of a six-pack as well has muscled biceps. His legs were thick and muscled, probably from spending so much time on his feet and she knew he ran every morning because she'd seen him on the beach several times. It was obvious he ate right and kept himself healthy. Sexy.

"Oh, umm. Gotta go." Isabelle dropped her phone on the arm

of the sofa and swallowed hard.

"I woke up to an empty bed, Tiger." Roman's voice was low and so damn seductive.

"Umm… sorry. I was… ah… thirsty." Isabelle stumbled over her words and wanted to kick herself for sounding so insecure.

"Did you have to order some water?" Roman chuckled.

"Huh?" She breathed when he lifted her hand to his lips and crouched in front of her.

"You were on the phone, Tiger." Roman nodded toward her cell.

"Stop calling me that, please." Isabelle groaned.

"Why? The name fits you." He leaned forward and kissed her shoulder.

"Why does that name fit me, Roman?" Isabelle whispered and closed her eyes.

"I've watched you every day since I started to work for you. Not only because you're incredibly sexy, that's just a bonus. From what I see, you meet every characteristic of a Tiger person." Roman nuzzled his nose against the side of her neck.

"What's that supposed to mean?" Isabelle snorted.

"You've got this air of authority when you walk into a room. I feel it every single time I'm near you. You're calm and warm but courageous, and fearless. You're always in a hurry to get things done, and I've noticed you like to work alone. You're sensitive, passionate, and I would bet my last dime you're a romantic at heart." He kissed the side of her face.

"Roman." She breathed his name.

It was impossible to think of a reason why what he was doing was so wrong. Somewhere in a small corner of her mind, she knew that it was meant to be, but she was terrified to admit that to herself.

Before she could even think about putting up a protest, he covered her mouth with his and she forgot whatever she was about to say as he eased her back on the couch and proceeded to rock her world again.

Chapter 4

Roman walked into *Jack's Place Pub*. Isabelle's family was celebrating her father's retirement and his election to Hopedale Mayor. It was a private party and he was kind of bummed that Isabelle hadn't been the one to invite him. He only found out because Nick mentioned it when they were running on the beach.

Isabelle was still hesitant to tell anyone she'd been spending time with Roman. He couldn't really call it dating because they never went anywhere outside the restaurant or her house. He only showed up at the pub because he knew Isabelle had a rough day. Not only was she coming down with the flu, but she was also refusing to take a day off to take care of herself.

The virus had hit almost everyone at the restaurant, including Roman. It was why he'd insisted she take a day to herself, but she showed up that morning. To top it off, she got another offer from *Landell Corp* that she refused again, but the gentleman who'd called her insisted she think long and hard about the offer. To Roman, it almost seemed like a threat.

For the rest of the day, she was short-fused. It was the first time since they'd started to get close that she treated him like he was an employee. Truthfully, he did work for her, but when she left to get ready for the party, she walked into the kitchen of the restaurant and gave him a list of what she wanted to be done before he left.

She hadn't even given him what they called the sneaky kiss before she left. It was a kiss she would give him quickly when they got a second alone at work. It had become a running joke between them of the places in the building they hadn't done a sneaky kiss. He was worried about her.

It was why he now sat next to the bar and waved to his best friend Ethan. A former pilot, Ethan Norris now worked as a part-time bartender and part-time pilot for Isabelle's cousin. Roman hadn't seen his buddy this happy in a long time.

"I thought you were blowing this off tonight?" Ethan placed a bottle of beer on the bar in front of Roman.

"I was, but I'm worried about Isabelle," Roman admitted as he lifted the beer to his lips.

"Don't worry about her, I told you there's nothing going on between me and her." Ethan rested his elbows on the bar and smirked.

"Not what I mean, fuckface." Roman narrowed his eyes. "But glad to hear it because I'm afraid she's grabbed hold of me, body, mind, and soul."

“Has the mighty Roman Young finally fallen?” Ethan feigned shock.

“Maybe, but I’m not sure if she wants anything more than casual.” Roman kept his voice low since all the O’Connor family were within five feet of him.

It was mid February and five months since Roman and Isabelle had ended up naked in her bed the first time. In the beginning, she’d seemed unsure, but she’d wait around after the restaurant closed and they’d talk until everything was cleaned and set up for the next day.

Roman walked her home every night because she’d stopped taking her car to work. He didn’t know if it was because Isabelle knew he wouldn’t allow her to walk home at night alone or she really did see it as a waste of gas to drive the short two minutes to her place of business.

“Have you told her how you feel?” Ethan asked.

“Not those exact words. We’re together practically every single night, so she’s got to know there’s more there than just a fling.” Roman took another sip of his beer.

When the music ended, he smiled as Wade Rivers got down on one knee and proposed to Jess. He knew about the proposal because Wade had enlisted Isabelle and the rest of the family to help make things perfect.

Wade and Jess had fallen quickly and were madly in love with each other. Isabelle had told Roman she'd never seen her sister so happy. She'd also joked about being the only single sister but Roman hadn't missed the sadness in her eyes. She was excited for her sister, that was evident.

How the hell Isabelle could be so excited over her sister's engagement but would completely steer clear of any conversation he wanted to initiate about dates frustrated him. Anytime he even hinted at going out to dinner or a movie, she'd completely change the subject.

Roman felt her eyes on him as he reached for the second beer Ethan had placed in front of him. Isabelle gave him a half smile but it suddenly disappeared and her expression changed. She looked as if she was in a complete state of panic and he had no idea why.

"Well, it's about time you showed up, Roman." A woman's voice caused Roman to turn toward it.

Isabelle's aunt placed her hand on his shoulder and gave him a huge smile. Cora Nightingale was Kurt's younger sister and for some reason, she always seemed to be happy to see him around Isabelle. Roman had no idea why but she always said the weirdest things to him.

She was a nice lady, but probably the oddest one out of the O'Connor family. Then again, Roman had only been in her presence a handful of times. She always made a point of telling him to have patience because he was the one. He'd heard hilarious rumors about the woman being a matchmaker but never really paid any attention to it.

"Everything's all tied up at the restaurant without any issues, I hope?" Cora smiled as she glanced over her shoulder.

"Yes, ma'am." Roman returned her smile.

"That's wonderful. You know you're perfect for her." Cora cupped his cheek.

"We work well together." Roman was a little uncomfortable with the way Cora touched him.

"I'm sure you do. That's why you'll be together for a long time." Cora turned and walked away.

"That was… Ummm… strange." Roman shook his head.

"You've just been tagged by Cora the Cupid." A voice from behind had him turn.

Another of Isabelle's cousins stepped next to him, grinning. Keith was the largest of the seven O'Connor brothers and if someone didn't know him, they would think he was completely serious and mean. Roman knew better because he'd seen Keith around his wife Emily and their kids. Keith would turn into a complete marshmallow around his two sons. Since his wife was pregnant again, the man was over the moon and Roman could understand why.

"I'm sorry, tagged?" Roman furrowed his brow.

"Didn't Ace tell you about Cora?" Keith said, using the nickname Ethan had received when he started to work for Newfoundland Security Services, the security company that Keith co-owned with Isabelle's brother in law.

"No, but I've heard the stories." Roman rolled his eyes.

"They aren't stories, Roman. She's never been wrong and she's predicted every couple in my family." Keith held up two fingers to Ethan.

"You're pulling my fucking leg." Roman chuckled.

"I wish, but as much as we poked fun at it over the years, she's always right on point." Keith slid a shot glass in front of Roman and picked up the other Ethan had placed in front of them.

"I need to stick to beer tonight." Roman started to push it away.

"If you're going to survive this family and convince my stubborn cousin that you're it for her, you'll need that shot of Screech." Keith pushed it back to him.

"This stuff is the reason I'm in this situation to begin with," Roman muttered to himself as he tossed the shot of dark rum down his throat.

"Look, most of us know there's something going on between you and Isabelle. Let me give you some advice. She's spent so much of her life doing things for other people and neglecting her own happiness that it's going to take a lot of patience to convince her she can take time to find it for herself." Keith lay the shot glass on the bar and turned to where Isabelle was slowly making her way toward them.

"You're telling me not to let her push me away." Roman watched the auburn-haired beauty walk toward them.

"That's exactly what I'm saying, but a word of warning, don't hurt her because Uncle Kurt may be former Chief of Police and new mayor, but he won't hesitate to kick your ass if you hurt his little girl. Plus, you'd have to deal with me and my brothers too." Keith chuckled and kissed Isabelle's cheek as she stepped next to him.

"I understand." Roman grasped Isabelle's hand and before she could resist, he tugged her behind him through the entrance of the pub.

"What are you doing?" Isabelle squeaked as he pulled her outside and pinned her against the door with his body.

"I'm going to say this once and once only. I want you, Tiger." He practically growled the words when her warm breath caressed his neck.

"I can't go. My family is all here and …" She began but Roman stopped her with a finger pressed against her lips.

"I don't mean for just sex. I'm not complaining about it, trust me, it's been incredible. I want more. I want to take you on a real date. I want to let people know you and I are more than an employee and boss. I don't want to be the secret you're keeping from your family and everyone else." Roman stared into her eyes as he slowly spoke so she wouldn't miss a word.

She stared for several minutes, with her mouth slightly hung open and breathing heavily. Roman was turned on, but he wasn't letting their talk turn into another night of hot and sweaty sex. Isabelle meant too much to him.

"Roman," Isabelle choked out his name.

"I know you're fighting it, Tiger, but I can tell you feel more between us than what happens between the sheets." Roman ran his knuckle across her soft cheek.

She closed her eyes and blew out a breath. He didn't know why she fought so hard to hide their relationship, but he'd find out if it killed him. Isabelle was worth it. He wanted everyone to know what a lucky son of a bitch he was to be with a woman like her.

"What did Aunt Cora say to you?" She opened her eyes and met his gaze with one equally intense.

"She said we're perfect together." Roman's eyes scanned the features of her face like he always did.

Roman knew every inch of her beautiful face. She had several faint freckles across her nose and cheeks. He'd watched her several mornings, covering them with some sort of makeup. She didn't wear much of the stuff and she didn't need to. Isabelle was a natural beauty. Her naturally curly auburn hair hung just below her shoulders and Roman loved tangling his fingers in her soft curls.

She blew out another breath, and her head fell back against the door. Roman glanced at her slender neck and it took every ounce of strength he had not to kiss his way up and down each side. He loved the soft coconut scent of the body wash she used. It stayed on her skin during most of the day. He'd told her once that anytime he had to make anything with coconut, it made him hard.

"Roman, you work for me. We shouldn't be doing this and dating would really start a wave of rumors. I adore my employees, but there's a couple who have big mouths." Isabelle met his eyes.

"What's wrong with people knowing we're dating?" He didn't understand.

"I can't discuss this now." Isabelle dropped her gaze but Roman was taking Keith's advice.

"You never want to discuss this, Tiger." Roman cupped the back of her head with his hand and pressed his lips against her cheek.

"Is everything okay, Isabelle?" A male voice from behind him caused Isabelle to almost shove Roman over the steps of the pub.

"Uncle Sean, ummm… yes, everything's fine. We're… just… talking." Isabelle pushed off the door and stepped aside for her uncle to go into the building.

"Hi, Dr. O'Connor." Roman nodded and rested against the railing.

"Roman, I think you can disperse with the formalities and call me Sean." Sean rested his hand on Isabelle's shoulder.

"You missed the proposal." Isabelle pulled open the door to the pub.

"I was just outside for a second. I saw it." Sean kissed Isabelle's cheek.

Sean was the father of the seven O'Connor brothers. He was in his early sixties, but like Isabelle's father, didn't look even close to that. He wasn't as stern-looking as Kurt and always had a pleasant smile.

"Okay." Isabelle glanced between Roman and Sean.

"I'm going to go inside now. I hope you two figure out what this is before Kurt finds out." Sean smirked and walked inside.

They were quiet as the door to the pub closed and Isabelle propped her hip against the railing next to him. Roman was about to speak, but Isabelle cleared her throat and raised her eyes to meet his.

"Look, I don't want to talk about this here. Go to my house and I'll be there as soon as I can get away." Isabelle took his hand and pressed her key into his palm.

"Tiger, every time I go to your house, we don't do much talking." Roman closed his hand over hers.

“I know, but we’ll stay in the kitchen.” Isabelle smiled shyly.

“That didn’t help last night.” Roman chuckled, reminding her of their hot session on her kitchen counter.

“Go.” Isabelle rolled her eyes and pushed him toward the steps.

Roman kissed her on the cheek then made his way toward Isabelle’s house. The walk would help him think and put together exactly what he wanted to say. Hopefully, it wouldn’t send her running and screaming from the house. He had a feeling if he told Isabelle he’d developed feelings for her, she’d do just that, but she needed to know.

The last thing Roman wanted was to lose what he had with her. The sex was great, but he enjoyed their talks and the time they spent together..

The other problem was someone was fucking with her and not in a good way. Roman noticed too many things go wrong with the kitchen over the previous few months. Most of the equipment Isabelle had was top-of-the-line and shouldn’t break down as often as it did.

It was clear to him she was concerned because of the loss in business, but Roman was worried about Isabelle. Since he’d spent practically every night with her over the last few months, he knew she didn’t sleep well and when she did, she would toss and turn. The stress of her situation was probably causing her to get sick and that wasn't good for anyone.

She'd made him promise not to say anything to her family, which was difficult because they were always close by. Isabelle was the typical oldest child and wanted to protect her younger sisters and her parents from worrying about her.

Roman was worried, though. Her employees were hard workers and asked him in passing if they should look for other jobs. Roman didn't say anything to Isabelle and tried to make his co-workers feel at ease. Isabelle didn't need the added stress of worrying about losing her staff.

Roman stopped outside Isabelle's house and looked down toward the restaurant. He could see the entrance from the sidewalk in front of her house. It was time he helped Isabelle figure out what was going on and convince her to ask for help from her family.

Chapter 5

Isabelle itched to leave the pub and get back to her house. She wanted to talk to Roman and see where they were going. Was it possible they could have a future? She wanted one, that was for sure but with the possibility of losing her business, it was hard to think about starting a relationship.

"You look tired, sweet pea." Her father tucked her under his arm and she smiled.

"I'm okay, Dad." She wrapped her arms around his waist and hugged him.

"I worry about you." Her father kissed her temple and smiled down at her.

"You worry about all of us, but I promise, I'm fine. I do need to head home. I've got to go to the restaurant early tomorrow." She wasn't actually lying.

"I thought you hired that chef to take some of the work off your shoulders?" Her father narrowed his eyes.

"Dad, he's taken a lot off my shoulders, but I'm still the boss." Isabelle kissed his cheek. "I love you and I'm so proud of you. I'll see you later."

"Maybe I should have a chat with that boy and make sure he's pulling his weight." Her father raised an eyebrow.

"Dad, I'm the boss of my business. You're now the boss of Hopedale. You worry about that and I'll take care of my restaurant." Isabelle shook her head as she pulled on her jacket.

"Get one of the boys to drive you home. It's late." Her father motioned for Mike to come closer.

"For God's sake, Dad. I literally live five minutes up the street." Isabelle groaned.

"A lot can happen in five minutes." He wasn't going to give in on that and she knew it.

She rolled her eyes as her father shouted to Mike. Since he was one of the designated drivers for the evening, her father wouldn't have an issue with him driving her home. Not that Isabelle would either, but she figured it was faster to walk.

"What's up, Uncle Kurt?" Mike asked.

"Can you dart Isabelle home?" Her father said using a term that meant *drive* to most Newfoundlanders.

"Sure." Mike smiled and wrapped his arm around her shoulders.

By the time Isabelle and Mike made it outside it was twenty minutes later. Between the innuendos from her cousins, and her Aunt Cora hinting at finding love in the kitchen, it was like maneuvering a landmine of things she didn't want to hear.

"I didn't see Roman with you tonight," Mike said as they pulled onto the road.

"Why would he be with me?" Isabelle rubbed her hands up and down her thighs.

"Cuz, you live between John and Kristy. Do you think neither of them has seen Mr. Chef leaving your house in the mornings?" Mike smirked.

Living in the house between her sister and her cousin made it somewhat difficult to keep her antics a secret. She thought she did a good job of it, but apparently she'd only been fooling herself.

"Gossip runs rampant in Hopedale." Isabelle rolled her eyes.

"It's not gossip if it's true." Mike reached across and pinched her cheek.

"Are the lives of all the married couples in my family so boring that they have to gossip about mine?" Isabelle slapped his hand away.

"Well, you and Pam." Mike winked and pulled into her driveway.

"It's not good for things to be fizzling at this stage in your marriage, Mikey." Isabelle pushed open the car door and stepped out.

"We're far from fizzling, cuz. As a matter of fact with this pregnancy, she's like a dog in heat." Mike wiggled his eyebrows.

"Oh, should I call Billie and tell her you compared her to a dog?" Isabelle smirked.

"You do and I'll tell Uncle Kurt to drop over to your house tonight." Mike nodded toward the open door of her house where Roman stood leaning against the doorjamb.

"Don't you dare. I'll castrate you," Isabelle warned and slammed the car door.

She heard Mike laugh as he waved to Roman and backed out of the driveway. She knew her cousin wouldn't say a word to her father unless Isabelle wanted him to. The last thing she needed was her dad arriving and asking what was going on between her and Roman. It would be hard to tell him when she didn't know the answer herself.

Isabelle made her way toward the steps and couldn't help but smile at Roman when he gave her a flirty wink. As she was about to make her way up the steps, her cell rang in her pocket. She pulled it out and tapped the screen.

"Hello." Isabelle answered.

"Hey, Boss. Sorry to call so late but I left my purse in my locker in the staff room." Cindy groaned.

"Do you have the keys to the restaurant?" Isabelle asked.

"Yeah, I just wanted to let you know I was running in there to get my purse." Cindy replied

"That wasn't necessary, but thanks for the heads up. Just make sure you reset the alarm." Isabelle reminded her.

"I will." Cindy said in her usual perky voice. "See you tomorrow."

Isabelle chuckled as she ended the call. Cindy often opened or closed the restaurant so she'd been given her own set of keys and the code for the alarm. No matter how dramatic the girl could be, Isabelle trusted her completely.

"Why exactly are you going to castrate Mike?" Roman laughed as she walked into the house.

"Because he's an ass." Isabelle shrugged out of her jacket and hung it up in the front closet.

"Remind me not to be an ass around you." Roman stood behind her and wrapped his arms around her waist.

He pulled her back into his body and she closed her eyes, relaxing into his embrace. He had a way of helping her calm down and stressing her out all at the same time. Roman seemed to read her every mood, which pissed her off because she could never read his.

"You're an ass all the time," Isabelle whispered as he nuzzled the side of her neck.

"That's not nice." He chuckled.

"Neither is trying to distract me from the fact that you let Mike see you here." She sighed as his lips feathered against the edge of her ear.

"I thought I heard someone on the front steps, but when I opened the door, nobody was there, then you guys pulled into the driveway," Roman said.

"You heard someone on my step?" Isabelle spun around in his arms and her heart started to pound in her chest.

"Hey, relax. I think it was just the wind knocking that tree branch off the overhang." Roman cupped her face in his hands. "Tiger, is there something you're not telling me?"

"No. I've just been hearing things around the house at night. Mostly when you're not here." She stepped back from him and turned toward the kitchen.

"I told you that you should get Keith to install a surveillance camera on the front of your house." Roman walked behind her.

"I told you I don't need it with John on one side and Bull on the other." Isabelle rolled her eyes.

Her cousin John was a police officer and was next in line to be the new Chief of Police. Dean "Bull" Nash was co-owner of

Newfoundland Security Services with Keith. He was also married to her sister Kristy and would snap someone's neck if they tried to get into Isabelle's house.

"You want a beer?" Isabelle pulled two bottles out of the fridge and held one out to Roman.

"No, I want my head clear when we talk." Roman took both bottles and put them back in the fridge.

"Seriously?" Isabelle glared at him.

"Yeah, seriously." Roman took her hand and dragged her out of the kitchen into the living room.

When he sat down, he tugged her down next to him. Isabelle watched him for a few seconds and it seemed as if he was at a loss for words. She'd never seen Roman speechless.

"I don't want to sneak around anymore," he finally blurted out.

"You make it sound like something torrid." Isabelle flopped back on the sofa.

"I don't mean to. Tiger, I really like you. A lot. I want more with you than what we've been doing." Roman rested back against the couch and linked his fingers with her.

"I like what we've been doing." Isabelle shoved him with her shoulder.

"I didn't say I didn't like that part, but I would like more." He reached across and turned her face so she had to look at him. "Isabelle, I don't want you to think that the only thing between us is just what happens in your bed."

"Roman." Isabelle sighed his name.

"I care about you and every time I look into those beautiful blue eyes, it steals my breath away. You make my heart race, and I'm not arrogant, but I know I make yours do the same." Roman gazed into her eyes. "I know we can build something. You just have to let down that guard."

Isabelle swallowed the lump in her throat. He always said such beautiful words when he talked to her and sometimes it was hard for her to think around him. He was right about the way he made her feel, but could what they have lead to something more?

Sexually they were perfect together, but it had been so long since she'd been in a serious relationship, Isabelle didn't know if she even knew how to be part of a couple. Over the last fifteen years, her life had been working her ass off getting her restaurant to where it was, and less than a dozen dates.

Roman was the first man in a long time to spend more than a night or two with her. Not that she slept around but she did have a few dates that ended up with her doing the walk of shame. Nothing to be ashamed of, it was just a way of letting off some steam with meaningless sex.

"What's going through that beautiful brain of yours?" Roman tucked a piece of hair behind her ear.

"Nothing, really," she lied.

"At least nothing you want to tell me, right?" Roman smirked.

"It's just… I've got to figure out what's going on with my restaurant." As much as she wanted to be on the same page with Roman, her business was in trouble.

"You don't have to do this alone. I can help, and if you'd talk to your family, maybe they could help too." Roman wrapped his arm around her shoulder and tucked her into his side.

"Do you know what my family has been through the last few years? Between crazy exes, sadistic serial killers, and assholes trying to hurt other people, it's a wonder all my family aren't in a mental hospital. The last thing they need is more crazy in their lives." She turned her face into his chest and inhaled his spicy scent.

Isabelle had watched her two sisters and seven cousins find love and start families, but it hadn't been easy for any of them. It was difficult to put any more stress into any of their lives.

"Then I'll help you figure things out, but only on one condition." He put his finger under her chin and gently tipped her head up so she had to look into his chocolate-brown eyes.

“What condition would that be?” Isabelle ran her hand over the top of his head and threaded her fingers in the hair on the back of his head.

“Let me take you on a date.” He smirked.

“And when exactly would we have time to go on this date?” Isabelle sighed.

With only three chefs in the restaurant, there was never an evening they were both off together. Sure, she could arrange the schedule to make sure that happened, but then they wouldn’t have a hostess for that night. She did need to take more time to herself, but how could she do that when her business was falling down around her?

“You know we can take at least one night together.” Roman brushed a kiss across her lips.

“Hmm… maybe,” she whispered as he gently nipped her lower lip.

“You can schedule us both off on a Tuesday night. It’s the slowest.” He ran a finger across her jaw.

“Lately, every night has been slow.” Isabelle kissed under his chin.

“Don’t worry, Tiger. It’s just a slump, it’ll pick up.” He tilted his head back as she kissed down the side of his neck.

“I hope so.” Isabelle shifted until she straddled his legs.

“What are you doing?” He smirked as she started to open his shirt.

“If you have to ask, then I must be doing something different.” She pulled open his shirt and lightly ran her nails down his chest.

“Tiger, I thought we were going to talk about us.” He slipped his hands under the back of her shirt and pulled her closer.

“We did.” She swiveled her hips and pressed her core hard against his growing erection.

“No, I talked and you sidestepped.” He grabbed her hips and held her in place.

“You aren’t going to drop this, are you?” In the last year, Isabelle learned how stubborn Roman could be.

“Not when I want something this badly.” He leaned forward and softly kissed the side of her neck.

“Hmm… you don’t play fair.” She moaned.

“Date?” Roman whispered against her ear.

“Yes,” she groaned as he sucked her earlobe into his mouth.

“Tuesday?” He practically growled into her ear.

“Yes,” she whispered as his hand slipped inside the bottom of her shirt and slid up to cup her breast.

"I'll pick you up at seven?" He pinched her nipple gently through her bra, sending sensations down to her pussy.

"God, yes." She moaned and threw back her head.

"Good." Roman lifted her off his lap and put her on the couch next to him.

"What are you doing?" She stared at him in utter confusion as he stood up and buttoned up his shirt.

"I'm going home. I've got to work in the morning and my boss is a ball buster." Roman pulled on his jacket and held out his hand.

"Are you serious right now?" Isabelle glared at him.

"Very. I'm going to do this right. No more upstairs at least until we've been dating for a few weeks." Roman wiggled his fingers out to her.

"You're just going to leave?" Isabelle stood up and slapped his hand away.

"Yes." He reached for her, but she walked by him to the front door.

A few seconds later, he walked in front of her and pulled her against his body. She pushed back and narrowed her eyes at him. How could he leave her turned on?

"I know you're pissed right now, but I told you, I want more than sex." Roman gave her a quick kiss on the cheek, then left closing the door behind him.

"Are you fucking kidding me?" Isabelle stood in her foyer with her mouth hung open and staring at the door.

Chapter 6

It took every ounce of strength and determination Roman had to walk away from Isabelle. His dick probably hated him at the moment, but he was determined to make his relationship with Isabelle more than physical. It definitely wouldn't be easy.

He strolled down the road where Isabelle's restaurant stood on the corner of Harbour Street and Beach Street. It would help him cool his desire while he walked home to the apartment he shared with Ethan.

Ethan rented an apartment over a beauty salon owned by Keith's wife, Emily, and Kim Newman. It was temporary until Roman could find a place of his own. It was a one-bedroom apartment with a kitchen and living room. Ethan slept in the bedroom while Roman crashed on the pull-out couch in the living room. Although, it had been a while since he'd slept there. Most nights, he'd been with Isabelle and only stopped back there to get a change of clothes.

He walked around the corner and looked up at the restaurant. It was a perfect location on one of the busiest roads in the town and across from the beach. The outside screamed elegant with large windows across the front and a glass entrance with the name of the restaurant etched into it.

Months earlier, Roman and Ethan discussed going into business together. They wanted to reopen the club under its original name and give it a better reputation. They'd made several offers on the property and received counter-offers that were still beyond their budget. Roman wondered if it was worth the aggravation.

Of course he didn't want to go into competition with Isabelle either. She mentioned she wanted to expand *A Taste of Hopedale* and looked into buying the building attached to her restaurant, but she'd given up the idea because the owners were asking too much.

The building was a former dance club that had closed up a couple of years earlier. *The Rock* had a sketchy past and the owners locked the doors one evening and never reopened. The building was bought by *Landell Corp* a short time later. It still remained vacant, and Isabelle even took a tour of the premises. It was shortly after that when things started to go downhill.

Roman doubted if she would consider the idea now, but he'd thought long and hard about offering her a deal. He had enough money from the sale of his family home and the inheritance he received after his mother died to buy into the business.

The thought of going into a partnership with Isabelle sounded like a good idea, but he had a feeling if he offered it to her now, she'd think he was seducing her to get what he wanted. Nothing was further from the truth. She was the reason he'd put the idea on the backburner.

Roman walked in front of the building that used to house the dance club. He glanced to where the name used to sit perched on top of the building. A huge rock with the name of the place carved into it. *The Rock* was a fitting name since Newfoundland was often called by the same name.

Roman was surprised to see it was gone, as was the *for sale* sign. *Landell Corp* had bought the building, but they were also looking to sell it again. His heart dropped. If someone bought it, it meant he missed his opportunity to buy it. So did Isabelle.

By the time he got to *Snippy Gals,* the salon that Ethan lived above, he was cold from the bitter wind that had started to pick up. He quickly walked around the side to the steps that led to the apartment. He wanted to get inside and check the website to see if the building was still posted on the real estate site. If it was sold, it might have something to do with why Isabelle was losing business.

Roman entered the apartment to find Ethan on the couch, shirtless and practically on top of a giggling woman. Ethan's head popped up and the girl squeaked in surprise. Roman tapped down the urge to roll his eyes

"Shit, I didn't realize you were coming back tonight." Ethan jumped up and the girl quickly adjusted her clothes.

“Sorry, I should’ve called.” Roman tried not to laugh at the way the woman struggled to pull her jeans up while trying to stay hidden behind Ethan.

“We’ll move this to the bedroom.” Ethan reached for the girl, but she looked completely panicked.

“I actually need to go.” She grabbed her purse from the coffee table and practically ran out the door.

“Wait.” Ethan ran after her and Roman chuckled as he slipped out of his jacket and pulled off his hat.

Roman grabbed his laptop from inside the bench Ethan used as a coffee table. He cursed when he realized it was completely dead. After plugging it in, he used his smartphone to find what he was looking for.

He’d just found the listing for the building when Ethan returned and glared at him. It was obvious the woman didn’t like the idea of another man in the apartment. He couldn’t blame her. Women had to be careful to begin with, and although neither of them would ever do something to harm anyone, the girl couldn’t know that for sure.

“She thought I was setting her up for a threesome,” Ethan grumbled as he flopped down in the armchair.

“Sorry, buddy. I don’t cross swords. Even with my best friend.” Roman laughed as he locked his phone.

He jumped up and tossed the couch cushions aside so he could pull out the fold away bed. It wasn't the most comfortable thing in the world, especially since he'd gotten used to Isabelle's king-size bed, but it would do.

"Did you think I'd suggest that?" Ethan snorted.

"No, but apparently your little friend wasn't so sure." Roman laughed as he collapsed down on the bed and tucked his arms under his head.

"I thought you'd be spending the night with Isabelle." Ethan raised an eyebrow.

"Not tonight. I need to pull back on that if she's going to believe I'm serious about building something with her." Roman never thought he'd ever uttered such a statement.

"You really like her, don't you?" Ethan leaned forward and rested his elbows on his knees.

"I do," Roman admitted.

"Good for you, buddy. She's great. I hope it works out." Ethan stood up and stretched his arms over his head. "Since I'm sleeping alone tonight, I might as well head to bed."

"Maybe you should start thinking about cutting down on the women you take home," Roman yelled after him.

"I'll keep that in mind, Mom," Ethan shouted back and then the bedroom door closed.

At thirty-eight, playing the field was getting old and Roman was tired. Ethan didn't seem to mind it, but once Roman laid eyes on Isabelle, he didn't want another woman, ever. Maybe Cora was right. Roman knew, after Isabelle, he'd never be happy with another woman.

Chapter 7

Isabelle ran like there was a lion chasing her. She had hardly slept all night and finally decided at five in the morning to get her daily run over with. Hopefully, the exercise would get her out of her pissy mood and she wouldn't feel as exhausted. When she looked outside, it only irritated her more to see the wet snow falling fast and hard.

It was why she ran on her treadmill and listened to *Work Bitch* by Britney Spears so loud that it was practically making her ears hurt. She wasn't like her sister Jess or Ian's wife, Sandy. They worked out all the time, but Isabelle only had time to run in the morning before work.

Her current workout was because she was sexually frustrated after Roman left her unsatisfied the previous night. Sure, she took care of herself, but that merely scratched the itch. It wasn't like she felt after sex with Roman. He always left her fully satisfied and happily exhausted.

"Leave me wound up, will you? This is why I've stayed single for so long." Isabelle panted as she started to slow down her run.

Ten minutes later, she hopped off the treadmill and headed to the shower. She had to shake her cranky mood before the restaurant opened. Isabelle was on hostess duty all day and it wouldn't be good for business if she was nasty with the customers. Her mood was also partly because she still hadn't bounced back from the stomach virus she'd had the previous week. With her energy level still on empty, it was difficult to get going, but she didn't have a choice.

She really needed to hire someone specifically for the hostess position, but with the way things were going, she didn't know if it was a good idea to hire anyone.

Then again, she would be able to spend more time doing what she loved if she did have a full-time hostess. That also meant she would have to work side by side with Roman. She probably shouldn't make that decision in her current mood.

By the time she'd showered and eaten, it was still way too early to go to work, but she didn't have anything left to do in her house and she was getting more irritated with the way Roman left the night before.

If she thought about it clearly, it was sweet that he wanted to do things right and start out with a date. Most women would think it was romantic, and she did, but the problem was they were way beyond the flirty first-date crap.

Isabelle pulled out the keys to the restaurant and unlocked the door. The sounds of the ocean crashing against the rocks on the beach echoed behind her as she pulled open the door. She was about to step inside when a hand fell on her shoulder.

Isabelle gasped as she spun around and dropped her open purse on the ground. Her head came to the shoulder of a tall man in running gear and when she looked up at the smirking man she wanted to punch him in his well-developed abdomen.

"Jesus, Mary and Joseph, Bruce. Why don't you just shoot me instead of trying to give me a heart attack?" Isabelle grumbled as she crouched to pick up her purse.

"Sorry, I thought you heard me call out to you. I wish you and your sisters would call me Hulk like everyone else. I hear that name and I almost turn around to see who you're talking too." Hulk crouched and helped her pick up her things.

"Nan calls you Bruce." Isabelle laughed. "You going to tell her to knock it off too?"

"That would be a huge no." Hulk chuckled.

"I was concentrating on the sound of the waves when you walked up. That's why you frightened me." Isabelle smiled as she stood up and shoved her things back into her bag.

"I wanted to stop by to see you later today, but when I saw you, I figured I'd see if you were available to chat now." Hulk handed her a lipstick.

"Sure, I just thought I'd get an early start today." Isabelle motioned for him to follow her inside.

"Do you always come in at seven in the morning?" Hulk asked as they stepped inside and Isabelle locked the door again.

Bruce "Hulk" Steel was one of the security professionals who worked for Newfoundland Security Services. Like the rest of the staff, he went by his nickname. The names had something to do with their personalities or because of something stupid they did. Isabelle had no idea why they all did that but assumed it had something to do with security.

Hulk was especially close to Nick and his wife. He had been put on security duty when Lora was being stalked a few years earlier. Hulk had been shot by the crazy guy and almost lost his life. He also had a soft spot for Lora's daughter, Molly. If Isabelle thought about it, the big man had a soft spot for all the kids in her family.

Hulk bought a house a couple of years earlier and only lived a few streets from Isabelle. She didn't know why a single man would want to purchase a four-bedroom, two-story house for just himself, but he did.

He was hot and in great shape, but to Isabelle he was the same as one of her cousins. Like the brothers she never asked for. Hulk was quiet most of the time, but he was always there when anyone in her family needed him. Just like all the guys who worked for Keith and Bull.

"You look like you could use some water." Isabelle pulled two bottles out of the fridge behind the bar and handed one to Hulk.

"Yeah, I should probably start taking a water bottle with me when I run. I usually get back to the house and down a gallon." Hulk chuckled as he twisted the top off the bottle.

"So, what's up?" Isabelle asked.

"Well, I was wondering if you were hiring?" He seemed embarrassed to ask.

"Keith not paying you enough?" She joked because Isabelle knew Keith's staff were paid very well.

"It's not for me. I've got a friend who's a single mother and her current employer has cut back on her hours. She has two young kids and her mom lives with her too. They're moving to Hopedale." Hulk didn't meet her eyes.

"Is this a girlfriend?" Isabelle teased.

Sandy was convinced Hulk was dating someone in the city but hadn't been able to find out for sure. It was strange for Sandy to come up with nothing because she was one of the best computer analysts in the country. Usually, nobody could keep anything from her.

"No, she's a *friend* who needs help. She's going to be moving into my house with her kids and mom." Hulk emphasized the word *friend.*

"That's going to take some getting used to for you." Isabelle rested her elbows on the bar.

"No, I'm moving into one of the bunk houses until she gets back on her feet." He glanced down at his hands.

The bunkhouses were basically small cottages that Keith had built on the back of his large property. When he first moved his company to Newfoundland, he wanted to have a place where his employees could be comfortable and feel at home. Most of the guys decided to settle in Hopedale and were buying their own homes around town. It left the cozy houses mostly empty.

"She doesn't know it's your house, does she?" Isabelle knew the answer before she asked the question.

"She won't accept charity. I'd rather you keep that little tidbit to yourself." Hulk looked up.

"I can, but you've met the rest of my family, right?" Isabelle laughed.

"I'll deal with that as it comes." Hulk steepled his fingers in front of his mouth and looked at her hopefully.

“Does she have experience?” Isabelle could tell this was important to Hulk.

“She’s been working at a coffee shop for the last ten years. The man she works for is giving her a hard time and cutting her hours because she asked him to not have her working late at night.” Hulk’s jaw clenched.

“Well, we’re open until nine.” Isabelle needed to make sure that he was aware of the hours.

“This guy has her working until midnight, and she misses time with her kids. The only help she has is her mom and since her mother babysits, she has to walk home, at night, in the city by herself. She leaves the vehicle for her mother,” Hulk explained.

Isabelle tried not to let him see her smile because by Hulk’s reaction, he definitely felt more than friendship for this woman. Sandy had said he seemed to spend a lot of time in town and when she’d checked into it, he’d rented a small apartment downtown. When Sandy mentioned it to Hulk, he told her it was for those days he didn’t want to make the drive back to Hopedale.

“What’s her name?” Isabelle asked.

“Caroline Baker.” His tone was almost reverent as he said her name.

“Tell her to drop by today around two. It will be slower, and I can have a chat with her. I can’t promise anything. You might want to check with Mom as well.” Isabelle smiled as Hulk stood up.

Isabelle's mom had a soft spot for people struggling. Especially a single mother raising two kids on her own. Isabelle knew of several waitresses her mother had hired over the years, even when she didn't need extra help. That was the O'Connor way and how Lora and Nick met.

"I'll ask Alice if you can't find a position for Caroline." Hulk walked toward the exit.

"Is there anything else I shouldn't let slip to your friend. I mean, you're hiding that it's your house she's renting?" Isabelle unlocked the door for Hulk.

"I'm not hiding it. It's just information she doesn't need to worry about." He winked.

"Should I tell her how you got the name Hulk?" Isabelle chuckled as he spun around and glared at her.

"No, that's another tidbit she doesn't need to know." He pointed his finger at Isabelle and then backed up a couple of steps.

Emily had told her the story of how Hulk got his nickname and she'd laughed so hard her stomach hurt. When Keith first hired Hulk, they'd found an old rundown building for the offices and sleeping quarters. They were painting the offices and the bedrooms, and there was a slight disagreement between two of the other guys about the color of the main room. The guys got physical over whether they should use green or blue.

Hulk had been in bed with a woman when he heard the argument and ran out of the room naked to see what the commotion was. He bumped into a ladder left in front of Hulk's bedroom door, and he knocked an entire can of green paint over himself.

They started calling him Hulk because he started growling and it took a long time to remove all the paint from his body. The fact that his name was Bruce just made the name stick better.

"Keith is an asshole for telling his wife that story." He waved as he turned and broke into a jog.

Isabelle chuckled as she closed and locked the door again. The little chat with Hulk distracted her for a little while and she didn't feel so pissed. She was about to push through the door leading to the kitchen when she heard a thud from the dining room. She glanced around as she walked through the dining area, but nothing was tipped over and all the chairs were still upside down on the tables.

Isabelle stepped next to the large row of floor-to-ceiling windows that ran along the front of her building, but the only things out there were the beach and a couple of people either jogging or walking up and down the road.

"What the hell?" Isabelle muttered to herself.

As she turned to make her way back to the kitchen, she saw one of the tiles on the ceiling pushed back and she stepped closer to look up inside. The tile was still up in the ceiling, but it was pushed to the side. She sighed as she turned around and made a mental note to get one of the guys to get up and fix it.

She'd just taken two steps when she saw exactly what made the thud. A large rat lay on the floor, but it didn't move. Isabelle screamed and ran back to the exit of the restaurant. She shook as she fumbled to unlock the door. When she heard the lock disengage, she yanked open the door and leaped outside.

She tripped as she practically ran down the two steps of the entrance. Isabelle flailed her arms to prevent herself from falling to the pavement, but before she hit the ground, two arms wrapped around her.

Chapter 8

Roman saw her bolt out of the restaurant as he stepped in front of the entrance. The distress on her face had him running toward her and catching her just before she hit the pavement.

"It's big, oh my, God. It's so huge," Isabelle said as he helped her to steady herself on her feet.

"Thanks, Tiger but I don't think it's that big." He forced a smile hoping his attempt at humor would calm her trembling.

"Seriously, an over-exaggerated penis joke?" Isabelle glared at him.

"Hey, I didn't over-exaggerate anything." He narrowed his eyes, but when she glanced at the restaurant again, he realized she wasn't in a joking mood.

"There's a huge rat in the middle of the dining room." Isabelle leaned into him and whispered.

"Rat?" He stared at her.

"Yes, I don't know if it's dead or alive but I heard a thump and when I went into the dining room, it was laying next to one of the back tables." Isabelle shuddered.

"I'll go in and check." He pulled on the door and stepped inside.

"I'm not going in there with you. If that thing attacks you, you're on your own." Isabelle wrapped her arms around herself.

"I'm touched by your concern." Roman chuckled as he made his way into the restaurant.

Roman grabbed the shovel next to the front door that they left there for clearing the step. As he slowly made his way into the dining room, he scanned the floor. He walked by each table, looking closely around every table. He couldn't see anything at first and was about to walk back out to let her know whatever was there was gone, but then he saw the dark-brown fur lying motionless next to the leg of one of the tables.

He poked it with the shovel, but it didn't move. He took a step closer to the large rodent and saw the eyes and the mouth were open. It was dead, but he wanted to know where it came from. In all the time working in the building, he'd never seen any sign of rodents. Isabelle had pest control come every six months as prevention.

"Is it still there?" Isabelle called from the doorway.

"Yeah, I think you should call pest control," Roman shouted back to her as he tipped his head back and looked up.

Roman noticed the opening in the ceiling. It looked like it had been shoved out of the way and not put back properly. It was probably where the rat came from. Roman wasn't an expert, but the rodent looked like it had been dead for more than a few minutes.

"God, they were just here like two weeks ago and said everything was clear. I hate calling them," Isabelle complained as she dug into her purse.

"It's better to get them in now to make sure there isn't an issue. Especially with the empty building next door." Roman walked toward her.

Isabelle crawled up on one of the bar stools and propped her feet up on another. She looked about ready to jump out of her skin as she explained to the pest control company what had happened. It was so damn cute.

When Roman placed a hand on her shoulder, she jumped and almost toppled off the stool. He smirked when she narrowed her eyes to glare at him. It seemed like Isabelle had a fear of rats. Not that he could blame her, he didn't like the things either.

She ended her call and climbed up to sit on the bar with her feet propped up on one of the bar stools. She nervously glanced around her as if she was waiting for something to jump out.

"You know rats can climb, right?" Roman rested his arms on top of the bar.

"You're not helping." Isabelle flicked her hand against his arm.

"Calm down, Tiger. For what it's worth, I don't think you have a rat issue. If you did, we would have seen droppings in the kitchen before now." Roman rested a hand on her knee and she flinched.

Isabelle covered her face with her hands and swiped them down until they dropped in her lap. He could see the tension on her face, and he understood. The last thing she needed was for word to get out that she had rats in her restaurant.

"I'm not going to be able to open today because of this. I can't have people coming in here until I know it's been cleaned top to bottom. Who knows where that thing was?" Isabelle shuddered.

"Are you afraid of all rodents, or just rats in general?" Roman stepped closer and slipped his arms around her waist.

"Not all rodents, I'm not afraid of you." Isabelle raised an eyebrow and gave him the sexiest smirk he'd ever seen.

"Oh, I'm a rodent now." He gripped her hips and pulled her to the edge of the bar.

"Maybe not a rodent, but you're a pain in my butt." She pulled back when he moved in for a quick kiss.

"Are you upset with me?" He tilted his head and carefully studied her expression.

"Not really, but you're the one who said you wanted to start with a date. We haven't even had a first date and you're trying to kiss me." Isabelle leaned back on her hands and he was sure she purposely stuck out her full breasts to drive him insane.

Before he had a chance to say anything, there was a knock on the door. He turned to see one of the guys from *O'Ryan Pest Control* waiting outside the door. Roman stepped away from Isabelle and let the older man into the building.

"Heard you had an unwanted guest." The man grinned.

"Yeah, over here." Roman led the man to the dining area.

The name Gerald was embroidered on the man's jacket, and as he crouched next to the rat, Gerald gave Roman a full view of a buttcrack. Roman stepped around him as Gerald poked at the carcass with a gloved hand, but when he picked up the dead rat and sniffed it, Roman almost threw up.

"The good news is this has been dead for a few days. I can tell by the smell." Gerald dropped the rat into the orange bag he'd carried in with him.

"I think it fell down from that corner." Roman pointed to the opening in the ceiling.

"It's possible. I'll put a few more rat boxes up in the ceiling there and I'll check the ones inside and outside. I'm a little confused because in the five years I've been doing this place, I've never seen any of the boxes disturbed." Gerald closed the bag and walked to where the ceiling was opened.

"The building next door is empty. Maybe they're coming in from there." Roman shrugged.

"It's possible, but the bad news is these guys don't travel alone." Gerald pointed a flashlight up into the ceiling.

"Can you check everything out? Isabelle can't open until we're sure that guy is the only one going to fall out of the ceiling." Roman glanced back to see Isabelle still on top of the bar.

"I'll be back in two shakes of a lamb's tail," Gerald said as he ambled around Roman and made his way outside to his truck.

"He's going to check everything," Roman told Isabelle as she pulled the phone from her ear.

"Good. I just called the staff and told them what happened. They're going to come in and help sterilize the place as long as Gerald makes sure it's not going to start raining rodents." Isabelle glanced up toward the ceiling.

"Well, if you stay up there, we won't get anything started." Roman held out his hand.

Isabelle stared at it for a second before taking it and jumping down to the floor. He brought her hand to his lips and kissed it quickly as he motioned for her to go ahead of him into the kitchen.

"Not a chance, buddy. You go in there first and make sure there's nothing in there." She stepped behind him and pushed him toward the kitchen entrance.

"First time I've ever seen a tiger afraid of a rat." Roman chuckled and dodged her when she swung her hand to slap his arm.

Once he did a full check of the kitchen, freezer, storage, and her office, Roman shouted to tell her everything was clear. While he did his check, he made sure to pay special attention to possible hiding spaces for pests. What he did notice was the lack of fecal matter.

If there was a rodent problem, there would definitely be droppings somewhere. There wasn't. So where did the dead rat come from and why did it suddenly break through the ceiling?

"Shit," Isabelle spat, bringing him out of his thoughts.

"What?" Roman responded.

"I promised Bruce, I mean Hulk, that I'd meet with a friend of his about a possible job here." She sighed and leaned against the counter.

"Didn't you say things were tight because of all the equipment you've had to repair and replace?" Roman knew she'd been stressed about finances.

"I know but we need a full-time hostess so I can come back to the kitchen." She pushed off the counter and headed toward the supply room.

“You just want to be back here with me,” Roman teased as he followed her.

Isabelle grabbed the knob of the closet but spun around at his words to give him that defiant glare. He loved to tease her but something in her expression concerned him. She seemed freaked.

“Let me make one thing clear right now, Roman. Our relationship, or whatever you want to call this, does not come inside this building. Here, I’m your boss and I don’t mean to make that sound like I’m a bitch, but I want to keep it separate,” she said and he understood.

“I get it.” He smiled.

He realized she was about to go into the supply closet and he’d forgotten to check the tiny room. Roman figured if there weren’t rats anywhere else that the room was probably clear as well, but he started toward her.

“Good.” She smiled and yanked open the door before he could stop her.

As the door swung open, her smile vanished, her eyes widened, and she turned completely white. Roman gently guided her back so he could see what had frightened her, but what he saw was the last thing he expected.

A body lay face-down on the floor in a pool of blood that appeared to have been there for a while. Roman guided Isabelle out of the entrance so she didn’t have to witness the scene any longer.

The last thing she needed after the start of her day was to add the image of a dead body to her nightmare.

Since Roman had worked as a paramedic before he changed careers, he knew by the waxy color of the hands and large amount of blood that the woman had been dead for a while. To be sure he took a careful step into the small closet and checked for a pulse, but he knew he wouldn't find one.

Roman had no idea who the poor woman was, and he couldn't move her to see her face. It didn't matter because suddenly, the rat was the least of Isabelle's problems.

Chapter 9

"Oh, God. Oh, God." Isabelle backed from the room as Roman closed the door.

Her heart pounded frantically in her chest and she found it hard to catch her breath. She slowly shook her head as if it could help clear the image she'd just witnessed. Did she really just see a body? A body. A bloody mess of a woman, and Isabelle had no idea who it was.

Isabelle had never seen a body before it had been cleaned up by a mortician. Her hands shook and she clasped them in front of her to try to control the trembling. She lifted her eyes until she met Roman's gaze. Even with the fact there was not only a rat in her place, but a deceased person as well, Roman's presence kept her from completely losing it.

"We need to call the police." Roman lifted the phone to his ear.

Why didn't she think of that? Her father was the former Chief of Police and her cousins were cops. It should have occurred to her to make that call.

"Yes, I'm sure the woman is dead." Roman sounded impatient. "I checked for a pulse. There's no sign of life and her body is cold."

His jaw clenched as he took Isabelle's hand and tugged her from the kitchen. Roman continued to talk to the operator as he hustled Isabelle outside the building. She didn't resist and allowed him to take control because her brain wasn't working at that moment.

A lump formed in her throat as she thought about the unknown corpse lying in her cleaning closet like a piece of trash. Isabelle hadn't seen too much, but she did know there was a lot of blood. The poor girl must have suffered tremendously.

"Gerald, we'll have to get you to come back to deal with all this. Right now, we've got bigger problems." Roman stopped the pest control man from entering the restaurant.

Isabelle's legs felt as if they were about to buckle under her and she sank down to the curb. She glanced up at Roman and saw his mouth moving, but she couldn't hear him. The only thing she could hear was the roaring in her ears. Her stomach lurched and she felt as if she was about to vomit as everything around her started to spin. She took several deep breaths as she closed her eyes to make it stop.

Warm hands cupped her cheeks and she opened her eyes to see Roman in front of her. She blinked her eyes several times to focus but he seemed to drift further and further away. She tried to reach for him, but her arms were heavy and right before everything went black, she heard him shout for help.

Isabelle opened her eyes and a familiar paramedic stared down at her. Bobby Tucker was an old schoolmate of Mike's and had remained a close friend with her cousin. She just couldn't figure out why Bobby seemed to be hovering above her.

"Hi there. It's good to see your eyes open." Bobby held his finger up in front of her face.

"I didn't know my eyes were closed." Isabelle tried to turn her head but everything spun.

"They were closed tight. You passed out." Bobby chuckled. "Can you follow my finger with only your eyes?"

Isabelle focused on his finger as he moved it from side to side, then up and down. He checked her pulse and nodded to someone she wasn't able to see. Isabelle realized that she was lying on gurney in the back of an ambulance when she started to glance around.

"I think she should go to the hospital to be safe," Bobby told the person behind her.

Isabelle turned her head and looked up. Roman seemed completely frantic with his hair mussed as if he'd ran his fingers through it. He looked unusually pale, which was odd because he always looked as if he had a nice tan. It only looked worse with the red and blue lights that reflected off his face.

Wait, red and blue lights?

“What happened?” She tried to lift her head but it wasn’t a real good idea.

“You fainted.” Roman held her hand between his.

“I don’t faint,” she grumbled.

“I think finding a dead body in your restaurant might have been a little too much for you, cuz.” Aaron’s voice caused her to glance out through the opened ambulance doors.

Aaron worked in the homicide division of the Hopedale division of the Newfoundland Police Department. He was the youngest of the brothers and everyone called him A.J. Except for his wife, Bethany. For some reason, she always called him Aaron.

“Who is it, A.J.?” Isabelle fought both Bobby and Roman so that she could sit up.

“I can’t confirm right now, Isabelle,” Aaron said.

Isabelle should have known he couldn’t tell her anything until the investigation was over. Thinking about the poor woman thrown in her cleaning closet like trash made Isabelle stomach sick. She had to know who the poor girl was and what happened to her.

“There was so much blood.” Isabelle swallowed the bile in her throat.

“Tiger, we need to get you to the hospital and make sure you’re okay.” Roman tucked a piece of her hair behind her ear.

“Seriously, there’s a woman dead in my restaurant and you want me to go see if *I’m* okay. I’m still alive. That woman is dead.” Isabelle dropped her head and covered her face with her hands.

“Isabelle, he’s right. There’s nothing we can do for that woman except to find out what happened. That’s my job. You need to go make sure you’re okay. You may feel fine, but you fainted and you could be in shock.” Aaron hopped up in the back of the ambulance and crouched in front of her.

“A.J., I need my phone. I’ve got to call my staff and let them know what happened.” Isabelle shook her head to try and clear her thoughts.

Roman put something in her hand and she glanced down to see her cell. She didn’t remember taking it, but she was in such a state of shock she couldn’t be sure. She hardly remembered walking out of the restaurant.

“I grabbed it off the bar when we were coming out of the building.” Roman squeezed her hand just before he released it.

Isabelle tapped the screen several times and brought up the folder that contained all her staff members’ information. What was she supposed to tell them? She basically called less than an hour ago to tell them she needed them to come in to sanitize the whole place. Now she had to tell them not to come in because a dead rat was the least of the problem. Isabelle held her finger over Milly's phone number and after a deep breath, she tapped it.

The phone rang several times before anyone answered, but it wasn't Milly. The only other person that would answer her phone would be her husband, but the male voice that answered seemed a little off to Isabelle.

"Ah, hello." It was Jake, but he sounded low and his voice sounded strained.

"Jake?" Isabelle had to make sure.

"Shit, umm... yeah." Jake cleared his throat.

"Jake, can I speak to Milly?" Isabelle asked.

There was silence, and for a moment, Isabelle thought the call might have dropped. When she checked the screen, Milly's name was still there. She heard Jake clear his throat again.

"She's… she can't come to the phone… not here." Jake sounded as if he strained to say the words and it made Isabelle sit up straight because it wasn't like Jake.

"Jake, for God's sake, give me the phone." The sound of Milly's voice gave Isabelle a huge sense of relief.

For a moment, the conversation between the couple was muffled and then Milly laughed. Isabelle hated to ruin that happiness, but she was about to do just that.

“Sorry, Isabelle. Jake and I were kind of in the middle of… something.” Milly chuckled.

“God, I’m sorry, Milly. This makes what I have to tell you that much worse.” Isabelle blew out a breath.

“What’s wrong?” Milly’s playful tone turned serious.

“Milly, the restaurant won’t be opened today.” Isabelle swallowed hard.

“Honey, you already called about that. Did that old rat freak you out that much?” Milly teased.

“Milly, the rat wasn’t the only thing we found this morning. Milly… we found a body in the cleaning closet.” Isabelle knew the only way to say it was fast and to the point.

“Dear, God, who was it?” Milly shrieked.

“I don’t know. All I know right now is it’s a woman,” Isabelle explained. “Can you do me a huge favor?”

“Sure, honey. Anything to help.” Milly was the best.

“Can you call the dining staff? I’ll call everyone else.” Isabelle pressed her hand against her stomach because it had started to churn once again.

“Isabelle, Jake and I will make all the calls. You sound freaked. Take care of yourself and we’ll deal with the staff,” Milly said.

“I can’t ask you to do that.” Isabelle sighed.

"You didn't ask, I offered. Just let me know what happens and I'll drop by your place this evening." Milly was in full mother mode.

The woman was only a few years older than Isabelle, but she always seemed to take it upon herself to mother everyone who worked at the restaurant. Milly and Jake had six children, so Isabelle figured it was just something she couldn't turn off.

When the call ended, she glanced outside the ambulance again. Another gurney was wheeled out of the restaurant with a body bag that obviously contained the deceased woman. The sight of it made Isabelle's head spin again and she grabbed Roman's hand. He instantly wrapped his arm around her and hugged her close to him.

The anxiety she felt almost instantly calmed, but she started to think it would be a good idea to go to the hospital just to be safe. Especially with the way her heart started to thud in her chest and everything around her spun once again.

Roman let Bobby know that Isabelle was going to go and be checked. Before the ambulance doors closed, she locked eyes with Aaron. She didn't like the expression on his face. Isabelle's stomach started to revolt, and it was everything she could do not to throw up all over herself.

"Tiger, we'll deal with that later. Right now, we're going to get you checked out. You don't look well." Roman cupped her cheek and forced her to turn away from the scene.

"That poor girl." Isabelle swallowed as Roman helped her lay back and the ambulance lurched forward.

Chapter 10

Roman sat in the uncomfortably hard chair next to Isabelle's hospital bed. He couldn't tear his eyes away from her beautiful face relaxed in sleep while he held tightly to her hand. It appeared the adrenalin rush had worn off and she hadn't been able to stay awake any longer.

Doctor Adam Cramer seemed to know Isabelle and her family well. When she was brought in, he did a very thorough examination of her. Roman did get a little annoyed with the way the charming doctor flirted with Isabelle. Roman was glad to see her simply roll her eyes and told Adam he needed a cold shower.

"She's probably going to sleep for a while." Roman glanced in the direction of the voice.

Isabelle's cousin Ian stood just inside the door. As a doctor, he had his own practice, but he did work in the emergency department one day a week. Roman didn't think he was working at the moment since he was dressed in old jeans and a sweater.

"I know." Roman gave him a faint smile and turned back to Isabelle.

"You know if Uncle Kurt comes in here and sees you like this, you're gonna have some explaining to do?" Ian walked into the room and leaned against the large windowsill.

"Exactly what do I need to explain? I'm just sitting with a friend." Roman shrugged.

"Roman, I saw the way you were looking at her when I walked in. I've no doubt in my mind that there's a little more than friendship between you two." Ian smirked.

"Can I be honest?" Roman sat back in the chair.

"Sure." Ian crossed his arms over his large chest.

All of the O'Connor Brothers were built like brick walls. Considering most of their jobs, it made sense, but Ian was a doctor and looked like he could knock off someone's head with one punch. Roman wasn't a small man either, but he was not close to the large man looking at him. Most people would probably be intimidated by Ian and the brothers, but Roman knew they were good men.

"I don't know what we are. I mean, we've spent a lot of time together, but she's resisting the idea of actually going out with me." Roman blew out a breath.

It sounded stupid when he said it out loud, but what was he supposed to say, s*he doesn't mind fucking but when it comes to romance, she puts up a wall*. He didn't know how comfortable he felt talking to Ian about that sort of thing.

"That sounds like Isabelle." Ian chuckled.

"What sounds like Isabelle?" Roman turned at the sound of her sleepy voice.

"Giving this guy a hard time." Ian walked around the bed.

"I'm not giving anyone a hard time, asshole." Isabelle shoved her cousin.

"That's not what he says." Ian kissed Isabelle's forehead.

"You believe everything he says?" Isabelle rolled her eyes.

"I know you well enough to know he's not lying about that." Ian picked up her hand and glanced at his watch.

"I didn't know you were on duty today." Isabelle pulled her hand away.

"I'm always on duty when it comes to my family." Ian grabbed her wrist again.

Isabelle glared at Roman while her cousin checked her pulse. She might be pissed off, but it was better than the look of terror he'd seen in her eyes earlier. That was a look he never wanted to see on her face again.

"You've got a big mouth." She poked Roman in the shoulder.

"Give the guy a break," Ian said.

"Bite me." Isabelle yanked her hand away from her cousin.

"How are you feeling?" Roman wanted to change the subject, quickly.

"I'm fine. It was stupid for me to come here in the first place." Isabelle sat up, but she seemed to get a little woozy and lay back down.

"Cuz, whether you admit it or not, you were in shock and since you fainted, it's always a good idea to make sure it's nothing serious," Ian reminded her.

"God, I almost forgot. That woman." Isabelle pressed her lips together.

Without a word, Roman jumped to his feet and wrapped his arms around her. The tears started as she gripped on to his shirt and pressed her head against his chest. He eased down on the bed next to her. She trembled in his arms for a few minutes and Roman pressed his lips against the top of her head.

"Shh… Tiger, we'll figure out what happened," Roman whispered.

"He's right, Isabelle." Ian smoothed back her hair.

For a few minutes, the only sound was her soft sobs. Roman hated that she'd seen the body because it probably wouldn't have been as traumatic if she hadn't. The dead rat was enough to upset her, but a dead girl would make anyone freak. The only reason he'd remained calm was because of his former career.

"Isabelle?" Roman didn't need to look toward the door to know the deep voice that broke the silence in the room.

“She’s all right, Uncle Kurt.” Ian stepped back as Kurt walked next to the bed and practically pulled Isabelle out of Roman’s arms.

“Sweet pea, are you really okay?” Kurt cupped Isabelle’s face in his hands.

“I’m good, Dad.” Isabelle smiled at her father.

“You’re not okay. You found a fucking dead woman in your restaurant.” Kurt’s voice echoed in the room then he turned to Roman.

Isabelle’s father stood up, pulled his phone from his pocket and tapped the screen several times. When Kurt lifted his head, and glared at Roman with pure rage in his eyes, it was unsettling. It was the first time he ever felt intimidated by Isabelle’s father. He just had no idea why the anger was directed at him.

Roman wasn’t someone who was easily browbeaten by anyone. He’d grown up with two older brothers who taught him to stand up for himself and their younger sister. The fact that Kurt made him feel ready to cow down didn’t sit well with Roman.

“You want to tell me what the hell you were doing at the restaurant last night?” Kurt practically growled the words.

“I’m sorry?” Roman stared at Kurt in confusion.

“I know I didn’t stutter. What the fuck were you doing at ten minutes past midnight in front of my daughter’s restaurant?” Kurt looked about ready to lunge at Roman.

“Dad, Roman wasn’t at the restaurant last night,” Isabelle snapped.

“Then why did A.J. send me this surveillance video of him in front of the building next to yours?” Kurt turned his phone around so they could see the screen.

Roman saw a video of himself from the night before. He was in front of the old dance club, looking up at the building. He’d been there but he hadn’t gone inside. It suddenly hit him exactly what Kurt was insinuating and it pissed him off.

“Hold on a minute.” Roman held up his hand

“Roman?” Isabelle looked at him her blue eyes wide with surprise.

“I walked by the restaurant last night on my way back to Ethan’s place. I stopped to look at the building because I got a weird vibe as I walked by, but I did not go inside. I was at Ethan’s place ten minutes later. You can ask him.” Roman tried to hold down his anger.

The idea that Kurt would even consider Roman could be involved in something so horrible hurt his heart. If Isabelle believed it, he’d be crushed. He glanced back and forth between Kurt and Isabelle to see a hint that one of them believed him.

“I’ll have a chat with Ethan to verify that.” Kurt narrowed his eyes and the old saying, *if looks could kill,* came to mind.

"You'll do no such thing." Everyone turned to the stern voice that floated into the room. "Kurt O'Connor, you're not a police officer anymore and I don't believe for one minute Roman had anything to do with what happened."

Isabelle's mother walked into the room, followed by Isabelle's grandmother. Roman relaxed when he saw the women because whatever anyone thought about him, he knew both women would be the voices of reason. He'd known the family long enough to know when Alice or Nanny Betty spoke, everyone listened.

"Dat's right. Now, my son, ya leave da lad alone," Nanny Betty snapped as she walked around Kurt and stood next to Roman.

"Mudder, we've got a video…" Kurt was stopped when his mother lifted her hand and pointed her finger.

"I don't care whatcha got. Dis lad would never hurt our Isabelle." Nanny Betty gently tapped Roman's arm and then sat on the bed next to her granddaughter.

"That's right. Now you stay out of the investigation. It's not your job anymore." Alice grabbed Kurt's phone and tapped the screen several times before she handed it back to him.

"What did you just do?" Kurt looked at his phone

"I deleted that video because you shouldn't have it." She poked Kurt in the middle of the chest and then turned to hug Isabelle.

"We'll chat later." Kurt glared at Roman.

"I hate to leave this little uncomfortable situation, but I've got to pick the girls up from school." Ian smirked as he made his way to the door. "I'm sure they'll release you soon, cuz. Love you."

"Love you too," Isabelle replied.

Ian had three daughters and a son with his wife Sandy. Two of the oldest girls were teenagers and were probably the sweetest kids Roman had ever met. He had two nieces and three nephews that were around the same age, but if Roman listened to his siblings, he'd think they were pure evil.

"Thanks, Ian." Isabelle smiled as Ian waved and disappeared out the door.

While Nanny Betty and Alice fussed over Isabelle, Roman stepped to the window and pulled out his phone. He wanted to text Ethan and see if he'd heard anything, but before he could Kurt snatched the phone out of Roman's hand.

"Don't you dare text your friend and have him back your story." Kurt kept his voice low but no less lethal.

"It wasn't a story, Mr. O'Connor. I was out for a walk and stopped for a few seconds before I went to Ethan's apartment." Roman replied and looked Kurt right in the eyes.

"Dad, for the love of God. Roman was at my house not five minutes before that video." Isabelle stood next to the bed.

"Isabelle." Kurt sounded like a bear.

"Dad, I'm a grown woman and I can have whoever I want at my house. Now stay out of this. Roman did not kill that girl." With that statement, Isabelle turned and stomped into the small bathroom off her room.

When the door slammed, Alice spun around and narrowed her eyes at her husband. Roman expected the three adults to rip into him for being at Isabelle's house, but Alice and Nanny Betty seemed annoyed with Kurt.

"Kurt, your daughter is right. For heaven's sake, she's thirty-seven years old. It's nobody's business who she has at her home and you growling like a bear at Roman because of what Cora said is not helping." Alice placed her fists on her hips and shook her head.

Apparently, Isabelle's aunt must have informed the rest of the family of her thoughts. If she'd told Kurt that Roman and Isabelle were meant to be together and Kurt didn't like the idea, Roman would have serious issues.

Before Kurt could respond to his wife, the doctor returned with a huge smile on his face. Dr. Cramer seemed happy to see the group in the room and greeted them as if they were all old friends. It seemed as if Kurt liked Adam much more than he liked Roman.

"Hey, if it isn't the new mayor of Hopedale." Adam shook Kurt's hand.

"How are you, Adam?" Kurt smiled.

Roman could see it wasn't a real smile. Especially when he glanced quickly at Roman before returning his attention to Adam. No matter how pleasant Kurt seemed to be with the doctor, Roman knew Kurt probably wanted to rip his head off.

"The only way I could be any better is if I had a wife as beautiful as yours." Adam winked at Alice.

"You're so sweet, Adam." Alice smiled as Adam turned to face them.

"And how are the two most beautiful women in the world?" Adam hugged Alice and Nanny Betty.

"I'm doing well, and you know Nanny Betty is better than us all." Alice smiled as Isabelle walked out of the bathroom.

"I'll have to find out what your secret is, Nan. How do you stay looking so young?" Adam winked at Nanny Betty.

"It's good genes." Nanny Betty laughed.

"Great genes, if you ask me," Adam replied then turned to Isabelle. "I hate to break up the little party here, but I'd like to talk to this lovely lady in private for a moment."

"Is something wrong?" Kurt's brow furrowed and Roman tensed.

"Just got to do the last check up before I give her the walking papers." Adam winked at Isabelle as she sat on the bed.

"Oh, okay." Kurt nodded.

Alice and Nanny Betty grabbed Kurt's arm and dragged him from the room. Kurt glanced back over his shoulder probably to see if Roman was following, but as Roman started to follow them, Isabelle stopped him.

"Roman, I'm sorry about my dad," she said softly.

"I'm good. Remember I deal with his daughter every day. He's a pussy cat next to you, Tiger." Roman blew her a kiss.

"Are you two a couple?" Adam glanced back and forth between Isabelle and Roman.

"Kind of." Isabelle smiled shyly.

"I see." Adam seemed unsure of what to say but Roman nodded and left the room.

He didn't want to leave Isabelle, but if he stayed while Kurt was there, the man would probably pop a blood vessel. Roman knew for sure when he stepped outside the room and Kurt scowled at him. As much as he wanted Isabelle's family to like him, the only thing he was concerned about was what the doctor was discussing with Isabelle.

Chapter 11

Isabelle felt slightly relieved to finally admit out loud that she and Roman were together. She sat back on the bed as Adam checked her heart and blood pressure. He didn't speak as he felt around her stomach making her feel slightly uncomfortable. It wasn't like Adam to be so serious.

"There's another reason I asked everyone to leave, Isabelle." Adam pulled a chair next to the bed and sat down.

"What's wrong?" Isabelle's heart felt as if it was about to jump out of her chest.

"We took some blood when you came in to make sure things were okay. I know it seems like overkill, but I know your family and they can be a little pushy." Adam chuckled.

"True," Isabelle agreed. "What's wrong with me?"

"Isabelle, everything came back fine, but we did find Human Chorionic Gonadotropin, or as we call it, HGC," Adam explained.

"I don't know what that means." Isabelle shrugged.

She heard the initials before, but she couldn't remember what it was. Unfortunately, she wasn't a doctor. It sounded bad and she clasped her hands together to prepare to hear bad news.

"Isabelle, you're pregnant," Adam said.

For several seconds, Isabelle stared at him as if he'd spoken another language. The words didn't register in her head and when she opened her mouth to speak, it was as if she couldn't get the words out.

"I'm assuming by your reaction this wasn't expected." Adam handed her a piece of paper.

Isabelle couldn't do anything but shake her head. Expected? The last thing she expected was to be told she was pregnant. They'd taken every precaution and the condom only broke once, but she was on birth control. Had been for a long while.

"This is a prescription for prenatal vitamins and folic acid. I've also sent a referral to an obstetrician. They'll get in touch with you for an appointment. Until they do, you should follow up with your family doctor." Adam must be talking to someone else.

Isabelle heard every word he spoke, but her brain wouldn't work and the only thing she could do was stare at the smiling doctor while he continued to instruct her about something that didn't seem possible. She wasn't even sure if this thing with Roman was going anywhere besides the bedroom. Maybe she should have thought about that before she jumped into bed with him.

“I’m not sure if the father is in the picture, but you do have options. If you have any questions, I’ve put my number on the back of that prescription. You can call me anytime if you’re not comfortable talking to Ian or Sean.” Adam stood up and smiled.

Since both her Uncle Sean and Ian were doctors, she never really thought about going to anyone else for medical issues. She did have a gynecologist that she would be sent to for her normal female things, but she was also a friend of her parents.

“You can also go home, but take it easy for a day or so,” Adam said.

“I’m… pregnant?” Isabelle wasn’t sure if she’d actually said the words out loud.

“Yeah, Isabelle. You may need a day or two to get your head around this.” Adam squeezed her shoulder.

“I’m pregnant,” she said again as if trying to see how it sounded coming out of her mouth.

“Yes, I’ll leave now so you can change and get ready to go home.” Adam turned to leave.

“Adam, please don’t say anything to my family outside.” Isabelle shot to her feet.

The thought of her father finding out she was pregnant, was bad enough, but to be pregnant for Roman would probably send her father into a fit of rage. For some reason, her dad didn’t seem to like or trust Roman. Isabelle didn't know why, but that was the least of her worries at that moment.

"I couldn't say a word, even if I wanted to. It's the whole doctor and patient thing." Adam winked and then left the room.

Isabelle slowly sat back down on the bed and stared at the closed door. There had to be a mistake, but Adam wouldn't lie to her. He wouldn't have a reason, and deep down, Isabelle knew there was no mistake.

She'd felt off for the last few weeks and blew it off as the flu that had been making its rounds through the staff. Roman had even been down with it for a couple of days. If Isabelle had paid attention, she would have realized that all her symptoms were not the same as everyone else.

She hadn't been feeling well for a couple of weeks, and she'd been overly emotional too. Isabelle blew it off as being exhausted from twelve to eighteen-hour days at the restaurant and mind-blowing sex at night.

"Now what am I going to do?" Isabelle sighed and dropped her face into her hands.

"You'll go home and let A.J. figure out what happened." Her dad's voice caused Isabelle to lift her head.

"I… yeah." Isabelle grabbed her clothes from the foot of the bed and practically ran to the bathroom.

She'd never succeeded to keep a secret from her father since she was a little girl. At least not any that concerned her. For some reason he could always see when she was at odds with something. He could always read her like a book. It was why she wasn't surprised when he caught her by the arm before she made it out of the room.

"Everything will be okay, sweet pea." Her dad tugged her into a hug and kissed the top of her head.

"I know, Dad." Isabelle swallowed the lump in her throat.

If he saw the tears, he wouldn't stop until he knew what caused them. It would be pointless for her to lie even if she had found a dead body in her restaurant. Isabelle managed to pull away and make it into the bathroom before the tears started.

She looked at herself in the mirror, but she didn't look any different. She still had her curly hair and her eyes looked the same. Her skin didn't seem to have that glow everyone always talked about.

As she stripped off the hospital gown and covered her flat stomach with her hands, she turned and checked out her profile. No bump. She still looked like herself.

Isabelle hadn't even asked Adam how pregnant she was, but she could probably figure that out. Especially when she thought about the last time she'd had a period. Maybe it was true what people said, pregnancy was contagious.

Between her sister and five of her cousins' wives being pregnant, maybe something was in the air. She wasn't stupid and knew the idea was ridiculous, but she wanted to find a reason as to why it happened to her. She couldn't even admit how she felt about Roman. Christ, her family didn't even know she spent practically every night with the man.

It also didn't help that her restaurant was probably on a downward spiral. Especially if the dead woman was murdered in her building. Who'd want to come to a place where someone was killed? There was no way the press would keep the name of her business out of their headlines.

"Well, girl. The creek is full of shit and the paddle is made of paper," Isabelle whispered as she stared at herself.

Isabelle walked out of the bathroom and stepped right into the middle of a heated discussion between her dad and Roman. She listened for a minute and quickly figured out that it was a disagreement on who was driving Isabelle home. This was the last thing she needed.

"Mr. O'Connor, I'll make sure she gets home safe. Ethan is on the way here now to drop off my car. I wouldn't do anything to hurt her." Roman spoke in his usual laidback demeanor.

"You aren't family and until I know for sure that you're not involved in what happened, there's no damn way you'll be alone with my daughter." Her father was his usual overprotective self.

“I think we should ask Isabelle.” Roman turned and suddenly all eyes were on her.

“Sweet pea, you should come home with us and stay for a night or two.” Her father glared at Roman.

“I think you’ll be more comfortable in your own bed.” Roman’s expression didn’t change, but it was as if he was in competition with her dad.

“She has a bed at the house she grew up in.” Her father growled and crossed his arms over his chest.

“Which she probably hasn’t slept in for a long while.” Roman turned back to her father and did the same.

The sight of his biceps bulging slightly under the sleeves of his T-shirt made her want to sigh. Although he wasn’t as large as her father, he wasn’t any slouch either. Her father dropped his arms and took a step toward Roman.

“Stop it.” Isabelle stepped in front of her father and glanced back and forth between the two men.

As they glared at each other over her head, Isabelle glanced at her mother and grandmother for some form of support in the situation. Her grandmother was busy texting something, which in another situation, would be comical if Isabelle wasn’t so irritated.

Her mother didn’t help either because she just rolled her eyes and sat down on one of the chairs. Why both women would not stop the ridiculous disagreement was beyond her, but she wasn’t in any mood for it. The last thing she needed was for her father and Roman to come to blows in the middle of her hospital room. She could see the headlines now, *Hopedale Mayor and Chef arrested for fighting*.

"Just stop." Isabelle huffed.

"Hey." Kristy walked into the room before Isabelle could respond to her father and Roman's behavior.

"Kristy, you're driving me home." Isabelle grabbed her purse and stomped out of the room.

"Okay," Isabelle heard Kristy draw out the word and then follow behind her.

Isabelle wasn't ready to tell Roman she was pregnant, and she definitely wasn't ready to tell her parents. How could she when she wasn't even sure she could get her head around the news? Isabelle needed advice and she knew just the people to help.

While she walked silently next to Kristy, Isabelle sent a quick text to her sister Jess and her cousin Pam. Between the four of them, Isabelle might be able to figure out what to do.

"I need you to stay for a bit when you get to the house," Isabelle said as she and Kristy stepped on the elevator.

"I got a text from Nan. I figured you'd need some sister time." Kristy smiled

Sister time was exactly what she needed. Although she loved and respected her cousins and their wives, she wanted to keep her pregnancy within the close circle of her sisters and Pam.

Isabelle: My house. Big problem. Need my girls.

Chapter 12

Ethan caught a ride with Nanny Betty because she needed him to go with her to pick up some packages. That meant Roman drove back to Hopedale in his Jeep, alone and aggravated. Kurt seemed convinced Roman had something to do with the death of the woman. Roman was hurt that anyone would believe that he would do something so evil.

He didn't know Kurt well and before things started with Isabelle, her dad was always friendly. It didn't make sense why he suddenly distrusted Roman.

Roman was more pissed at himself. He never should have put Isabelle in a situation where she had to pick between him and her father. If he wanted a relationship with her, that was the worst way to start. He was almost relieved when Kristy showed up and Isabelle escaped the uncomfortable situation.

She wasn't present when Kurt told him to stay away from his daughter or when Roman told him that wasn't going to happen. That was probably a clue that Kurt knew more than he admitted. Maybe they weren't as secretive as they thought. It was one of the reasons he headed right to Isabelle's house.

Roman immediately hopped out of his Jeep as he stopped in the driveway. The only car that was there was Isabelle's, which made him think she was home alone. Before he was able to make it to the door, it opened and Jess stepped into the doorway.

"She's resting, Roman." Jess blocked his entrance.

"I need to talk to her for a moment." Roman wanted to apologize for his behavior at the hospital.

"Roman, she's upset. She just found out the name of the woman found in the restaurant." Jess pulled the door closed behind her as she stepped outside.

"Who is it, Jess?" A knot formed in his stomach.

"It was Cindy." Jess spoke in a quiet voice.

"Fuck." Roman stepped back and plowed his hand through his hair.

Cindy was a sweet girl and Roman couldn't believe someone would hurt her. Sure she could be a little over-dramatic, but he knew everyone at the restaurant loved her. Most customers tipped her well because she was a great waitress. He mentally kicked himself for not recognizing it was her laying facedown in the closet.

"A.J. was in the driveway when we got here." Jess shoved her hands into her front pockets.

"Jess, I need to see Isabelle." Roman didn't care that he sounded as if he was begging.

"Roman, I don't think it's a good time right now." Jess sounded almost apologetic.

Roman was about to push a little, but the front door opened and Isabelle appeared. Her eyes were red, obviously from crying over Cindy, but she looked fragile. It shook him to his core because he had never seen Isabelle look that way. It reminded him of how his sister looked when their parents died.

"It's okay, Jess." Isabelle moved back and motioned for them to come in.

Roman stepped inside and Isabelle closed the door. Jess looked at her sister for a moment. It wasn't until Isabelle gave a slight nod that Jess left them alone in the foyer. For a moment, Isabelle simply stared at the floor and folded her hands in front of her.

"I'm so sorry about Cindy," Roman whispered.

"She was stabbed." Isabelle sniffed and Roman couldn't take it anymore.

Instinctively, he tugged her into his arms and held her tightly in his embrace. She trembled as she fisted his shirt and buried her face into his chest. He could feel the wetness of her tears through the material of his T-shirt but he didn't care if he had to wring it out when she was done.

“Shhh… I’m here for you, Tiger,” Roman whispered against the top of her head.

After several minutes she took a deep breath and blew it out slowly as she lifted her head. Without looking up at him she played with one of the buttons on his shirt, and it bothered him that she seemed to avoid eye contact.

“God, I feel like all I’ve been doing the last twenty-four hours is bawling.” She sniffed as she smoothed her hands across his chest. “I’ve soaked your shirt.”

When she finally lifted her eyes to meet his, he could see the anguish. Losing someone you care about wasn’t easy, and he hated that she was going through it. Cindy may not be part of her family, but she’d worked for Isabelle for a long time.

“It’ll dry and it’s normal to cry after the day you had. Are you okay?” Roman cupped her face between his hands and used his thumbs to wipe the tears from her cheeks.

“I’m not really sure.” She closed her eyes.

“You’ve had a very traumatic day.” Roman pressed his lips against her forehead.

“I need to talk to you about something,” she blurted out.

“Look, I know what happened at the hospital between me and your dad was stupid. I don’t know why he doesn’t trust me all of a sudden, but that’s the least of my worries. As long as *you* know you can trust me, that’s all I care about.” Roman gazed into her eyes.

"I do, but it's not about what happened at the hospital. At least not what happened between you and Dad." She lowered her eyes as if she was unsure of herself.

"Isabelle, what are you talking about?" Roman tensed.

He hated hospitals for one reason. Anytime someone he loved went to one, they would end up sick or dead. The thought of something being wrong with Isabelle made his stomach turn. He couldn't stand if she was sick, but Roman knew if she was, he'd sit by her side until she was well, and he wouldn't care what Kurt said.

"Before I left, you know, when Adam made you all leave the room?" Isabelle still wouldn't meet his eyes.

"I remember." Roman was trying hard not to panic.

"Well, when I arrived, they did some routine blood work. Apparently, they do it for everyone who's brought in by ambulance." Isabelle played with the one button at the opening of his shirt.

"Isabelle, are you sick?" It made him want to throw up to think that she could have a serious illness.

"Not at this minute." She sighed.

"What…" Roman's question was interrupted when the door opened and Kurt stepped inside.

"I'm sure I told you to stay out of here." Kurt narrowed his eyes.

“Dad, I asked him to come here and this is my house.” Isabelle turned and glared at her father.

“Sweet pea, you need…” Kurt began but Isabelle held up her hand to stop him.

“Look, let's get this straight. Roman is welcome here any time he wants. This is my house and he’s my guest. I’ve got no idea why you seem to have it out for him, but it’s going to stop. We’re seeing each other, and you better get used to it.” Isabelle fisted her hands and placed them on her hips.

Kurt stared at his daughter wide-eyed. Roman had to fight back the grin that threatened to show because she’d just let the cat out of the bag. He didn’t like the way Kurt’s face turned red as he raised his eyes to glare at Roman.

“Dad, you don’t know him and you haven’t even given him a chance.” Isabelle sounded more hurt than angry.

Kurt didn’t speak as he glanced between his daughter and Roman. For some reason, Roman wasn’t intimidated and he actually felt a kinship with Isabelle’s father. After all, Kurt was only looking out for his daughter. He was right about one thing, he didn’t know Roman, but that would be fixed very soon.

“Dad, why are you being harder on him than you ever were on Dean or Wade?” Isabelle’s voice trembled.

“They didn’t sneak around for months.” Kurt glared at Roman.

That was it. He and Isabelle hadn't been keeping things hidden as well as they thought. He finally realized Kurt probably thought Roman was only using Isabelle for sex.

"Look, Mr. O'Connor, …" Roman started, but Isabelle stopped him.

"I was the one who wanted to keep this quiet, not Roman. As a matter of fact, I finally agreed to go out on a public date with him this week. Dad, he's a good guy and the sooner you stop treating him like he's the devil, the sooner you'll find that out." Isabelle stepped back and linked her hand around Roman's arm.

Kurt stared at Roman as if he was trying to choose his words carefully and not piss off his daughter any further. If there was one thing Roman had figured out, it was that the men in the O'Connor family didn't like to piss off the women. Especially Nanny Betty.

"Mr. O'Connor, I promise you I'd never do anything to hurt Isabelle. I care about her very much." Roman felt the need to say it out loud not only for Kurt but for Isabelle's sake as well.

"I'm going to be honest with you, Roman. I don't like the fact that you've been leaving my daughter's house at all hours in the night. I know she's an adult, but I don't want her to get hurt by someone who's just using her for one thing." There was one thing about Kurt, he was straightforward.

"Dad," Isabelle snapped.

"Mr. O'Connor, I promise you that's not what it is. Isabelle is an amazing person and the more I get to know her, the more I want to know. Yes, I work for her and I've spent more than a night or two here, but I swear I would never treat her with anything but respect." Roman made sure he kept eye contact with Kurt and didn't waver.

"I'll hold you to that, but my father was Mr. O'Connor. Call me Kurt. That doesn't mean I'm not keeping my eye on you. My daughters are my pride and joy, so if you mean what you say, prove it to me." Kurt slowly lifted his hand and held it out.

Roman took his hand and shook it firmly. He also tried not to cringe at the way Isabelle's nails were digging into the crook of his arm. He knew it was because she was concerned but when her father released Roman's hand, Kurt pulled Isabelle into a hug and kissed her temple.

"I love you, sweet pea. I'm only making sure this guy deserves to have your company," Kurt said softly.

"Dad, I love you too, but you've got to stop treating us like we're still little girls." Isabelle tipped her head back and looked up at her father.

"You'll always be my little girls." Kurt winked and after another quick hug, he released Isabelle and made his way further into the house.

"I'm so sorry about him." Isabelle turned back to Roman.

“Don’t be sorry for a father that loves you. I just want to make sure I don’t do anything to really piss him off.” Roman chuckled.

Isabelle’s smile vanished and she looked as if she was going to puke all over him. Before he could reach for her, she bolted up the stairs. He was about to follow her, but Kristy stopped him and made her way up the stairs.

Kristy was one of six of the O’Connors who were currently expecting and from what Roman heard, they were all due somewhere between April and May. He envied the O’Connor family. They were close and all of them lived within ten minutes of each other. Unlike his siblings, who were spread all over the country and only saw each other once or twice a year.

“Would you like to come in further, or are you just going to stand there?” Pam smirked as she peeked out of the kitchen.

“Is Isabelle okay?” Roman asked Pam as he glanced back at the top of the stairs.

“She’s had a pretty upsetting day. It can play havoc with your system.” Pam gave him half a smile then turned to go back into the kitchen.

Pam was right. The only reason Roman wasn’t shaken by the situation was because he was so concerned about Isabelle. The start of her day had been the huge dead rat and ended with the murder of her friend.

Roman pressed his back against the wall and slid down to the floor. He rested his elbows on his knees and rubbed his hands against his face. The adrenalin of the day had worn off and he was exhausted.

He draped his arms over his knees and stared at the wall in front of him. Isabelle had her family to help her through the situation but except for Ethan, Roman had nobody to turn to. His mother's death had been hard on him because she'd always been the one he went to for advice. It had been three years and he missed her just as much as he did the day she passed.

"I think you'd be more comfortable if you came in and sat on the sofa." Kurt crouched in front of him.

"Yeah." Roman blew out a breath.

"You know, Isabelle wasn't the only one who got a shock today. Are you sure you're okay?" Kurt asked and Roman could see the genuine concern in the man's eyes.

"I'm fine. I was thinking about my mother." Roman stood up.

"My fadder's been gone for fifteen years now and I find myself thinking about him at least once a day. I don't think you ever really stop missing those who've passed on." Kurt placed a hand on Roman's shoulder.

"Kurt, I hope you believed me when I said I care about Isabelle," Roman said.

"I believe you, but I'm going to give you the same warning I gave Wade and Bull. Don't hurt her and we'll get along just fine." Kurt raised an eyebrow.

It was odd how most people in the family referred to Kristy's husband by his nickname, Bull, but it seemed most of the women called him by his given name, Dean. If people didn't know the difference they might think he was two different people.

"I promise." Roman nodded.

"That's all I need to hear." Kurt smiled and for the first time all day, it didn't look forced.

Roman felt some of the tension leave his shoulders with the realization that he made a step in the right direction with Isabelle's father. After all, it wouldn't work with Isabelle if her family didn't get along with him. What kind of life would that be?

It was the first time he realized that he wanted a life with her. Isabelle was it for him. It was more than sex, more than fun. He wanted to spend the rest of his life with her and hopefully someday have a family.

Chapter 13

Isabelle had felt stomach sick since she'd gotten home. She'd managed to keep the nausea at bay for a short while, but suddenly her stomach clenched and she barely made it to the bathroom in time.

"Isn't this supposed to be happening in the morning?" Isabelle choked out as Kristy handed her a damp face cloth.

"Honey, with Decker I was sick morning, noon, and night for the first trimester. This little button made me sick after supper." Kristy rested her hands on her pregnant belly.

"I don't like this already." Isabelle sighed as she sat back on her feet.

"Pregnancy is not for the faint of heart." Kristy snorted.

"Especially when you didn't expect or plan for it." Isabelle looked up at her sister from the floor.

"That's the problem with you. You plan everything, but trust me, big sister, when you hold your little baby for the first time, you forget all about days like this." Kristy's smile seemed almost euphoric as she ran her hand over her swollen belly.

"How am I going to tell Roman? I almost had it out when Dad showed up." Isabelle stood up and grabbed her toothbrush from the holder.

"Isabelle, he needs to know." Kristy reminded her.

Isabelle brushed her teeth, glad she wasn't able to make a snarky comment about Kristy being Mrs. Obvious. Isabelle would never keep something like a baby from Roman. Even if they didn't work out, he deserved to know he was going to be a father.

"I'm going to go down and let you get yourself together, but I would probably wait to break the news until we're all gone. Especially Dad." Kristy smirked as she closed the bathroom door behind her.

"Dad," Isabelle sighed as she wiped her face.

She shuddered with the thought of telling her family about her condition. Telling Roman made her nervous enough, but the thought of informing her family made her cringe. Isabelle hated to think about how disappointed they would be in her.

Eventually, they would be happy about a new baby in the family, but they'd expect her to be in a committed relationship or married. She wasn't sure where she and Roman were headed, although, she knew where she wanted it to go.

“We’re heading out, Isabelle,” Kristy shouted from downstairs. “Dad said he'd drop by in the morning to check on you.”

“Okay, love you.” Isabelle figured that was Kristy’s way of letting her know the coast was clear.

“Love you too,” Kristy said right before the front door closed.

“Well, it’s now or never. Just rip the Band-Aid off. That’s it. Rip it off. It will only hurt for a second. I hope,” Isabelle whispered to herself.

Isabelle walked into the kitchen and found Roman chopping something with his back to her. Music played through her small countertop radio and he hummed along with some pop song. She sighed at the realization that he’d actually turned the radio off her favorite country station.

The radio was ancient, and it took forever to get it on the right station. It was why when she finally got it to the music she liked, she left it on the counter and never touched it. When she wanted to turn it off, she unplugged it.

“Hey.” Roman smiled as he turned down the music.

“You do realize that radio is a bitch when you’re trying to change the channel?” Isabelle stepped into the kitchen and walked over to the counter.

“Not anymore. I tightened the screws. It happens with these old radios.” He demonstrated how well it worked.

"Son of a bitch." Isabelle tested it herself. "Do you know long I've had that thing?"

"I don't know how long you've had it but from what I can see, it's probably around sixty years old." Roman went back to chopping up an onion and peppers.

"How do you know that?" Isabelle tilted her head and watched him.

"My dad used to repair old electronics and he collected a lot of antique radios over the years. I helped him and I guess it rubbed off." Roman placed the knife on the counter and seemed suddenly focused completely on her. "Are you okay?"

The concern in his eyes made her feel bad for making him worry. She also felt like shit for what she was about to tell him. The weight of the world felt like it was on her shoulders with the thought of a baby. It made her wonder how well Roman would handle it.

"I'm fine." Isabelle held out her hand and he stepped toward her.

"It's the first time I've ever seen you like that." Roman smoothed her hair back from her face.

"I'm not used to everything that happened to me today." She relaxed at his gentle touch.

"I guess finding Cindy today shook me a little today too." Roman kissed her forehead and started to step back.

“Roman, I’ve got to tell you something.” Isabelle grabbed his hand before he could reach for the knife again.

“Okay.” He looked at her quizzically.

“I think you better sit down.” Isabelle motioned toward the kitchen chair.

“I don’t need to sit. Tiger, what’s wrong?” Roman held her hands in his.

“Okay. I’m…” Before she finished, Roman interrupted.

“Jesus, you’re sick, aren’t you? Isabelle, you don’t have to worry. I’m here for you…” Isabelle interrupted him before he could finish.

“No. No, I’m not sick. At least not at the moment.” Isabelle’s stomach had finally settled.

“You’re going to get sick?” Roman asked.

“Can you stop talking so I can get this out?” Isabelle sighed.

“Oh, okay, sorry.” Roman pressed his lips together.

For several seconds, Isabelle stared down at where their hands were joined. A chill ran up her spine at the thought that he would leave once he knew the truth. She didn’t want to think about Roman not in her life, but she would never force him to do something he wasn’t ready for. She also didn’t want him to stay just because of the baby.

"Tiger, you can tell me anything. You know that, right?" Roman said, and she lifted her eyes to meet his.

"I'm pregnant." Isabelle whispered the words and she hoped it was loud enough for him to hear.

At first, the words didn't seem to register with him, but she saw the second they did. His eyes grew big and his mouth dropped open. His hands dropped to his sides as he loosened his grip on her fingers.

Roman opened and closed his mouth several times as he stared at her with an expression she couldn't quite distinguish. Was he upset? Was he scared? Did he even understand what she'd said? Isabelle was about to ask if he heard her when he finally spoke.

"I think I might want to sit down after all." Roman slowly made his way to the kitchen chair.

He sat down and placed his hands on top of the table as if he needed to do that to keep himself upright. Roman didn't lift his head for several seconds and Isabelle was afraid to say anything. She crossed her arms over her stomach as nausea started again.

"Pregnant?" Roman whispered the word, but he didn't look at her.

Isabelle's heart pounded in her chest as she waited to find out for sure if she would have to raise this child on her own. He started to shake his head and she figured it was his answer. She swallowed hard as he lifted his eyes to meet hers.

"Pregnant?" He repeated the word.

Isabelle nodded and he dropped his gaze down to his hands again. He seemed to focus on his ring. He'd told her that his father had made it for him when he was a teenager and it took several years before it actually fit. It was made out of a nut and all his siblings had them as well.

Isabelle's eyes blurred with tears because she was sure it was over at that point. Roman wasn't happy about the news. If he wasn't ready, there was nothing she could do about it. She'd just have to raise the baby on her own.

"Roman, I only told you because you deserve to know. I don't expect anything from…" Before she could finish, he was on his feet and had her wrapped in his arms.

"I never thought I'd be a father. Especially, at my age. I mean, I'm thirty-eight years old I should have kids in junior high by this point. I'd given up on becoming a dad." Roman held her so tightly she could barely breathe.

"You're not upset?" Isabelle whispered the words into his neck.

"What? Tiger, no. I wasn't expecting this. I'm sure you weren't either, but my mother always said you'll have what's for you, when it's for you. I'm assuming she meant that I would have a kid when I was ready for one but… Wow… A baby." Roman pulled back and cupped her face in his hands. "I knew the day I met you that you'd change my life for the better."

"I don't know if I'm ready for this. I mean, we only just decided to let people know we're seeing each other." Isabelle covered his hands with hers.

"Isabelle, I know for a fact that you're it for me. I'm falling in love with you, but I get the feeling you believed I was only coming to you for one thing." Roman gazed into her eyes.

"It crossed my mind," Isabelle admitted.

"I'm not going to lie. Sex between us is incredible, but I love spending time with you. I love talking, laughing, and working with you. Tiger, you're the most amazing, strong, beautiful woman I've ever met. The longer I know you, the further I fall. Why do you think I wanted do start doing this right?" Roman's eyes never moved from hers as he spoke.

His words were beautiful and looking into his eyes, Isabelle knew Roman wasn't the only one falling in love. She wasn't ready to say the words out loud, but it felt a lot better to know it was mutual. She was also relieved that he didn't run away when she told him about the baby.

"So, in case what I said didn't get my point across, maybe this will." Roman smiled.

He dropped his head and immediately his lips met hers. Roman's kiss was slow, tender, and matched the words he'd said completely. Isabelle melted into his embrace and she knew from his kiss he wasn't going anywhere.

Isabelle woke up curled next to a softly snoring Roman. He'd carried her to bed after their kiss and to her surprise, wrapped his arms around her as they fell asleep. It wasn't the first time they fell asleep that way, but it was usually after they'd had sex.

Before she had a chance to enjoy the warmth of having his shirtless form next to her, she felt the unwelcome bile rise in her throat. Isabelle jumped out of bed and ran to the bathroom.

After a few minutes of emptying her stomach into the toilet, she groaned. She managed to wet a cloth and hold it against her forehead as she prayed for the queasy feeling to fade. It was going to be a long pregnancy if she had to deal with this the whole time. She really needed to find out just how far along she was and when to expect their little bundle.

"Can I get you anything, Tiger?" Roman's hand gently caressed her back.

"Why did Eve eat the damn apple?" Isabelle groaned.

She remembered a church lesson about God increasing the pain of childbirth because Eve disobeyed him. Obviously, morning sickness was part of that pain, or at least Isabelle now believed that. Who cared if it was true or not?

"I wish I…" Roman started but Isabelle stopped him before he finished the sentence.

"If you say you wish you could do it for me, I will punch you." Isabelle lifted her head and glared at him.

"I wasn't going to say that. I was going to say I wish I had something to make you feel better." Roman chuckled as he pushed her damp hair back from her face.

"Oh. Okay." Isabelle stood up and prayed it had passed for the time being.

"My sister-in-law used to eat dry crackers when she was pregnant." Roman wrapped his arm around her shoulder as she made her way back to bed.

"I think it's passed for now, but I'll remember that." Isabelle sighed.

As she sat on the bed, the realization that she wouldn't be going into work that day hit her like a ton of bricks. What was she going to do? She had to reopen but how was she going to walk into the place again?

"Why don't you take it easy and let me take care of you today?" Roman pulled the blankets back and motioned for her to get into bed.

"I can't. I've got to see what's going on with my building." She sighed.

"Tiger, we won't be going near that place today." Roman pointed to the pillow.

"Are you going to be bossy like this all day?" Isabelle asked as she crawled into bed not because he said but because she was really tired.

"If I have to." He smiled as he pulled her heavy quilt up over her.

"I don't listen to bossy men." Isabelle yawned.

"I'm fully aware of that. I've seen you with your father." Roman chuckled as he closed the heavy drapes.

"I used to listen to him, when I was little." Isabelle tucked her hands under her cheek.

"Sleep, Tiger." Roman kissed her temple.

The last thing she heard was the soft click of the bedroom door as she drifted off to sleep.

Chapter 14

Roman sat in Isabelle's living room with the phone to his ear as he listened to Ethan complain. The real estate agent who had put in their last offer on the club had called back with another counter offer from the owner.

It wasn't that Roman lost interest in the plan because he wanted to partner with Ethan and reopen the dance club, but at the moment, he had more important things on his mind. A bar could be a huge risk and at first, he was all in, but he had a kid to think about.

He was going to be a father and started to wonder if it was a good idea to invest all his savings into a club. Then again if it was a success, he'd be able to take care of Isabelle and the baby. If it was a failure, he'd have nothing for his child.

"What's the problem with him now?" Roman asked.

"He's just nickel and diming us. He said if we want to keep the equipment inside the building that it would raise the price," Ethan said.

"Tell him that we don't want it," Roman returned.

"I would if it didn't cost more to get all new. I asked Alice what it would cost for new coolers, the taps for the draft beer, and so on. She said she could probably help us get a discount, but it's still pricy." Ethan went on.

"I don't know what to tell you. Maybe it just wasn't meant to be. Bud, I don't have time to deal with it now. I'm worried about Isabelle." Roman sat back on the couch.

"Shit, I'm sorry. How's she doing?" Ethan asked.

"She's got a lot to deal with." It was the only thing he could think to tell Ethan.

Roman wasn't sure if Isabelle would be okay with people knowing about her condition before her family. He felt like shit for keeping it from his best friend, but he wasn't going to betray her.

"I can't imagine how she's dealing with the death of her employee and finding her must have freaked her out," Ethan said.

"Yeah, I'm pretty freaked out myself." Roman admitted, but he was more worried about becoming a father.

"I'm sure, but you've seen shit like that before. I don't think she has," Ethan replied.

It reminded Roman of all the times he'd come to a scene where there was nothing he could do. After six years of being a first responder, Roman decided it was time to do what he loved to do. Cook. He enrolled in culinary school and never looked back. Sure, he still had nightmares of some scenes or something would remind him of a particular person he'd responded to, but cooking always made him feel happy.

He and Ethan chatted for a couple more minutes before Roman ended the call. He tossed his phone on the coffee table and dropped his head back until it rested against the back of the couch. He hadn't slept much because his mind wouldn't shut off. After he finally drifted off for an hour or so, Isabelle had started to get sick.

The last twenty-four hours had gone from being excited about Isabelle agreeing to a date, to discovering a dead body, to finding out he was going to be a father. Talk about a rollercoaster ride.

"Your first priority is Isabelle and the baby," Roman whispered to himself.

Before he had a chance to put together a plan on what he had to do, he heard the front door open and close again. He assumed it was one of Isabelle's sisters and went to greet them. He stopped in his tracks when Nanny Betty scurried into the living room and shoved several large containers into his arms.

"Put dat in da fridge and come help me and Tom bring da rest inside." Nanny Betty turned and disappeared out through the door again.

"If you know what's good for you, then you better do as she says." Isabelle smirked from the middle of the stairs.

“She does know we’re both chefs, right?” Roman turned to make his way to the kitchen.

“That doesn’t matter to Nan.” Isabelle laughed.

She followed behind him and opened the fridge. Roman spent several minutes trying to make the large containers in among all the other food. If anyone else checked the refrigerator, they would think Isabelle was preparing for a food shortage.

“Come on, get out ta da car and bring in da rest.” Nanny Betty placed a tin container on the counter.

Tom entered the kitchen with a huge smile and carrying a box. For a man in his eighties, he was pretty spry, much like the tiny woman chattering on about having enough food until Isabelle was feeling better.

Tom Roberts was one of the richest men in the province and was still the owner of one of the biggest communication companies in the country. He was also Nanny Betty’s life companion and they were a very sweet couple. Although, Tom definitely wasn’t the dominant in the relationship.

“Dere’s no need for ya ta be cookin’ when ya don’t have ta.” Nanny Betty scurried around the kitchen, putting things away.

“Nan, I’ve got lots of food in the house.” Isabelle hugged her grandmother.

"But ya gotta cook dat. Ya only gotta warm dis stuff up." Nanny Betty cupped Isabelle's face in her hands and narrowed her eyes.

"What's wrong, Nan?" Isabelle asked.

"Ya look different. Almost, … oh dear." Nanny Betty stepped back.

"Nan?" Isabelle glanced at Roman then back to her grandmother.

"Nan, do you need to sit down?" Roman found out a long time ago never to call Nanny Betty by Mrs. O'Connor.

For some reason, she didn't like it and it had something to do with her disliking her mother-in-law. Roman got that lecture once and that was enough for him.

"No, but I tink Isabelle might need ta be takin' it easy." Nanny Betty placed her small hand on Isabelle's stomach.

Isabelle's eyes widened in surprise and Roman stared in shock. Was it possible the woman knew? Roman didn't see anything different when he looked at Isabelle.

"I'm fine, Nan." Isabelle stepped back.

"Are ya now? I'm guessin' probably a little nauseous." Nanny Betty raised one of her eyebrows.

"Why would you think that?" Isabelle choked out the words.

“Ducky, yer nan has been ’round long enough ta see dat special glow.” Nanny Betty smiled and gently patted Isabelle’s cheek.

“Nan, please don’t say a word to anyone else. I’m not ready for everyone to know yet,” Isabelle begged.

“Lassie, I’d never tell a secret dat wasn’t mine ta tell.” Nanny Betty smiled.

When she turned to Roman, he fully expected her to give him a lecture on accepting responsibility. He was sure he was going to get that conversation once Kurt found out, but he never thought about how the rest of the family would react.

“You’re gonna be dere fer her and dats why I’m not worried.” Nanny Betty held out her hand to Roman.

“I most definitely will.” Roman took the woman’s hand and she squeezed his gently.

“My Kurt will give ya a hard time when he finds out, but don’t let him intimidate ya.” Nanny Betty smiled again. “He’s jus’ being a dad.”

“I understand,” he replied.

He did. Roman didn’t even know the sex of their baby, but he already felt protective of the little one. He couldn’t imagine how he’d feel once the Little Tiger was born. He already loved the baby more than he thought possible.

"What do we have to do next, my darling? Tom smiled down at Nanny Betty with a look of love that was hard to miss.

"I got dese two straightened away. I gotta drop off da rest over ta da orphanage." Nanny Betty turned back to Isabelle.

"The orphanage?" Isabelle seemed surprised.

"Oh yes, Hannah's volunteering over dere with dat nice Fire Chief." Nanny Betty nodded.

Bull's older sister Hannah had moved to Hopedale shortly after Kristy and Bull got married. She didn't work, mostly because Bull's family were very wealthy, so she didn't have to. Roman wasn't sure what her story was, but he did know the woman did a lot of volunteer work and that the Hopedale fire chief was pretty smitten with her.

Nanny Betty released his hand and turned back to where Tom had made himself busy. When Nanny Betty gently touched the man's arm, he stopped what he was doing. Roman watched the older man lean down and kiss the older woman's cheek.

It was the sweetest thing Roman had ever seen. Even at their age, they still showed tender affection for each other. He turned his eyes to Isabelle to see she was watching the couple with a smile on her beautiful face.

When she glanced toward him, he finally saw what Nanny Betty had been talking about. Isabelle's cheeks seemed brighter and her eyes sparkled more than they usually did. She really was glowing and once again, her beauty took his breath away.

Chapter 15

Isabelle stepped shakily inside the door of her restaurant for the first time in almost a week. She'd sent out a press release to let her customers know her place would be closed until further notice. It took her a long time to gather the courage to step into the building again.

The investigation on what happened to Cindy was still opened and Aaron was frustrated with it because there were no new leads. The only thing they were able to find was security footage of when Cindy entered, and when Roman walked by about an hour later. Cindy entered the building alone and never exited nor did anyone else.

Aaron was in the process of going through the footage from the security inside the restaurant, but the only thing on it was Cindy headed into the kitchen and a dark figure behind her.

"Tiger, you don't have to do this right now," Roman whispered behind her.

"I can't stay closed forever." Isabelle squeezed his hand mostly to make sure he didn't let go.

Roman had helped her father close off the cleaning closet a couple of days earlier. She told them she'd never be able to walk into that room again. When they finished, she knew it was time to get back to her business.

"The staff should be here shortly," Isabelle said as she pushed the door leading into the kitchen.

Her eyes immediately went to where the door of the closet once was. If she didn't know the difference, Isabelle would never know there was a room behind the wall. What she did notice was a small gold plaque on the wall with a picture of Cindy.

"Milly brought it in and asked to put it up in memory of Cindy," Roman explained.

"That's so sweet." Isabelle smiled as her eyes filled with tears.

"Milly and Jake have been here almost every day this week, helping to get things ready to re-open." Roman stepped behind her and wrapped his arms around her.

Isabelle felt a wave of guilt run through her. Her employees had shown up every day once the building was cleared, but it took her almost a week to come back inside. Roman told her she didn't have to rush anything because nobody expected her to forget what happened.

She did have to deal with the media for a few days. They wanted to know all about what happened and if she'd reopen.

Isabelle had avoided them and her father had Aaron's wife Bethany give a statement to the press. It stopped the calls and Isabelle could relax.

Her heart broke for Cindy's family. Cindy was the baby and to see her parents and siblings at the funeral was so difficult to watch. Isabelle expected them to be angry with her, but they weren't, and Cindy's mom had told her how much Cindy loved and respected Isabelle.

Isabelle leaned back against Roman and breathed in his clean scent. The warmth of his embrace made her feel safe as it always did. It gave her the strength and the courage to get back to work. After all, she needed to for the baby's sake.

"Everything is going to be fine, Tiger." He kissed the top of her head and she closed her eyes.

"I hope so. I guess we'll find out for sure when we open Saturday." Isabelle turned into his embrace and wrapped her arms around his waist.

"Everything is ready and with all the social media blasts and the commercial on the radio, we'll have so many here that we won't be able to keep up." Roman cupped her head between his hands.

With the way he stared into her eyes, she could see he really believed what he was telling her. He was so positive that he made her feel like he could be right. Especially when his lips quirked up into that sexy grin and his eyes crinkled at the corners.

She'd discovered over the last week that Roman kept her sane while she tried to figure out what to do. He'd sent her pictures and videos of puppies when he wasn't with her. They always made her smile.

With the restaurant closed for so long, she'd had to move some of her savings into her business account. She made sure she had enough to make the payroll while the place was closed, but if she didn't get enough customers in the next two weeks, she would have to borrow, and that was the last thing she wanted to do.

"Do I need to pull out that picture of the Husky again to make you smile?" Roman winked and reached for his phone.

"Not right now, but you might want to keep that picture close. That's my favorite type of dog. I always wanted to get one when I moved out on my own, but with the restaurant, it wouldn't be fair to a dog to be stuck in the house all day long." Isabelle stood up on her toes and kissed his cheek. "Thanks for the distraction though."

Roman smiled and motioned for her to go ahead of him into her office. They'd come in with the intention of preparing the menu for the next two weeks and do up the purchase list. She'd tried to tell him she could do it on her own, but Roman insisted they'd get it done faster with two of them and they'd have the evening to chill at home.

By the time they finished everything, it was almost lunchtime. Her stomach had been upset that morning and she could only manage to get down a couple of dry crackers and a cup of herbal tea. So by the time she'd sent off her orders, her stomach started to growl like she hadn't eaten in a week.

"I'm starving," she stood up and stretched out her back.

"Do you want me to make some lunch?" Roman asked.

"How about we go to *Jack's Place* and let my mom feed us?" Isabelle reached for his hand as they walked out of the office.

Jack's Place was the combination diner and pub that was owned by her parents, although her father was more of a silent partner. Mostly because his suggestions always got silenced. A lot of people asked what it was like to be in competition with her mom, but she didn't feel that way. Her restaurant was completely different from *Jack's Place*.

"Sounds good to me. I love your mom's partridgeberry pie." Roman grinned.

"I think you should have more for lunch than pie." Isabelle laughed as they stepped outside.

"Ms. O'Connor, I was just coming to see you." A male voice startled her.

Isabelle turned around to see an attractive man in a black pinstriped suit. His thinning dark hair was impeccably groomed and although his smile seemed genuine, something about him made her take a step toward Roman.

"I'm sorry, do we know each other?" Isabelle didn't remember the man at all.

"I would hope so. We've had several conversations over the phone and email." He winked after his vague statement.

"I speak to a lot of people on the phone and email. You'll have to be more specific." Isabelle felt slightly annoyed by the way he leered at her in front of Roman.

"I thought you would recognize my voice." He seemed annoyed that she didn't know who he was.

"Look, buddy. My girlfriend doesn't know you, so either tell her or move on." Roman wrapped his arm around her shoulders.

Roman probably seemed a little over-the-top caveman, but it didn't upset Isabelle. It actually made her feel warm and fuzzy because he referred to her as his girlfriend. As juvenile as it was to feel that way, Isabelle couldn't help it.

The man glared at Roman for a moment then turned back to Isabelle as he reached into his pocket. Roman's grip tensed on her shoulder and he pulled her behind him. The movement seemed to amuse the stranger and he chuckled as he held out a card.

"Good to see a man protective over his woman, but I don't think this business card is very dangerous." He held out the card and Roman snatched it out of the man's hand.

"Bryce Landell of *Landell Corp.*" Roman read the card and handed to Isabelle.

Isabelle remembered the name. Bryce had been contacting her for almost a year to convince her to sell him her building. She'd turned him down several times, but he'd been relentless. She'd thought he'd gotten the hint, but to have him show up in person didn't make her feel confident.

"Mr. Landell, what are you doing here?" Isabelle stepped around Roman.

"I was told that your restaurant was out of business and I wanted to make you an offer on the building." Bryce held out a folded piece of paper.

"Figured you'd get it for a discount price, did you?" Roman said sarcastically.

"*A Taste of Hopedale* is not out of business. I had to close up for a week because of an unfortunate situation, but we're reopening on Saturday." Isabelle knew he had to have heard about the murder.

"Oh, even with all the bad press, you're still going to reopen?" Bryce seemed shocked.

"Yes, she is. Now if you don't mind, we were heading to lunch." Roman snapped.

Roman kept himself between Bryce and Isabelle as he guided her around the obnoxious man. It seemed as if Roman wasn't giving Bryce a chance to get too close.

"Mind if I join you?" Bryce asked and Isabelle pressed her lips together to keep from laughing at the way Roman growled.

"Yes, we do mind," Roman said as he and Isabelle kept walking away from Bryce.

"I wasn't asking you." Bryce snarled.

"Maybe not, but I'm answering. Goodbye, Mr. Landell," Roman shouted over his shoulder and they made their way to *Jack's Place*.

Isabelle took one quick glance behind her as they walked into the parking lot of the diner. Bryce was still in front of her building, staring at them with his phone to his ear. The look made her shiver and Roman pulled her tighter against his side, probably thinking she was cold.

"That guy is a fucking ass," Roman grumbled as they walked into the diner and made their way to the booth at the back.

"He's pushy, that's for sure." Isabelle shrugged out of her jacket.

"Yeah, and it's not a coincidence that he just shows up when you're about to reopen." Roman reached across the table and took her hands in his.

He seemed to do it whenever they were sat within arm's reach of each other, he always had to be holding her hand. It was sweet and she loved it. Not only that, she loved him. She hadn't told him, but she'd come close to saying it a couple of days ago.

Roman wasn't wrong about Bryce's timing. Something about the way he showed up out of the blue had her on edge. He'd been relentless with the calls and emails, but never had he actually shown up. It was why she hadn't known who he was.

"What can I get you?" Sabrina, one of the newer waitresses at the diner, stepped next to the booth.

"I'll have a turkey sandwich and a cup of camomile tea." Isabelle smiled up at the pretty woman.

"And you?" Sabrina turned to Roman.

"I'll have a burger with cheese and fries and a black coffee." Roman ordered his lunch and then immediately turned back to Isabelle.

It gave her butterflies when he gave her his full attention. She prayed it would never change. He'd also taken to keeping his hand on her stomach when they slept in bed together. She'd asked him why and he said he wanted to make sure he felt it when the baby kicked for the first time. Isabelle had laughed and explained that since she was only a little over eight weeks that it would probably be several months before he could feel that.

The only other issue was he seemed to think they needed to hold off on sex. It didn't bode well since her hormones were in overdrive. No matter what she said to him, he said he wanted to wait until the next doctor's appointment to make sure it was safe. How a man of his age didn't know sex was okay during pregnancy was beyond her. It was sweet, but she was sexually frustrated.

"Hey, guys." Sandy slid into the seat next to Isabelle.

"Hey." Isabelle tried to pull her hands from Roman's but he wouldn't let go.

"I was looking for you at the restaurant," Sandy said as she pulled out an iPad and started to tap the screen.

"We don't open until Saturday. What's up?" Isabelle wasn't used to seeing Sandy look so serious.

"I've been going through all the security videos from your restaurant and outside, as well as the harbor security. Aaron asked me to dig in and I've spent the last four days doing just that." Sandy turned the iPad toward Isabelle and pointed. "Do you know this guy?"

Isabelle leaned in to get a better look at the fuzzy image on the tablet. The only thing she could see was someone dressed in dark clothes with a baseball cap and the face hidden.

"I can't see the face." Isabelle shrugged.

"Yeah, the little fucker seemed to know where all the cameras were." Sandy tapped the screen a couple more times and turned it back to Isabelle again.

The image was a little clearer but still, the person had their face turned from the video. Isabelle studied the clothing, but none of it looked familiar. What did draw her attention was that the person was entering the building next to her restaurant.

"Does he come out and go into my building?" Isabelle asked.

"That's just it. He doesn't come out until way after Roman walks by. Then he runs like a bat out of hell with his head down and out of view of any more cameras.," Sandy explained.

"It can't be him then." Roman shrugged.

"Are there any connecting doors to your building and the club?" Sandy asked.

"No. The whole thing used to be one whole building, but it was divided up years ago and the owners sold it as two separate buildings. All access to the other building was closed off with a brick wall." Isabelle had been told that when she bought the building.

"That's why the blue print from twenty years ago showed it all as one building." Sandy huffed.

"I guess this means the police are no closer to finding out who killed Cindy," Roman said solemnly.

"We'll catch him." Sandy winked and gave Isabelle a quick hug before she stood up.

"Thanks, Sandy," Isabelle replied.

"No problem, it's part of my job." Sandy waved as she walked away.

For a few minutes, Isabelle stared out at the windows at one of the fishing boats as it bobbed up and down next to the dock. Being that it was the last week of February, the boats were being prepared for the upcoming crab fishery. It reminded her that she'd have to set up a menu to include fresh crab for the season.

She always tried to keep her menu up to date with the local fishing seasons. Then again, would she even have a business by the end of April? The thought of getting a loan to pay the bills made her stomach turn, especially with a baby coming. The last thing she needed was to be in debt.

"Want to share what's going through that beautiful head of yours?" Roman's quiet question pulled her from her thoughts.

"Nothing." She turned and gave him her best fake smile.

"Tiger, you're not a good liar." Roman brought her hand to his lips and kissed it gently.

"I'm just thinking about how different it's going to be without Cindy." Isabelle sighed.

It wasn't really a lie. It was hard to think about not seeing Cindy's smiling face every day. Even with the daily drama that often came with Cindy, the perky waitress would be missed by everyone.

"Did you call Hulk's friend?" Roman asked.

"I did. She's going to drop by tomorrow and I'm pretty sure I'm giving her the job. She's got a great reference." Isabelle nodded toward where Hulk had entered the diner.

"I think Caroline is more than a *friend* to him." Roman smirked.

"I think you're right." Isabelle laughed and sat back as Sabrina placed their food in front of them.

They sat eating in comfortable silence, Isabelle's mind going a mile a minute on what she had to do over the next few days. She knew Roman wasn't going to be happy if she overdid it and it was nice to have someone look out for her that way. She'd been a hardworking woman for so long, she hoped it was possible to sit back and allow Roman to take some of the weight off her shoulders. Could she actually do that? She had to for the sake of her child.

Chapter 16

Roman had plans and a huge surprise for Isabelle, but in order to do that he had to make sure she wasn't home alone. He had a bad feeling from the moment they ran into Bryce. There was something about the way the man leered at Isabelle that made him think the asshole was after more than just Isabelle's restaurant.

Then there were the noises that he'd heard a few times outside her house. When he'd rush out to investigate there was never anyone around. When he told Isabelle that he was going to mention it to John and Bull, she told him not to bother. She was convinced it was that stupid tree in front of her house. Roman didn't believe that, which was why he sent a text to Kristy.

Roman: I was wondering if you could drop by and keep Isabelle company for a couple of hours?

Kristy: Sure. Is she okay?

Roman: She's fine but I hate to leave her alone with everything she has going on.

Kristy: You're too sweet. I'll be by in about thirty minutes. I have to wait for Dean to get home so he can watch Decker.

Roman: Thanks.

Kristy: My pleasure, but if she figures out you called me over to babysit, I'm not covering your butt.

Roman: Noted.

Roman chuckled as he shoved his phone into his pocket and headed into the kitchen to let Isabelle know he had to run out for a bit. She was sat at the kitchen table and seemed to be completely zoned in to her laptop.

"Whatcha doin, Tiger?" Roman stepped behind her and gently squeezed her shoulders.

"Nothing, really. Just looking for some new ideas for crab dishes." Isabelle tilted her head back and looked up at him.

"Trying to get ahead of the game, huh?" Roman leaned down and kissed her lips softly.

"Yeah, hopefully I'll still be open by then." She sighed against his lips.

"Don't worry, Tiger. Things will be fine." He pressed his lips against her forehead.

Isabelle told him about some of the dishes she usually served for different seasons. Roman had only started at the restaurant the previous summer, so he never saw any of the menu for that season.

He liked what she showed him, but he looked forward to showing Isabelle some of his own recipes he'd put together over the years. Maybe between the two of them they could come up with something unique to her restaurant.

"Hello. Your favorite sister is here," Kristy called from the foyer.

"Hi, Jess." Isabelle smirked.

"Not funny." Kristy stepped into the kitchen and narrowed her eyes at Isabelle.

"You know I love you." Isabelle chuckled.

"Of course you do." Kristy eased down into one of the kitchen chairs and rested her hands on her belly.

Roman glanced at Isabelle and tried to picture the woman he loved with a swollen belly filled with his child. It made him even more sure of his feelings for her. He hoped the surprise he planned showed her how much he cared about her and that he'd give her everything she ever wanted.

"I have to run out for a bit. Do you need anything while I'm out?" Roman asked.

"No, I'm good." Isabelle smiled and he gave her a quick kiss on the cheek before heading out.

"Okay, I'll be back before you know it." Roman started to leave.

"I'll be fine. The babysitter you hired knows me well." Isabelle raised an eyebrow.

"Busted." Kristy snorted.

"I'm gone, bye." He should have known he would never get away with that.

Roman hopped in his car and pulled out of Isabelle's driveway. As he made his way out of Hopedale and headed into the city to pick up the special surprise for Isabelle, he realized he hadn't called his siblings in a while. He knew Isabelle had told her sisters and Nanny Betty knew about the baby. Maybe he should probably tell his brothers and sister as well.

He was about to pull off the highway into St. John's when his phone rang through the speaker of the car. He tapped the button on the wheel to answer the call as he turned off onto the exit ramp.

"Hello," he said.

"Roman, it's A.J." Aaron's voice echoed through the car. "I was wondering if you could come into the station?"

"Sure, I'm in town right now, but I could be there in about an hour. What's this about?" Roman had already given Aaron a statement.

"I want to confirm a few things with you. An hour will work. When you come in let reception know I'm expecting you," Aaron replied.

"Will do," Roman answered.

Roman had told Aaron everything he knew, which wasn't much. He didn't know that much about Cindy except she'd worked for Isabelle for a while. Roman didn't have much interaction with the dining staff during work hours because he spent his time in the kitchen.

Since he'd been so open with Aaron about what he knew, Roman found it unusual to be called into the station. The only thing he could think of was that they found something and they wanted him to break it to Isabelle.

As his thoughts ran through the reasons that he'd been summoned to the police station, he made his way through the city of St. John's and the bottom of a hill that brought him to an area of the city known as Shea Heights.

He was making his way to see a lady who had Isabelle's surprise. Roman was excited to do something for her that she'd always wanted. He hoped it wasn't going to end up being a huge mistake and something that stressed her out more than she was.

Chapter 17

Isabelle was happy to spend time with Kristy. After all, her sisters, Nanny Betty, and Tom were the only other people besides Roman who knew about the pregnancy. It was amusing to her that she was turning to her youngest sister for advice.

"It's normal for your breasts to be sore and the worst part is they get so big." Kristy held her hands out in front of her own breasts.

"Great because my boobs are not already big enough." Isabelle pulled out her shirt and looked down into her cleavage.

"Dean says he didn't think my tits could get any bigger. Asshole." Kristy laughed

"You're just making this sound like heaven," Isabelle said sarcastically.

"It's not all bad. The first time you get that little flutter of the baby moving, it's a feeling like no other." Kristy smiled.

"I'm scared," Isabelle admitted as she picked at the fruit on her plate.

"That's normal. I was terrified when I was pregnant with Decker, but you know what?" Kristy reached across the table and covered Isabelle's hand with hers.

"What?" Isabelle met her sister's eyes.

"You've got nothing to worry about. You're going to be the best mom in the world." Kristy squeezed Isabelle's hand.

"Thanks." She forced a smile.

"Next to me, of course." Kristy grinned.

"Of course," Isabelle laughed.

The truth was, Isabelle was scared that it would be all too much for Roman. They were doing everything completely upside down. In her family, it was date someone, get married, and then have babies. Then there was the keep the other person from getting killed or kidnapped, but that was a whole other thing Isabelle didn't want to have to deal with. After all, who'd want to kill her?

Maybe her parents. She still had to tell them and although her father had become more civil with Roman, she figured when her dad found out, Roman would be on the enemy list again. If her dad didn't kill Roman on the spot.

"You know you're going to have to take it easier than you have been, right?" Kristy smirked.

"If things don't get better at the restaurant after we open, I may not have to worry about working." Isabelle sighed.

"It's a slump, honey. If you need help, we'll all pitch in. Don't try to do this all by yourself," Kristy ordered.

She'd talked to Kristy several times about the issues she had at work. In true sister style, Kristy didn't say a word to anyone other than Jess and Pam. Then both sisters and her cousin handed out flyers for the restaurant whenever they had a chance.

Isabelle didn't know if it had helped, but it definitely wouldn't hurt. Pam and a partner ran a fashion store both online and in Hopedale called *Cupid's Closet*. They sold accessories, lingerie, formal dresses, casual clothing all for women. Pam had placed a small ad on their website for Isabelle's restaurant as well and offered a discount to anyone who brought in a receipt from a meal there.

Jess owned a flower shop in St. John's and had done something similar. She'd offered a contest to anyone looking for a romantic evening with their spouses, she'd give them a free bouquet, and have it delivered to the restaurant during their meal. It was all great until Cindy's murder.

"I haven't had a chance to ask. How are Jess' wedding plans going?" Isabelle wanted to change the subject from anything to do with her or the restaurant.

"Maybe if Wade and our sister would set a date we could actually start plans." Kristy rolled her eyes.

"If my sisters didn't keep getting pregnant, maybe I could set a date." Jess chuckled

Isabelle glanced toward the kitchen doorway as Jess walked into the room. Kristy stuck out her tongue at Jess and Isabelle could only roll her eyes.

"Maybe you should too, that way we can all go together." Kristy snorted.

"First of all, you're going to pop in less than a month and Isabelle is due what, October? Even if I get pregnant tonight, I'll be months behind you two." Jess plopped down in the chair next to Kristy.

"I don't think I even have less than a month." Kristy rubbed her hand over her belly. "This baby girl is ready to come out any day. Dean already has plans on beating up any man who comes near her."

"That should be interesting." Isabelle laughed.

Her two sisters went quiet for a few minutes and Isabelle watched them as they glanced at each other. She didn't need to ask to know they had something on their minds.

"What?" Isabelle asked.

"We were just wondering…" Jess stopped and looked at Kristy.

"Spit it out." Isabelle huffed.

"When are you going to tell everyone?" Kristy asked.

"Nan already knows." Isabelle almost laughed at their shocked expressions. "I didn't tell her, she looked at me and knew."

"Why does that not surprise me?" Jess snorted.

"I think the only one that you have to worry about being pissed at you is Sandy. She hates when people know something she doesn't." Kristy laughed.

"What about Mom and Dad?" Jess asked.

"I'm going to have to do it soon. I know that, but I don't want them to be disappointed with me." Isabelle sighed.

She was a grown woman and felt like if she told her parents that she was pregnant out of wedlock, that they would think less of her. In her head, she knew it wasn't true. Isabelle never wanted to see that look on their faces.

For the next hour, her sisters grilled her on Roman, the restaurant and when she would announce her pregnancy to the family. When she heard his voice, Isabelle breathed a sigh of relief.

"Tiger, I'm back." She couldn't hide the smile when his voice echoed through the house.

"God, you got it bad." Jess stood up and helped Kristy to her feet.

"I know." Isabelle groaned and stood as well.

"Come out here. I've got a surprise for you," Roman shouted.

Jess motioned for Isabelle to go ahead of her and Kristy. She couldn't even imagine what Roman could have gotten for her. Maybe something for the baby. The thought had her hurrying out to the living room. He was in the doorway and held up his hand.

"Wait there." He disappeared into the foyer and when he returned, he was holding something in his arms.

"Roman, what did you do?" Isabelle gasped when the small furry dog lifted its head and stared at her with huge bright blue eyes.

"Her name is Cobalt." Roman grinned.

"You got her a dog?" Jess laughed.

"A Husky." Roman still had a huge grin on his face but when he looked at Isabelle, it faltered a little.

"She's adorable." Kristy waddled toward Roman and gently scratched the puppy's head.

"Well, we're going to leave and let you deal with this." Jess snorted as she pointed at Roman.

Isabelle heard the click of the front door and the muffled laughter of her sisters as they left her house. She hadn't moved, and Roman stood stock-still in the doorway holding the puppy who was licking Roman's face.

"She's beautiful, Roman." Isabelle slowly walked toward Roman.

"But?" Roman's smile fell.

“Why did you get me a dog?” She giggled as Cobalt turned her attention to Isabelle.

“You said you always wanted one, so I asked Nick where I could get a Husky. He told me about this breeder who trained K9 dogs for the Newfoundland Police Department. She breeds Huskies, and when I called her, she sent me a picture of this little girl.” Roman seemed so proud of himself.

“She’s so cute.” Isabelle was getting sucked in deeper by the minute.

“Barb said she’s fourteen weeks old and kennel trained. We have to leave the kennel opened, except for the times we have to put her inside the cage. If we want her to go outside, we put a puppy pad in front of the door we want her to use.” Roman went on with the instructions, but Isabelle was a goner.

The young Husky was white with black curved around her beautiful blue eyes. It looked like a mask and the name Bandit came to mind, but Roman said the dog's name was Cobalt. Which suited the pretty puppy completely.

“So, Cobalt. Do you think I should thank Roman for bringing you to me?” Isabelle smiled as the dog frantically wagged her tail.

“I’m thinking that tail wag is a definite yes.” Roman winked.

Isabelle looked up and met his eyes. How could she not fall in love with the man even more after he’d gone and made one of her dreams come true? Sure, it was just a puppy, but it showed her how much he actually cared and listened to her.

"Thank you, Roman. I love her," Isabelle said softly then took a deep breath. "And…"

"And?" Roman tilted his head at the same time the dog did.

"And you're making me fall for you." Isabelle smiled.

Roman didn't speak or move for a moment and Isabelle suddenly wanted to take back what she said. Her heart thudded in her chest as he placed Cobalt on the floor and Isabelle held her breath.

Roman took a step closer and cupped his hand around the back of her head as he gazed into her eyes. She was sure at that point he could probably hear her heart pound. She barely heard the soft whine from the puppy as Roman leaned closer.

"I've been waiting for you all my life, Isabelle. I've been falling hard and fast for you since the first day I met you." Roman pressed his forehead against hers.

With those sweet words Roman gently brushed his lips against hers. Isabelle rested her hands on his hips as he slowly made love to her mouth with his. Her heart started to pound for another reason and she reached for the buttons of his shirt.

Before she could do any more, Roman pulled back and covered her hands where they lay against his chest. There was no doubt in her mind that he was as aroused as she was, but he took a step back and blew out a breath.

"When do you have to go back to see the doctor?" He practically growled.

"Why do you have to go to the doctor?" The sound of her father's voice made her gasp and Roman slowly turned around.

Her father and mother stood in the foyer with the door still open. Cobalt moved in front of Isabelle and started to whine as she wagged her tail back and forth.

"Dad, Mom. I didn't hear you come in." Isabelle stammered over her words.

"I could see why." Her mother winked at Roman as Isabelle bent over and picked the dog up in her arms.

"This is Cobalt." Isabelle smiled but it faltered when she met her father's suspicious glare.

"She's adorable. You've always wanted a Husky." Her mother didn't seem to be bothered by her father's reaction and scratched the dog's head.

"Roman got her for me." Isabelle laughed when the dog started to lick her mother's face.

"The doctor, Isabelle. Why are you going back to the doctor?" Her father was like a dog with a bone. "Are you sick?"

Isabelle glanced at Roman and he looked steady as a rock. She knew her parents had to find out sometime. Maybe she should just pull off the proverbial Band-Aid with them like she did with Roman. When Roman gave her a slight nod, she knew he agreed.

"Let's go to the living room and sit." Isabelle made her way to the couch and sat down.

She didn't want to put the dog down on the floor, but the minute Roman sat next to her, Cobalt decided she wanted to be between them. Her father didn't sit. He stood behind the armchair next to the fireplace where her mother eased into the chair.

It was obvious by the grip her dad had on the back of the chair that he was anxious. Isabelle felt terrible because he probably thought the worst, like Roman did. Her mother seemed concerned as well.

"Isabelle?" Her father pushed.

"I'm not sick," Isabelle blurted out.

"That's good to know," her mom said.

"I'm…" Isabelle stopped and glanced at Roman.

"We're pregnant," Roman finished.

Isabelle held her breath as she waited for her parents' reaction. Her mother had a huge smile, but she didn't seem surprised. Her father was a different story. He didn't move and his face didn't show any emotion.

"That's so exciting. Another baby in the family." Her mother jumped to her feet and hurried across the room to sit next to Isabelle.

Her dad didn't move but his focus moved to Roman. Isabelle did her best to keep her eyes on her dad as she hugged her mother. The last thing she needed was her father to turn on Roman again.

"Isn't it wonderful, Kurt?" Her mom leaned across Isabelle and gave Roman a tight hug.

"Wonderful," Her father said through clenched teeth.

"Dad?" Isabelle stood up as her father started to walk toward Roman.

"I want to talk to *you* outside. Now." Her father put a hard emphasis on the word *you* and walked out of the house.

Roman stood and was about to follow, but Isabelle grabbed his arm. The last thing she wanted was for her father to beat the hell out of Roman, because the look on her dad's face said he just might do that.

"Tiger, I respect your dad. If he wants to talk to me alone, I'll do that. I need him to know how I feel about you and that I'm not going anywhere." Roman gave her a quick kiss on the lips and then he disappeared through the door.

"Mom, it's not going to be good if the Mayor of Hopedale goes to jail for murder." Isabelle groaned and sat next to her mother.

“Honey, your father isn’t going to kill him. He’ll find out what his intentions are. That’s what dads do.” Her mother smiled.

“I hope you’re right.” Isabelle rested her head on her mother’s shoulder. “I don’t want to have to tell this baby his grandfather killed his father.”

Chapter 18

Roman stepped out onto the front porch of Isabelle's house. Kurt stood on the top of the steps with his arms folded in front of his chest, staring out at the beach. Roman didn't know if it was an intimidation tactic, but he wasn't about to stand down. He loved Isabelle and although he hadn't told her those exact words yet, he knew it was true. Roman stepped next to him and watched the waves crash upon the rocks.

"Before you say anything, Kurt. We weren't keeping it from you. Isabelle wasn't ready to tell anyone yet and I had to respect her wishes." Roman turned to look at Isabelle's dad.

"What are your plans?" Kurt's voice sounded strained.

"My plans are to stand next to your daughter every day that she allows me to." Roman wasn't about to say he was going to marry Isabelle just because she was pregnant.

It wasn't that he didn't see it in the future, but he knew if he asked, Isabelle would believe he only wanted to do it because of the baby. When he asked her, and he knew he would one day, he wanted her to know one hundred percent that he loved her and wanted to spend the rest of his life with her.

“You can’t ask her to marry you.” Kurt seemed to have read Roman’s mind. “Not now.”

“Because she wouldn’t believe it was because I wanted to spend my life with her,” Roman replied.

“Exactly. You love her?” Kurt finally turned to look at him.

“I do.” Roman had never spoke anything with more conviction.

Kurt stared at him for several minutes before he turned back to the beach. Kurt might put off as being a tough former police officer and Chief of Police, but to anyone who saw him with his wife, daughters, or grandchild, they’d know the true heart of Kurt O’Connor. Roman saw him swallow several times before he spoke again.

“She’s my first little girl.” Kurt’s voice cracked.

“I’m sure she’ll always be a little girl to you.” Roman understood that.

“Yes, but she’s also the one who hates to worry us. She was always the one that didn’t let us see when she was stressed, hurt, or sad. Not that we couldn’t see it, but we always had to drag it out of her. She’s like me that way.” Kurt turned back to face Roman.

“She tries that with me too.” Roman smirked.

“I want two things from you, Roman.” Kurt met Roman’s eyes.

“What are the two things?” Roman asked.

“Don’t ever hurt her.” Kurt narrowed his eyes.

“I’d never hurt her,” Roman admitted.

“Good.” Kurt nodded.

“What’s the second thing?” Roman asked.

“Tell me what’s going on with her restaurant.” Kurt lowered his voice as if he wanted to make sure nobody heard him.

“We’re getting everything ready for Saturday.” Roman shrugged.

“I know there’s been stuff happening and Isabelle has been keeping it from us. Is there someone trying to sabotage her?” Kurt asked.

“Honestly, I don’t know, but there’s something sketchy going on. That’s what I told A.J. today when I dropped by the station. He asked me the same thing,” Roman replied.

Before he came back to Isabelle’s house, he’d talked to Aaron and John. They’d asked him if he’d noticed anything around Isabelle’s house over the last few weeks. Apparently, Bull and John had security videos outside their homes and one of the cameras caught someone lurking around Isabelle’s house. It was then that Roman told him about the noises he’d heard.

"Is that the reason you got the dog?" Kurt's lips quirked up in a grin.

"Partly," Roman admitted.

Cobalt might be only a puppy, but Roman could train her to be a watchdog. He'd gotten some advice from the breeder, and Barb told him that if he had any questions, she'd be happy to help.

"She's always loved Huskies." Kurt shook his head.

"Yeah, she told me." Roman relaxed a little, mostly because Kurt didn't look like he was about to kill.

"I want to give you a heads up. My gut tells me something's going on and it's aimed at Isabelle and her business. Promise me you'll keep your guard up too." Kurt held out his hand.

"I promise, I'll do my best to keep her safe." Roman shook Kurt's hand.

"That's all I can ask." Kurt nodded and released Roman's hand.

"Can I be honest with you, sir?" Roman asked.

"I appreciate honesty." Kurt shoved his hands into his jeans' pockets.

Roman took a few moments to put together what he wanted to say. He didn't want to betray Isabelle's confidence, but he knew that her father would want to know what was going on. Roman also wanted to make sure Kurt knew about the asshole who stopped them outside the restaurant.

"Look, I told A.J. about this guy, but I know they aren't exactly letting you get involved in the investigation." Roman gave him a sympathetic smile.

"Yeah, Alice has made sure of that." Kurt grumbled.

"There's a guy, Bryce Landell. He was waiting outside the restaurant this morning when we left. Kurt, the guy seemed a little pushy. I didn't get a good feeling from him," Roman said.

"What do you mean, pushy?" Kurt raised an eyebrow.

"He seemed to think *A Taste of Hopedale* was closed for good and basically said he'd take the building off Isabelle's hands. He tried to hand her a piece of paper, I'm assuming with an offer, but she told him she wasn't closed for good. He tried not to show it, but he was annoyed." The way the guy accosted them outside the entrance of the restaurant still didn't sit well with Roman.

"What did A.J. tell you?" Kurt's shoulders looked tense and his jaw clenched.

"Said he'd check the guy out," Roman explained.

"Then he will, but thanks for telling me. I still have other ways to help." Kurt winked and gave a sly grin. "Just don't tell anyone."

“My lips are sealed.” Roman chuckled as they made their way back into the house.

Roman could see the stress all over Isabelle’s face when he walked into the living room. At first, he thought something had happened while he was outside with Kurt. At least until her mother laughed.

“See, I told you he wouldn’t kill Roman.” Alice smiled and gave Isabelle a side hug.

“Nah, killing is too easy. I like to torture the men involved with my daughters. Psychological torture is the best kind.” Kurt laughed when Isabelle rolled her eyes.

Isabelle stood up from the sofa and made her way toward them. Roman held out his hand and she took it as she stood up on her toes and kissed her father’s cheek. The love was so evident in Kurt’s expression that it wasn’t hard to see how much the man loved his daughter.

“I love you, sweet pea. I would never do anything that would make you sad. I think killing the chef here might do that.” Her father wrapped his arm around her and kissed the top of her head.

After the discussion, Roman offered to cook supper for Isabelle and her parents. Kurt wouldn’t hear of it and after a quick call to Jess and Kristy, they were off to St. John’s to have supper with Isabelle’s family.

Roman was a little sad that he wasn't about to do the same with his parents and siblings, but it did remind him that maybe he should make more of an effort on his part to talk to his brothers and sister. After all, with video calls, it would be like being with them for just a few minutes.

As if Isabelle recognized his thoughts, she reached over and placed her hand on top of his at the table. He smiled at the woman next to him. He didn't think it was possible, but he fell in love a little more.

After supper, Isabelle went shopping with her mother and sisters. Kurt, Bull, Wade, and Roman happily declined the offer to go with them and made their way back to Hopedale in Kurt's truck. Jess offered to drive the women home after their shopping trip.

After a couple of beers with the men at *Jack's Place*, the pub that was the second half of Alice and Kurt's diner, Roman made his way back to Isabelle's house. He decided to call his brothers and sister and tell them all about Isabelle and the baby.

Maximus, or Max was the oldest brother and lived just outside of Ottawa, Ontario. He was married and they had three children who were all in their teens. Demetrios was the second brother, also married, and he lived in Alberta with his wife and two pre-teens. Marcella was the youngest of them all and still single. She lived in Montreal and didn't seem to have any intentions of tying herself down.

The last time Roman had gotten together with his family was Christmas when he flew up to Ontario for the holidays. Isabelle always closed down the week of Christmas and although he hated to leave her, she'd insisted he go.

When his family asked if he'd been seeing anyone, he'd lied and told him it was nobody serious. He knew even those few months ago that Isabelle wasn't just any other woman. Luckily, his brothers had moved on to Marcella and he was off the hook.

Roman opened his phone and tapped his brother's number. He waited for Maximus' face to appear on the screen and calmed himself. He had no idea why he was so nervous to tell them he'd finally found the love of his life.

"Who died?" Maximus answered.

"Jesus, is the only reason I call you to tell you someone died?" Roman laughed.

"Usually," Maximus replied.

That answer hit Roman directly in the chest. It was true. The only time they called each other was when there was bad news. How did a family that was once so close end up like that? His father was probably rolling over in his grave.

"We need to change that, Max," Roman said.

"We do." Maximus smiled.

“I actually called to tell you some good news.” Roman grinned.

“Yeah, did some girl finally knock you off your feet?” Demetrios’ face appeared behind Maximus.

“Dem, what are you doing there?” Roman was surprised.

“Got laid off in Alberta and Max got me an interview with the construction company he works for,” Demetrios replied.

“Sorry you got laid off but it’ll be great if you move close to Max.” Roman felt a twinge of jealousy that his siblings were together without him.

“Yeah, so what’s the good news?” Demetrios pushed.

“I’m in love.” Roman grinned.

“What?” Maximus’ eyes almost popped out of his head.

“Stop fucking with us.” Demetrios laughed.

“Not fucking with you. Her name is Isabelle O’Connor and she’s the most amazing woman I’ve ever met,” Roman said. “You guys will love her.”

“I thought when you were here Christmas you weren’t seeing anyone seriously.” It figured Maximus would remember that.

“Actually, I wasn’t sure what it was then. I guess I was afraid to admit how special she’d become to me. Scared I’d fuck it up somehow,” Roman admitted.

"When do we get to meet her?" Demetrios asked.

"Well, probably after the baby is born." Roman almost choked with laughter at the shock and confusion on their faces.

"Baby?" They shouted together.

"Oh, didn't I say that? We're having a baby in October." Roman grinned.

"Holy shit. Congrats, Roman," Maximus shouted.

"Hang on, I'm getting Cella on the line," Demetrios said as he glanced down.

A few minutes later, Roman heard Marcella's voice. He wished he could see her, but it didn't seem like any of them were good with technology and would probably end up breaking something if they tried a group video chat.

"Who died?" Marcella's voice echoed through the speaker of Demetrios' phone.

"Jesus." Roman laughed.

"See, I told you." Maximus pointed to the phone.

"Nobody died, but Roman is in love and he's gonna be a dad," Demetrios shouted into his phone.

"First of all, stop shouting at the phone. It's on speaker, Idiot, you don't have to shout. Second of all, you're full of shit." Marcella scoffed.

“No, he’s not, Cella.” Roman knew if he didn’t speak, Marcella wouldn’t believe Demetrios.

“Yeah, right.” She snorted.

“I’m serious. Her name is Isabelle O’Connor.” Roman laughed.

For a few minutes, his sister was quiet. They could hear what sounded like computer keys clicking but they had no idea what she was doing.

“She’s your boss, asshole,” Marcella said finally. “She owns the restaurant you work at.”

“Yes, that’s where we met.” Roman shook his head and he saw Maximus roll his eyes.

“You’re serious?” Marcella said.

“Yes, I’m serious.” Roman laughed.

“Wow, that’s great. I can’t wait to meet her.” Marcella turned into her regular chatterbox after that.

Roman was happy to answer anything his siblings had to ask. Hopefully, when the baby was born, Roman and Isabelle could make a trip up to meet them, or maybe they would come back to Newfoundland.

With all the time he spent in Hopedale and with the O’Connors, Roman started to miss his siblings more and more. The chances of them moving back to Newfoundland was slim, but he certainly wouldn't let so much time go by before calling them again. He wanted them to be as close to Baby Tiger as Isabelle's family would be. If things went the way he hoped, they'd all be family someday.

Chapter 19

Isabelle was frustrated beyond belief. Her restaurant had reopened a few days earlier and the place was packed every night. It was no different tonight and it was reserved completely every day for the rest of the week. Anyone would think she'd be relieved, but the problem was, she'd lost several of her staff.

Her sous chef Gwen, Milly and Jake returned to work, but only one of her busboys had returned. The other two found other jobs and Angelina moved to Labrador to be with her boyfriend. That meant she was left with only two waiters.

Hulk's friend Caroline joined her staff but Isabelle had to put her on the floor as a waitress, which left Isabelle out of the kitchen and on hostess duty, again. To top it off, Bryce, his father and a brunette with over-inflated boobs and an underdeveloped IQ walked into the restaurant with no reservation.

"Ms. O'Connor, it's so good to see your wonderful restaurant opened again." Stanley Landell smiled.

Stanley was a tall, slim, and bald, or at least he would be if he didn't do the most horrible comb-over. He was probably in his early fifties, but time had not been good to him. He seemed like a nice man for the most part, but a prickle skittered up the back of her neck when he grabbed her hand and kissed it.

"We hit a little bump in the road but we're on track now." Isabelle tried to reclaim her hand without being rude.

"I see you're pretty full tonight." Bryce smirked as he glanced around.

"Yes, we're booked up all week." Isabelle stepped behind the podium and Stanley finally released her hand.

"I'm sure you could fit our little group in for supper." Stanley grinned.

"I honestly can't. All our tables are full right now. I've got another party waiting at the bar and as you can see behind you, we have another group coming in for their *reservation*." Isabelle put emphasis on the word reservation as she nodded to the four businessmen watching her.

"Even for an old friend?" Bryce purred.

"Not even for any of my family," Isabelle replied, but of course that wasn't true.

Where Bryce got the idea that they were old friends, she had no idea. She'd known the man less than a year and would never describe him as a friend. Annoyance maybe.

Isabelle motioned for the group behind Bryce to come around the Landells and explained there would be a few minutes' wait. She pointed them to the bar, and assured them the waitress would let them know when their table was ready. She hoped when she turned back to the podium Stanley, Bryce and the woman would have left.

"Do you think if we wait we could squeeze in?" Stanley pushed.

"I'm sorry, Mr. Landell, I just can't do it." Isabelle was getting annoyed and she had to pee.

"What a dump," the woman mumbled as she tossed her hair over her shoulder and pouted.

"If you want, you can make a reservation for next week, but we're booked up until next Wednesday." Isabelle opened the reservation book and picked up her pen.

"We'll have to call. I have to check some things before I do that." Stanley smiled, but it wasn't hard to see he was pissed.

"Okay, have a good night." Isabelle returned.

Caroline luckily pulled her away from the podium before the trio could say another word. She did notice the way Bryce and Stanley leered at Caroline, and she chuckled to herself because if they even tried a move on the woman, Hulk would knock them out. Although, both he and Caroline still didn't admit they were more than friends.

"I've got a free table for one of the groups at the bar," Caroline told her.

"Can you go let them know?" Isabelle asked.

"Of course." Caroline spun around and hurried to the bar area.

She really was an amazing worker and Isabelle thanked her lucky stars Hulk had brought her to Hopedale. She would have been in a really bad situation if he hadn't.

As Isabelle waved to the last group to leave for the evening, she glanced at her watch and blew out a breath. She was tired and all she wanted to do was go home and crawl into bed. That wasn't possible since she was short-staffed as it was and everything needed to be prepared for the next day.

She was on her way into the kitchen when she heard someone knock on the door she'd just locked. Isabelle was about to ignore it, but when she glanced out the window, she was surprised to see several of her family outside.

In a panic, she hurried to the door and yanked it opened. Before she could ask what they were all doing there, Nanny Betty shoved by them and motioned for her to go inside.

"What da ya need? We're here ta help." Nanny Betty waved to the group of people behind her.

Her mom, dad, her Uncle Sean and Aunt Kathleen, her Aunt Cora and Uncle Brian, Pam, Jess, James, Marina, Sandy, and Tom started to pull off their coats and hang them in the coat room off the front entrance.

"Why are you guys here?" Isabelle stood there in shock.

"We got an anonymous text saying you might need some extra help with the cleanup tonight." Sandy winked and nodded toward the kitchen.

Roman.

"Yeah, there are enough of us, that we can get this done in no time." Jess smiled as she linked her arm into Isabelle's.

"Since Sandy, Jess, Pam, and I are the only ones not pregnant, we figured you could use the help." Marina smiled.

Marina was married to James and they had five children. They had a blended family and had met when Marina's sister married John. She and James had both lost their previous spouses and for a long time fought their attraction to each other.

"We're here to help too." Isabelle leaned around her dad to see another bunch of smiling faces.

Ian and Sandy's two oldest daughters, Lily and Evie, and Wade's daughter, Ocean, grinned at her. James and Marina's two oldest boys, Mason and Danny, stepped inside the door and quickly pulled off their coats.

Isabelle couldn't stop the tears if she tried. She always knew her family would move heaven and earth for her, but she never needed the help before, at least not that she'd admit. To see them all filing into her restaurant ready to be put to work filled her heart with joy.

"It's the hormones," Marina whispered as she shuffled by Isabelle.

Roman had appeared in the door of the kitchen and smirked when she turned and pointed her finger at him. She couldn't love him more if she tried. As tired as she felt at that moment, when they got back to her house, she was going to show him just how much. Especially since she'd been to the doctor and he assured Roman it was perfectly safe to make love.

"Come on, you go into the office and get that stuff done and we'll deal with everything else." Roman tugged her into the kitchen and back to her office.

When they stepped inside, she spun around and wrapped her arms around him. To her, he was the most amazing man in the world. She couldn't love or trust anyone as much as she did him, and when Roman smiled down at her and kissed her forehead, she knew he loved her too.

"Thank you so much," Isabelle whispered as she hugged him tightly.

"You're welcome, Tiger. I know the last week has been exhausting and you're not getting enough rest. This way, we can get you back to your house and to bed." Roman tried to step back but she held tightly.

"I want you tonight," she whispered against his lips.

"Isabelle," Roman breathed against her mouth.

"I need to be with you, and you heard the doctor yesterday." Isabelle brushed her lips across his cheek and pressed her body against his.

"I did, and God, I want you too." Roman practically growled the words as he covered her mouth with his.

His kiss told her everything she needed to know. He wanted her and if half of her family and her small staff weren't just outside her door, she probably would have jumped him in her office. She couldn't wait to be alone with him.

Isabelle practically ran into her house with Roman close behind her. It took less than an hour for everyone to get the dining room and kitchen cleaned and set up for the next day. The hardest thing was trying to get everyone to leave so she could lock up and get Roman back home.

Roman closed the door and locked it. He turned around and in a flash, had her swept up into his arms and headed upstairs. He kicked the bedroom door open and eased her down on the bed as he quickly struggled out of his clothes.

"I need to feel you next to me." Roman growled as she eased back on the bed and watched him strip.

"Are you saying you want me to undress myself?" Isabelle raised an eyebrow and smirked.

"I'm saying those clothes are coming off one way or the other, and if I have to strip you, I may just tear them off." Roman dropped his dress pants and underwear.

He stood there in all his naked glory with his smooth muscles contracting as he stalked closer. His cock was hard and pointed right at her, and she sat up as he stepped next to the foot of the bed. Isabelle reached out and slowly ran her fingers across his stomach and flicked her tongue against the tip of his swollen head.

"Fuck, Tiger." Roman moaned.

"I want to taste you. You've kept me waiting for way too long," Isabelle purred and then quickly sucked the head of his cock into her mouth.

Roman gasped and fisted her hair in his hands as she slowly slipped his long, hard length into her mouth. Roman wasn't the largest man she'd been with, but he was still above average in length. He could also do things with his tongue that made her scream more times than she could count.

"Damn, Tiger. That feels so damn good." Roman groaned and started to thrust his hips forward.

She loved the way she could bring him to his knees just by using her mouth. Roman had told her once that nobody had ever made him come with a blow job. It was like a challenge to her and she had done it several times since they'd been together. Once he'd even fell to his knees because he'd orgasmed so hard.

It had been weeks since they were intimate. Roman wouldn't even let her touch him because he said it wouldn't be fair for him to get off without her. She'd rolled her eyes but it had been the sweetest thing she'd ever heard. They were about to make up for it and there was no rushing it.

"I want you… Fuck… Naked, Tiger." Roman pulled back and grunted when she released him with a pop.

"Is that my new nickname, Naked Tiger?" Isabelle licked his cock once more.

"If it gets those damn clothes off, I'll call you whatever you want." Roman growled.

Isabelle stood up and yanked her shirt over her head. While she removed her bra, Roman fell to his knees and tugged down her slacks and panties. He slid his hands up her legs and around to the back of her thighs while he placed soft kisses across her slightly swollen belly.

Over the last week, Isabelle noticed that her tummy wasn't completely flat anymore, and the small bump was hard. She still hadn't felt any movement, but they'd heard the baby's heartbeat the previous day and the doctor said the baby had a strong beat.

"You're so damn beautiful." Roman licked down to the top of her sex and slid his hands up to gently squeeze her ass.

His tongue slipped between her wet folds and he quickly found her sensitive nub. It seemed like months since he'd touched her, and her legs trembled as he slowly circled her clit with his long talented tongue.

"I love the way you taste. Fucking delicious." Roman growled as he lapped at her.

Isabelle tangled her fingers into his hair as her head fell back. He moved a finger between her folds and slipped it slowly inside her throbbing pussy. Roman sucked her clitoris into his mouth and rapidly flicked his tongue against it as he fingered her.

"Roman. God, yes." Isabelle held on to him so she wouldn't fall.

She was close and Isabelle didn't want him to stop, even if her legs did give out. His hot breath, wet tongue and long fingers brought her close to an intense orgasm.. When Roman started to hum as well, she knew there was no holding back as he brought her to the brink.

"Oh… oh… Roman." Isabelle gasped as her legs trembled and the orgasm slammed through her body like a bolt of lightning.

As her body shuddered in ecstasy, Roman didn't stop his wonderful pleasuring. He inserted a second finger and gently bit down on her sensitive bundle of nerves, making another shock wave crash through her body.

"Roman," she called out, and her legs collapsed under her.

Roman caught her before she hit the floor. He quickly covered her lips with his and swirled his tongue against hers. She could taste herself on his mouth as he sucked her tongue and lowered her to the floor. Isabelle lay on her back and he rolled on top of her. She could feel his hard length pressed against her belly and she froze for a moment.

"Condom," she moaned.

"Tiger, I'm clean. I promise." Roman lifted up so she could see his face.

"I know but… shit. Never mind." Isabelle rolled her eyes when she realized she didn't have to worry about getting pregnant.

"I can use one…" Before he could finish, she wrapped her hand around him and guided him where she wanted him most.

"Make love to me, Roman," she whispered against his lips.

Roman pushed into her and his eyes rolled into his head as he slipped deeper. It felt so damn good. Isabelle had never had sex without a condom, for safety reasons. To have Roman inside her bare felt better than she could have ever imagined. She hoped that the expression on his face was because it felt good to him as well.

"Fuck, Tiger. Being inside you like this is fucking heaven." Roman groaned as he slowly pulled out and pushed back in again. "Fuck."

Isabelle wrapped her legs around his thighs and lifted her hips up to meet his thrusts. It felt so good to be with him again and she knew that it would probably be a very long night. She highly doubted one time would satisfy either of them.

Roman wasn't a one-and-done guy. The times they were together, he would be ready to go again ten minutes after he ejaculated. It was refreshing for her because she'd never been with a man like that before. Normally, they'd pass out or go home.

"Come for me, Tiger." Roman growled into her ear as he sucked her earlobe into his mouth.

Isabelle was close, and she could tell by the way his body shook that he was almost there himself. Roman pressed into her, putting pressure on her clitoris. After a few seconds, she screamed out his name and he pounded into her two more times.

"Isabelle, yes." Roman plunged deep and she could feel his thick cock pulse inside her.

For several minutes, they lay on the floor with him on top of her as they both tried to catch their breath. Isabelle didn't want him to move, but Roman pushed up on his elbows and smiled down at her.

"We didn't make it to the bed," Roman said.

"I'm aware." She giggled.

"I'm not complaining but I have to do a replay up there on that bed." He wiggled his eyebrows up and down.

"Oh, really?" Isabelle smirked.

"Oh, Tiger, really." Roman moved and she felt him slip from inside her.

He helped her to her feet and walked her backward until her legs hit the edge of the bed. Roman cupped her face between his hands and gazed into her eyes. His brown eyes sparkled in the soft light of the lamp. There was something different in the way he looked at her and she wasn't sure how to feel about it.

"I know things are going a little fast for us and we aren't going to have a lot of time with just me and you because of Baby Tiger, but I want you to know, I'm not going anywhere," Roman whispered.

Isabelle swallowed the lump in her throat as she reached up and ran her hand down his cheek. A year ago, she never thought she'd find someone to make her feel the way Roman did, let alone be having a baby.

"I can't imagine my life without you in it…" Isabelle stopped when she felt a small flutter in her belly, and she gasped.

"Tiger, what's wrong?" Roman stepped back as she dropped her hands to her stomach.

"I… I think… I think the baby just moved." Isabelle giggled.

"Really?" Roman fell to his knees and pressed his hand against the top part of her stomach. "I can't feel it."

“It’s like a flutter. I don’t know if you could feel it from the outside but it’s almost like… butterflies.” Isabelle sniffed as a tear slipped down her cheek.

“That’s amazing. You’re amazing.” Roman stood up but kept his hand over her tummy. “I can’t wait to meet you, Baby Tiger.”

“Is that what we're calling him or her?” Isabelle laughed.

“Until we know if it’s him or her. I guess we should discuss if you really want to know before the birth or after.” Roman sat on the bed and pulled her onto his lap.

“I’d like to know. I’m kind of a control freak and want to be prepared.” Isabelle snorted.

“That is true.” Roman grinned.

“Hey.” She playfully slapped his arm and he lay down on his back, pulling her over until she lay on top of him.

“I’ll do whatever you want. It’s your body and Baby Tiger might be my baby, but until he vacates his current living area, you’re in charge.” Roman rolled over until she was on her back and he hovered over her.

“You’re amazing.” She smiled.

“Can I show you again just how amazing?” He winked.

“I’d never say no to that,” Isabelle whispered.

Roman lowered his head and kissed her slow and tender. His hands slid around her belly as he started to show her again just how incredible he was.

Chapter 20

Roman was on cloud nine as he sat next to Isabelle holding her hand while the doctor showed them the small blip on the monitor that was their baby. She'd just reached eighteen weeks and she was showing even more.

It was early March and in most places, people would be excited for Spring, but in Newfoundland, they were expecting a lot of snow that evening. It wasn't uncommon but since most of the snow had melted, it was depressing to find out they were about to get slammed again.

All his depression disappeared when he saw the baby's heart beating on the screen. Roman swallowed hard and his eyes blurred with tears. He couldn't believe that this little thing was his baby and the woman he loved was carrying it.

"Is everything okay?" A tear slipped out of the corner of Isabelle's eye and Roman's chest tightened.

"Yes, everything looks great, but this little button isn't going to make it easy to find out the sex." The doctor smiled.

"Figures, Baby Tiger would be stubborn." Isabelle laughed.

She'd started using the name whenever they talked about the baby and he'd even caught her a few times talking to her belly. He did as well and her face would light up every time she felt movement.

"Maybe that's someone telling us to wait." Roman chuckled.

"Let me try one more thing and if it doesn't work, we'll have to wait until the next ultrasound." The doctor moved around and pushed the wand on the other side of Isabelle's belly.

"Does that hurt?" Roman whispered.

"No, but I do have to pee." Isabelle laughed.

For several minutes, the doctor poked and prodded to get the baby to move. Roman was about to tell her to give up because he could see Isabelle was getting more uncomfortable the more the doctor moved the wand around her stomach.

"There we go." The doctor grinned.

"Don't tell us." Isabelle and Roman said together and then they both laughed.

"I thought you wanted to know." The doctor said with confusion.

"Can you put it in a sealed envelope so we can have a reveal party?" Isabelle asked.

“That’s become quite common, actually.” The doctor printed off several pictures and tucked them into an envelope.

When she sealed it, she handed it to Roman and he looked at what she wrote on the front. *Baby O’Connor-Young*. Again, emotion-filled his heart and he blinked back the tears that formed. It seemed as if when Isabelle got pregnant, Roman became an emotional mess whenever things with the baby came up. He was going to be a complete basket case when the baby was born.

The doctor told them the baby was healthy and she set up another appointment for the next checkup. Roman didn’t hear most of the conversation because he couldn’t look away from the name on the envelope.

It was the first time it actually became real that he was going to be a father. He was going to be responsible for another life, with Isabelle of course, but it was sobering to think about it. Roman had great parents growing up and if he could be half the father his dad was, Baby Tiger would be okay.

“Roman?” Isabelle interrupted his thoughts and he looked up to see her smile at him.

“Sorry, did I miss something?” He glanced around but the doctor was gone.

“Yes, the doctor said we’re having twins.” Isabelle grinned.

“What?” Roman almost fell over.

“Kidding.” Isabelle laughed.

“Don’t do that to me.” Roman blew out a breath.

“You did miss the doctor say bye, but you were zoned into the envelope. Did you want to open it?” She was sat on the edge of the bed.

“No… it’s… it’s what she wrote on this.” Roman handed it to Isabelle.

“Did you not want the baby to have your last name?” Her smile disappeared.

“Are you kidding? Of course, I want that. It just hit me that I’m going to be a dad. It’s real.” Roman stepped in front of her and took her hands in his. “You’re making me a dad.”

“Well, not me exactly. Baby Tiger is doing that.” Isabelle giggled.

“True. Let's go back to Hopedale and figure out who’s going to be the first one to know what we’re having.” Roman helped her down from the bed and they walked out of the hospital.

Nothing could wipe the smile off his face as he made his way back to the town that had become his home and the people who were like his family. One day they would be because there was no doubt in his mind one day Isabelle would be his wife.

Roman stood next to the large grill and swirled the vegetables around the pan, flipping them several times before placing it back on the burner and reducing the heat. Gwen, the sous chef, chopped the rest of the peppers on the other side of the kitchen while Isabelle pulled the chicken off the rotisserie.

Isabelle's mother and Jess had come to help out in the dining room because of the huge dinner party booked for the evening. They worked in comfortable silence with only the voices from the dining room coming through the door when one of the staff entered the kitchen.

They had twenty-five dishes to prepare before they could close the kitchen down and he couldn't wait. He'd asked Kurt to drop by the restaurant after closing so they could ask him to do the gender reveal. He and Isabelle had discussed it when they got home from the doctor and Isabelle agreed that Kurt would be overjoyed to be the first to know.

"That's the last of the veggies. I'll start preparing the desserts." Gwen placed the large bowl of peppers next to Roman.

"Thanks, Gwen," Isabelle called from across the room.

"It's just great to be busy again." Gwen smiled.

"It really is." Isabelle grinned.

Roman didn't disagree. It not only took the stress off Isabelle financially, but he didn't have to be concerned about Isabelle being overworked. He and Ethan had also decided not to purchase the club next door. The current owner would not come down on the price. It was a relief, and Roman put the majority of his savings into a fund for the baby.

The rest, he wanted to invest in Isabelle's restaurant, but he hadn't found the right time to bring it up. He hoped she liked the idea of him buying into her business but he wasn't sure if she would even want him to do it. Isabelle had started the business on her own and she was proud of that. She'd told him the day she opened was her proudest moment.

He glanced over his shoulder to see her stare at him with a sweet smile on her beautiful lips. Roman winked and blew her a kiss as he turned back to the job at hand. They still kept things professional at the restaurant, but every now and then they would slip. He didn't care because he wanted everyone to know he was Isabelle's man.

In less than three hours, the customers were fed their appetizers, main dishes, and dessert. When the party left, they gave a generous tip to the staff and filed out with huge smiles on their faces. Several of the group even told the staff they would be back again and would have no issues recommending the place.

"Everything in the kitchen is spic and span." Jess walked out of the kitchen, followed by Gwen and Alice.

"You guys didn't have to do that." Roman smiled at the three women.

"We know but all that's left to do is the tedious paperwork. That's been left on your desk, sis." Jess pulled on her jacket.

"Your father said he'd meet us at your house. So we'll meet you there." Alice followed Jess out through the exit.

The rest of the staff were right behind them, leaving Roman and Isabelle alone. He laughed when Isabelle shrugged and dragged him behind her back to her office. The pregnancy seemed to lower her control issues or she was just too tired.

"If you help me, we can get the cash and receipts done faster." She chuckled when he groaned.

Roman sat on one side of the desk with Isabelle on the other. While Roman added the cash receipts, Isabelle completed the deposit slips. It took them about thirty minutes to finish and he was ecstatic when she shut off her computer. As she pulled on her coat, she asked him to grab the envelope with the baby's gender from the top of her desk.

Roman was about to reach for it when he heard her curse. When he turned, he saw Isabelle struggle to open the door out of the office. The door had a hydraulic mechanism on the top which allowed the door to close automatically.

Roman stepped next to her and gave the door a shove but it didn't budge. He pushed against it with his shoulder but the only thing that happened was a rattle on the other side. It seemed as if something had the door jammed, but he couldn't figure out what could be outside the door that would do that.

"Something must have fallen across the door." Isabelle groaned as she walked back to her desk.

"Give your sister a call and get her to come back and let us out of here." Roman grabbed the handle and jiggled the door again.

"What the hell?" Isabelle's gasp caused Roman to turn around.

"What's wrong?" He saw her hold the phone to her ear.

"The phone isn't working." She held out the cordless phone.

Roman checked the cord that ran from the base, but it was secure. He checked the phone again, but still no dial tone. Roman got a chill running through his body as he reached into his back pocket for his cell phone. He cursed under his breath when he remembered he'd shoved it in his locker in the staff room.

"Do you have your cell?" Roman asked.

Before she could answer, the shrill sound of the smoke detectors echoed through the office. Isabelle covered her ears and Roman glanced up at the sprinkler heads. He expected the system to come on, but nothing happened and that concerned him.

"Your sprinklers aren't working," Roman shouted over the loud blare of the alarm.

"They'll only come on when they sense heat. That's what the guys told me when the system was installed," Isabelle yelled.

Roman turned around in the office and looked up at the small window above her desk. He was sure she could fit through it and he'd manage to squeeze through it as well, but the problem was it was about five feet from the floor.

Roman pushed the file cabinet across the room and under the window. He grabbed the end of the desk and slid it in front of the cabinet. The alarm was next to the window and it hurt his ears as he climbed up on the desk. He tried to pull the window open, but it wouldn't budge.

"I don't think that even opens." Isabelle sounded panicked.

Roman turned to say something and his blood ran cold. In the window above the door, he could see flames licking up the wall outside the office. He glanced down to the door to see smoke seeping in from under it. Isabelle must have noticed it too because she moved as far away from the door as she could.

"We got to get out of here. Now," he shouted.

Roman jumped down and grabbed the wooden coat hanger next to the door. He hopped back up on the desk and beat the window out. He did his best to clear the sharp pieces of the glass away from the edges, but if they got cut getting out, that would be minor compared to dying from smoke or fire.

"Come on," Roman yelled.

He grabbed Isabelle's hands and pulled her up on the desk. He held her as she climbed up on the file cabinet and she placed her coat on the window ledge. She managed to sit up on the ledge and turn over. Roman held her hands as she shimmied out.

"Careful of the glass, Tiger," Roman reminded her.

Roman helped her through the window. The problem was even when he hung out to lower her, she still couldn't touch the ground. She still had about a foot drop and when he released her hands, she managed to land on her feet.

"Roman," she screamed his name.

Roman was about to climb up, but he remembered the envelope that meant so much to both of them. He couldn't leave it there. He jumped down to grab it, but most of the papers had fallen on the floor when he moved the desk and climbed up on it.

"Come on," he heard Isabelle shout through the window.

Roman frantically searched the floor for the envelope but the room had started to fill with smoke and it was hard to breathe. Roman got down on his hands and knees and shoved the papers out of the way. He coughed as the smoke started to burn his lungs, but he couldn't leave without the envelope.

"Roman." Isabelle sounded hysterical.

"Damn it." Roman coughed and reluctantly stood up.

His heart sank as he turned to see the fire burning under the door and flames flicking into the room. He jumped up on the desk and out of the corner of his eye spotted the envelope on the corner of the desk.

"Got ya." He snatched it up and shoved it into the inside pocket of his jacket and zipped it up.

"Roman, answer me, God damn it." Isabelle's screaming echoed outside.

"I'm coming," he shouted back as he hopped up on the file cabinet and climbed out of the window.

Roman was about to make the jump to the ground when there was a loud explosion. He wasn't sure what the noise was, but it felt as if someone shoved him hard and he flew out of the window. Roman heard Isabelle scream as his body smashed against something.

Roman groaned and rolled to the ground. He tried to take in a breath but it felt as if something was wrapped around his chest, constricting, and it was impossible to take in air. When something warm touched his face, he looked up at Isabelle.

"Roman. Oh my God. Help… Help, he's hurt." Her voice faded out as everything went black.

Chapter 21

Isabelle clung to her father as Roman was wheeled into the trauma room. She couldn't get the memory of him flying across the road as an explosion blew through the restaurant. When she saw him land on top of a car on the other side of the street and roll to the ground, she was sure he was dead.

By the time she knelt next to him, she realized he was alive but hurt, badly. It seemed like forever before the emergency response arrived, but luckily, they were able to stabilize Roman and get him to the hospital quickly.

She didn't know what to do, so she just clung to her father and prayed harder than she ever had before. He was the love of her life and she couldn't live without him. She hadn't even had a chance to tell him those three words and if he didn't make it, she never would.

"Sweet pea, he's going to be fine," her father murmured as he kissed the top of her head.

Isabelle hoped he was right. She couldn't even think of what her life would be like without Roman in it. It was heart-wrenching to think about their baby growing up without his dad. God couldn't be that cruel to take him away right when she found him. Could he?

"Isabelle," Ethan called as he ran up the corridor toward her. "Is he okay?"

"They have him there." Isabelle nodded toward the door in front of her.

"What the fuck happened?" Ethan asked.

Isabelle really didn't know. The only thing she did know was that Roman saved her life by getting her out of the restaurant before the explosion. She didn't know why he'd taken so long to get out himself, but he'd almost been killed in the process.

As her father explained the situation to Ethan, Isabelle's eyes were glued to the door of the trauma room. It wasn't that long ago that she'd been here with her sister Jess when Wade was hurt.

Her family seemed to be spending a lot of time at the hospital lately. At least once a year, one of her family or friends were brought in for one reason or the other. Some of them had almost lost their lives and the family had gathered around just like they were doing again.

Isabelle shuddered at the thought of not seeing Roman again. How would she go on if something happened to him? It was impossible to picture anything but a life with Roman. Her heart hurt so much that she was sure she would never be able to survive the pain.

"I've called his brothers and sister. They want me to keep them posted. His sister is going to come home on the next flight out of Montreal," Ethan told her.

"I haven't met her or his brothers," Isabelle murmured mostly to herself.

"Apparently, he's told them about you." Ethan gave her a small smile.

"I don't know if they know about the baby." Isabelle choked out the words and tears blurred her vision.

"Isabelle, he's strong and healthy. He'll get through this," her father told her.

"Dad, he was thrown across the street like a rag doll." The heavy sobs started at the memory of Roman's body slamming into the car and then rolling to the ground.

"Your dad is right. We don't even know how bad it is." Ethan rested his hand on her shoulder.

Isabelle wiped the tears from under her eyes with her fingers. She'd never been such a mess in her life and it seemed like she'd opened the flood gates. Isabelle pressed her hands against her belly as she felt a small thump from inside.

"Oh my God." Isabelle sobbed and laughed at the same time.

"What? Is the baby okay? Are you in pain?" Her father's eyes widened.

“I’m… I’m fine. The baby… I think the baby just kicked.” Isabelle choked out.

Her father placed his large hand on Isabelle’s stomach and Ethan grabbed a chair from the waiting room. He held it behind her and her father eased her into the chair.

They acted as if she was about to go into labor, but it was bittersweet to feel such a firm kick and not share it with Roman. The thought that he could be fighting for his life made her sit up straight. It was as if their baby thumped her to tell her she needed to be strong for his or her daddy.

Isabelle started to stand, but her legs trembled, and she sat back on the chair as the doctor walked toward them. It was Adam and for the first time since she’d known him, he wasn’t smiling.

“Adam.” Her father’s voice came out like a warning.

“Kurt, I was told that Mr. Young’s next of kin was here.” Adam looked around.

“I’m here.” A tall slender woman ran toward them.

Isabelle had no doubt the woman was Roman’s sister. Marcella was like a female version of Roman. The same dark eyes and hair with olive-colored skin that looked flawless. She was tall, slender, and dressed in black jeans with a dark green sweater.

“I’m here,” she repeated as she stopped in front of Adam and held out her hand.

“Ms. Young?” Adam shook Marcella’s hand.

“Please, call me Cella, everyone does.” Marcella turned as Ethan placed his hand on her shoulder.

“I’m Dr. Adam Cramer. I’m the ER doctor on duty tonight,” Adam said.

“Is Roman okay?” Marcella choked.

“If you want, we can talk in private.” Adam motioned toward one of the quiet rooms off the corridor.

“Are you kidding? These people are like family to my brother. This woman is having his baby, for crying out loud.” Marcella pointed to Isabelle.

“Of course.” Adam nodded.

Marcella reached down and grabbed Isabelle’s hand as they waited for Adam to tell them what was going on with Roman. Isabelle squeezed Marcella’s hand as Adam began.

“Your brother is on his way to surgery. He had several broken ribs and one punctured his lung. It’s a large puncture and needs to be repaired surgically,” Adam explained.

Isabelle knew it had to be serious if Adam wasn’t his normal cocky self. He went on to explain that Roman had some superficial burns on his arms and back. Adam didn’t seem concerned about the burns, but what worried Isabelle was the tension in his jaw.

“You’re not telling us everything.” Isabelle stood up.

"He's bleeding internally, and they need to find where it's coming from." Adam met Isabelle's eyes and she knew it was bad.

"Roman and I have the same blood type. Will you need blood?" Marcella appeared calm, but Isabelle knew by the way she held her hand that Roman's sister was scared.

"It won't hurt to have extra." Adam nodded.

"My brothers are on the way, but I'm not sure if they're the same. I do know for sure that I'm compatible with Roman." Marcella told them.

Isabelle envied Marcella's strength while Adam explained what needed to be done in order for Roman to receive his siblings' blood. It was hard to understand because she wasn't really listening. The only thing she could concentrate on was breathing.

"I wish we'd met under better circumstances." Marcella turned her attention to Isabelle.

"Me too." Isabelle nodded.

"My brother didn't do you justice." Marcella pulled Isabelle into a tight hug. "He loves you," she whispered into Isabelle's ear.

Isabelle pulled back slowly and stared at Roman's sister. She wasn't sure she'd heard her properly, but when Marcella smiled and nodded, Isabelle realized she did hear the words.

"He told you that?" Isabelle swallowed the lump in her throat.

“Yes, he didn’t know if you were ready to hear those exact words.” Marcella tugged Isabelle to the chairs inside the waiting room.

“Oh,” Isabelle sniffed.

“He’s never been in love and I can tell by the way he talks about you that you’re it for him.” Marcella’s eyes filled with tears.

“We’re having a baby.” Isabelle blurted it out because she didn’t know what to say to Marcella’s words.

“I know.” Marcella smiled.

“Good.” Isabelle pressed her lips together.

“Ms. Young.” Adam stuck his head into the waiting room.

“Yes?” Marcella shot to her feet.

“We’re ready for you.” Adam motioned to a lady in a lab coat next to him.

“Oh, good.” Marcella crouched in front of Isabelle. “I’ll be right back. Think positive thoughts and pray.”

With those words, Roman’s sister hurried out of the waiting room and disappeared from sight. Isabelle clasped her hands together and started to pray harder than she ever had in her life.

Isabelle sat in the corner of the waiting room. She’d been offered tea, food, water, but she knew she couldn’t keep anything down even if she tried. It had been more than two hours since they’d brought Roman into surgery and nobody had come out to update them.

Considering the number of people in the room, it was surprisingly quiet. Her cousins and their wives were sat in their perspective couples, her parents were on either side of her, and her aunts and uncles were quietly talking on the other side of the room.

They weren't only there because they cared about her, but because they cared about Roman, too. He was like family to them and hopefully, someday he would be.

Chapter 22

Roman stood in the middle of a large kitchen. It was familiar, but for some reason, he couldn't remember why. The yellow walls and white cupboard doors with flowers etched into the center drew him nearer. It was almost as if he couldn't stop himself from moving toward the center cupboard.

His hand raised as if on its own and he pulled the door open. The cupboard was empty except for a white china cup, a blue baby blanket, and the gold chain that he carried in his pocket with his mother's engagement ring. He was about to reach for it, but a voice stopped him cold.

"Don't you break my favorite cup, Roman." The soft voice of his mother echoed behind him.

Roman turned slowly and looked into the dark eyes of his mom. She was just as he remembered her the last time he'd seen her. She was dressed in a white blouse and blue jeans. Her orange apron tied around her waist and she was stirring something in a bowl.

"Mom?" Roman whispered.

"Heavens, Roman, you look like you've seen a ghost." His mother pushed him aside and proceeded to pour the contents of the bowl into two cake pans.

"Mom, you're… you died." Roman choked on the words.

"Don't be silly." She scoffed and brought the filled cake pans to the wall oven.

Roman could only watch her as she popped the cake pans into the oven and turn back to him with a smile. All he could do was stare at her as she scurried around the kitchen as if nothing happened. Like she'd done so many times before. He realized the kitchen he stood in belonged to his childhood home.

"You better go get cleaned up. Isabelle will be here soon, and you don't want her to see you in such a mess. Don't forget to give her that chain." His mother waved her hand up and down at his clothing.

Roman looked down at himself. He was covered in soot and blood. He didn't know what happened, but when he raised his head, his mother had something in her arms wrapped in a blue blanket. The smile on her face lit up when she spoke softly to whatever she had.

"He's just like you. I'll keep this little angel safe until he's ready to be held in your arms." His mother swayed back and forth while she smiled down at the bundle in her arms.

"Who are you keeping safe, Mom?" Roman tried to step closer but it was as if he was glued to the floor.

"Your baby boy, of course." His mother didn't look up.

"My what?" Roman looked down to his mother's arms.

The most beautiful baby he'd ever seen stared at him with blue eyes. Isabelle's blue eyes. The dark hair and chubby cheeks had Roman hypnotized, and he reached for the child.

"He's going to be fine. You're going to be the best father this little boy could have." His mother's voice started to fade as the room filled with smoke.

"Mom? Come back," Roman shouted.

"You'll be fine." The voice was faint but it didn't sound like his mother anymore.

As the room engulfed in flames around his mother and the baby, Roman tried to go to them, but something held his hand tightly. He couldn't figure it out and he tried to turn around to tell the person to let him go. He had to save his son.

"You're going to be fine." Isabelle stood behind him with a huge smile and the gold chain from the cupboard around her neck.

"What's happening?" Roman tried to speak, but it was as if something prevented him.

It was as if he couldn't hear his own voice and he started to panic. He stared at Isabelle and she squeezed his hand. He closed his eyes, but when he opened them again he wasn't in the kitchen.

"It's okay, Roman. It's a tube to help you. Don't fight it." Isabelle's touch was gentle on his cheek but for the life of him, he couldn't figure out why she was talking about a tube.

Roman blinked his eyes and when he opened them again, he was looking up into Isabelle's blue eyes, but her smile was gone. She looked worried. Her hair was mussed and it looked like she'd been crying.

"Hey." She choked out the words.

Roman tried to speak, but she stopped him and Isabelle lifted his hand up to show him why he couldn't speak. There was a soft plastic tube in his mouth and a soft rhythmic beep made him turn toward the sound.

It was a heart monitor like his mother had been hooked up to the night she died. That strong smell of antiseptic surrounded him and he wrinkled his nose. It was a hospital, and he was the patient.

"It's to help you until your lung heals." Isabelle smoothed her hand over his hair.

Roman was about to ask what she was talking about when the pain started to radiate across his chest and abdomen. He lifted his other arm and placed his hand over his chest. He was covered in something, but it wasn't a blanket.

“You had surgery, Roman.” He heard Marcella’s voice and turned toward it.

Why was his sister here? None of this made any sense and for some reason, there was something shoved into his mouth to help his lung and he hurt all over. He needed them to stop the pain he had all over, not shove things down his throat.

“Your brothers are outside. I’m going to go out and let them come in.” Isabelle tried to pull her hand from his but he gripped it so hard, he was sure he probably hurt it.

“It’s okay. I’ll go out. I think he wants you to stay.” Marcella kissed Roman’s cheek and smiled. “I’m so glad you’re going to be okay.”

With that, she nodded and left the room. Roman turned back to Isabelle and he wanted so bad to ask her what the hell happened to him. He couldn’t remember anything but his mother holding a baby in the middle of a fire.

Fire.

The memory of the restaurant filling with smoke and him helping Isabelle out of the window flashed in his head. He went for something and then climbed out himself, but he didn’t remember anything after he’d sat on the edge of the windowsill.

“I was so worried.” Isabelle clasped his hand between hers and a tear ran down her cheek. “I know this is not the most romantic time to say this, but I need you to know. I can’t take a chance that you never hear the words from me. Roman, I love you. I love you with all my heart."

He tried hard to tell her the same, but she stopped him and told him she knew how he felt. She leaned down and kissed the corner of his mouth and sat next to him on the bed.

Maximus and Demetrios walked next to the bed and he met their concerned eyes. He'd never seen them look like that and he reached out with his hand to Maximus. His brother grabbed his hand and squeezed it.

"You're fucking lucky you survived this," Maximus said.

"I'd hate to have to kick your ass for dying before you got to meet that kid of yours." Demetrios dropped his hand over Maximus' and Roman's hands.

Roman struggled to mouth what he wanted to say, but Maximus stopped him. His brothers and his sister were here for him. He wanted to tell them how good it was to see them, but all he could do was grip on to them.

"You can bullshit us when that tube comes out. Right now, get better. Fast. I want to find out what you did to get this gorgeous woman to fall for an ass like you." Maximus winked at Isabelle and Roman stuck his middle finger up to his oldest brother.

"That's the brother I remember." Demetrios laughed.

For a few minutes, the only sounds were the beep of the monitor and of people outside the room. Roman's eyelids felt as if they had a lead weights on them, and he fought to keep them open. He was scared to close them, but when he met Isabelle's gaze, she leaned into him.

"Sleep, baby. I'm not going anywhere," Isabelle whispered next to his ear.

The last thing he heard was a quiet conversation between Isabelle and Maximus. It was soothing to hear them, and he had a feeling that there was some kind of medication involved in his groggy feeling. He relaxed and fell into a deep sleep.

Three days was long enough to have that tube down his throat, and he couldn't be happier to have it removed. It was weird and made him want to vomit as they pulled it out, but it was a relief to have it gone.

Roman's throat was irritated, and it was a little difficult to get used to breathing on his own again. Isabelle stood by his side as he took the first breath on his own. The doctor told him to take his time and if he felt any discomfort or shortness of breath, he needed to let them know. If he couldn't manage to breathe on his own, they'd have to reinsert the tube. He didn't want that.

"It's good to talk." Roman almost didn't recognize his own voice.

"It's the best thing I've ever heard." Isabelle smiled.

Roman had a little trouble hearing on his left side because of the explosion. It wasn't completely gone, but when someone spoke to him on that side it sounded as if he had his finger in his ear. The doctors assured him that his hearing should return.

"I love you too." He smiled up at her. "I wanted you to hear me say it back to you, but it was hard with that damn thing down my throat."

"It's good to hear it." Isabelle sniffed.

"I'm sorry." Roman choked.

"For what?" Isabelle asked.

"For freaking everyone out." Roman cleared his throat.

"I just don't know what took you so long to get out." Isabelle lifted his hand to her lips.

Roman stared at her as he tried to remember what happened and after a few minutes trying to access the memories, it hit him. The envelope. He went back to get it so he could give it to Kurt.

"My coat," Roman choked out.

"I think the ER staff put it in a bag. I'm not sure where they brought it." Isabelle seemed confused by his request.

"Can you find out, please?" Roman begged.

"Okay." Isabelle gave him a quick kiss on the cheek and disappeared out through the door.

Roman lay back on the bed and enjoyed that he didn't have a piece of plastic jammed into his mouth. His body ached from head to toe and it was painful when he yawned, coughed, or laughed. Of course, with several broken ribs, a lung that had been punctured and surgically repaired, it was a wonder he wasn't in more pain. Then again, his injuries could be much worse.

Isabelle told him that Kurt and Aaron didn't have any new information on the fire but did know it was set intentionally. The fire department inspector had not filed his final report, but Roman found it hard to believe that someone would set a fire on purpose. They did discover why he and Isabelle weren't able to get out of the office though. Someone had jammed a large board into the handle of the door and braced it against the wall. Roman couldn't understand why they didn't hear something.

Aaron believed that the fire was related to Cindy's murder as well. Apparently, Isabelle had told him about all the stupid shit going on at the restaurant and Aaron believed it was all connected. It killed him that someone destroyed everything that Isabelle had worked so hard for. He was terrified to think about what would have happened if he hadn't been there.

"You're looking much better." Kurt said as he entered the room.

"Feeling a little better," Roman replied as he glanced at the other man with Isabelle's father.

"That's good to hear." Kurt nodded. "Roman, have you met Garrett Sellers?"

“Not officially.” Roman shook the older man’s hand.

“Garrett’s the Director of Regional Fire and Emergency Services,” Kurt explained.

“Or for people who don’t want to confuse other people, I’m the Fire Chief.” Garrett chuckled.

“Either way, it’s nice to meet you.” Roman smiled.

When Roman glanced toward Kurt, his smile faded. Isabelle’s father’s jaw was clenched and his forehead was furrowed. The look told Roman that Garrett wasn’t just there for a visit.

“What’s wrong?” Roman asked.

Kurt and Garrett exchanged a look that had Roman even more concerned. For Isabelle’s father to bring the fire chief in to talk to Roman, it meant that something was really bad.

“Roman, as you know, the fire was definitely arson.” Garrett handed Roman a large yellow envelope.

“What’s this?” Roman asked as he opened the top.

“It’s a couple of things the inspector found,” Garrett explained.

Roman pulled several photos out of the envelope. The first one was the burnt-out remnants of the kitchen in the restaurant. It made his stomach turn to look at it and he shuffled through the next picture. He could see the door that led to Isabelle’s office and the board that jammed the door.

"The inspector said the plank was jammed between the door and the edge of the wall," Garrett continued.

"Isabelle told me." Roman shuffled to the next photo and his stomach clenched.

He wasn't sure what he was seeing, but something told him that the explosion that almost killed him came from the shattered pieces on the picture. He'd seen pictures of bombs in magazines and on television and he had a feeling it was what he was looking at.

"Whoever set the fire knew what they were doing. They were able to jam your door, set the fire, and set the propane tank to explode. Forensics are trying to figure out exactly what the arsonist did," Garrett explained as he pointed to the picture.

"Roman, do you remember seeing anything strange before you and Isabelle went into the office?" Kurt asked.

"As far as I know when we went into the office, all the staff was gone. We were doing the deposit for the night." Roman continued to shuffle through the pictures.

"I know Isabelle has been having issues for a while, and I'm pissed she didn't tell me about it," Kurt grumbled.

"Dad, don't start." Isabelle entered the room.

Isabelle held up his jacket and he blew out a breath as she handed it to him. He immediately opened the pocket and pulled out the crumpled envelope. When he held it up, Isabelle stared at him as if he lost his mind.

“This is why I had to go back,” Roman told her.

“You put your life in danger for a fucking envelope,” Kurt snapped.

“It’s not just an envelope.” Roman held it out to Kurt. “It contains the gender of the baby and we wanted you to be the one to reveal it.”

Kurt glanced between Roman and Isabelle for several seconds before he lifted his hand and took the crumpled paper from Roman. He held it in his hand as if it were going to explode.

“Why would you want me to do that?” Kurt’s voice sounded strangled.

“Dad, why wouldn’t we? You’ve been a constant support to me and I know the way this baby is coming into the world is not what you expected to happen for me, but we’d be honored for you to be the one to reveal it.” Isabelle wrapped her arms around Kurt’s waist and rested her head against his chest.

“I’m honored, but before we deal with that, let's find out who the fuck destroyed your business.” Kurt hugged Isabelle into his side and kissed the top of her head.

Roman tried to concentrate on the conversation as he lay back on the bed. He’d managed to make it through most of the day without pain medication and he didn’t want to give in to it, but it started to get intolerable.

He didn't want Isabelle to know because she worried so much and stress wasn't good for the baby. He'd begged her to go home and rest but it was like beating his head against a brick wall. When she got something in her head, there was no way to change it.

"Are you okay?" Isabelle touched his cheek.

"Yeah, I'm just tired." Roman covered her hand with his.

"Get some rest, son." Kurt dropped his hand on Roman's shoulder. "You need to be one hundred percent to look after my daughter and grandbaby."

"Dad," Isabelle groaned.

Kurt smirked as Garrett retrieved the photos from Roman. Isabelle rolled her eyes as her father started to head out of the room. When Garrett walked out, Kurt turned back to them.

"Thank you for trusting me with something so important." Kurt held up the envelope then put it inside his coat. "It means the world to me."

With that, Kurt turned and left the room. Roman smiled as he turned back to the woman he loved. She had tears in her eyes when she gazed down at him.

"We could have called the doctor and asked for a copy of the ultrasound. I can't believe you risked your life to go back for that." Isabelle cupped his face between her hands.

"I wanted your father to like me." Roman smiled.

"He does like you." Isabelle laughed.

"I think I'm growing on him." Roman started to reach up to touch her face but the pain worsened.

"I'll get the nurse," Isabelle said but he stopped her.

"I'm fine. I don't want that shit they give me." Roman closed his eyes and took a few breaths until the pain passed.

"Baby, you had a major injury and surgery. If you're in pain, you should take something." Isabelle pressed her lips against his cheek.

"I will if it gets too bad." Roman smiled. "Right now, I want you to lay down here with me and that will make all my pain go away."

"I don't want to hurt you." Isabelle pulled back.

"You won't. I miss having you in my arms." Roman slowly moved over in the bed to make room for her.

Isabelle eased down next to him and it may have been in his mind, but the pain eased slightly. Roman closed his eyes and tried to concentrate on the warmth of her body next to him. The pictures he'd seen flashed through his head. He pulled Isabelle tighter into his side as the thoughts of what could have happened to her if he hadn't been there filled his head.

"I love you, Roman," she murmured.

"I love you too, Tiger." He breathed the words against the top of her head.

He loved her more than his own life and he would jump in front of a moving train to keep her safe. It was hard to believe that it had been less than a year since he'd started to work for her, but in that time, she'd grabbed hold of his heart and he never wanted her to let go.

Roman relaxed as he listened to Isabelle's breathing become deep and even. It wasn't long after that he drifted off to sleep, feeling content with Isabelle in his arms.

Chapter 23

Isabelle stood in front of her restaurant wishing it was all a dream. She wanted to burst into tears, but thankfully Cobalt, her father, and Roman's brothers were with her for support.

The insurance adjuster had called out of the blue and asked her to meet him there. Roman's brothers seemed to think it was their duty to watch out for her, but she didn't mind. The last thing she wanted to do was meet this guy alone.

Roman was still in the hospital and not enjoying it one bit. It had been almost a week since the fire and he was healing slowly. The doctor had even told him that once the last drainage tube came out that he'd probably release Roman.

She felt Cobalt rub against her leg and let out a soft whine. Isabelle looked down to see the pup staring past Maximus and Demetrios at two men headed toward them. When the men got closer, Cobalt started to growl, and Isabelle had to hold tightly to the dog's leash because the pup seemed ready to attack.

“I don't blame you for growling, girl. Insurance adjusters can be bastards,” Maximus scratched Cobalt's head.

Demetrios punched his brother but Isabelle had no idea why. It must have been a joke between the brothers because Maximus thought it was amusing.

"Ms. O'Connor." One of the men held out his hand and she regretted shaking it the minute his hand touched hers.

His hand was sweaty, and she didn't like the way he squeezed hers. His eyes immediately dropped to her breasts and Isabelle wanted to slap the creep, but she held her tongue since the guy could probably screw up her insurance settlement.

"Mr. Strang." Isabelle pulled her hand back and tried to wipe it on her jeans without anyone noticing.

"You can call me Archer, and this is our photographer Terry, um… Howe. He's going to take some photos around the building." Archer nodded toward the mousy-looking man holding the camera.

"I'm sure the fire department and the police department sent you their photos," her father said.

"And you are?" Archer glared at her father and Isabelle wanted to laugh.

"I'm Kurt O'Connor, Isabelle's father, former Chief of Police and the current Mayor of Hopedale," her dad responded.

Archer visibly swallowed hard and Maximus chuckled at the sudden change in the insurance adjuster's demeanor with her father. Isabelle met Maximus's eyes and pressed her lips together to keep from laughing with him.

“I’m so sorry, Mr. O’Connor… er... Mayor.” Archer stammered over his words.

“Mr. O’Connor is fine, but as I said, you should have had several pictures sent to you that were taken by the fire department as well as the forensics department. If you didn’t get them, I do have copies with me.” Her father pulled a folder out of his briefcase.

“No, we have them, but policy dictates that we take our own pictures as well.” Archer nodded toward Terry.

“Must be a Newfoundland policy because my wife is an insurance adjuster in Ontario. I’ve never heard of her needing to take her own pictures when she got them from the authorities.” Demetrios interjected, and Isabelle realized why he’d hit Maximus.

“I’m sorry, I forget your name,” Archer said.

“Probably because I didn’t give it to you,” Demetrios replied sarcastically.

“Anyway, the faster we can get the photos, the faster we can get Ms. O’Connor’s claim pushed through.” Archer walked away without another word to Demetrios or Maximus.

He also kept glancing back at her dad as he pointed out different areas he wanted the photographer to take pictures of. Something about the way Terry squirmed made Isabelle uneasy, and he didn’t seem to even know how to hold the camera.

“Why do I get the feeling those guys are not legit?” Maximus whispered.

"Because they're not." A familiar voice said from behind them.

Isabelle turned to see Bryce stood behind her, glaring at the men with their backs to them. He looked about ready to kill as he stepped between Maximus and Demetrios.

"Bryce, what are you talking about?" Isabelle asked.

"They work for the guy who wants to buy this property," Bryce said through clenched teeth.

"Why did they call and say they were from my insurance company? How did they even know?" Isabelle glanced back to Archer, who had turned to see Bryce.

"It's not hard to find out that stuff. Insurance companies have the names of adjusters on their websites." Bryce crossed his arms over his chest.

"Let me handle this." Her father stalked toward Archer and Terry.

Both men turned ghostly white when they saw her father and started to walk the other way, but Maximus and Demetrios blocked their escape. Isabelle glared at the two imposters and then back to Bryce.

"I'm telling you now, that fire was meant to burn down this whole building." Bryce pointed to the part of the building that was vacant.

“Why do you think that?” Isabelle asked.

“Someone is trying to ruin my deal.” Bryce growled.

“How is burning down my restaurant going to destroy your deal, Bryce?” Isabelle tapped down the urge to roll her eyes.

“We own the building next to your restaurant. We’ve been trying to convince you to sell us your building so we could sell the entire property. We have an interested buyer who wanted to build a condo complex.” He said.

Bryce didn’t seem to realize what he’d let slip, but Isabelle turned to him, and tried hard not to punch the asshole. That was the reason Bryce was so desperate to get her restaurant.

“To me, that sounds like *you* have the motive to get rid of my business.” She tried to keep her voice calm as she poked him in the chest.

“I know you don’t like me or my family, but we’d never stoop to that level. We were very generous with our offer.” Bryce seemed genuinely insulted.

“You wanted to sell this property to a developer who would throw up a condominium complex. In Hopedale? You really don’t think that would have gotten passed, especially with my father as mayor?” Isabelle snorted.

If there was one thing about the small town, it was that it didn’t want big city developers putting up cold-looking buildings to take away from the beauty of the area. Her dad would definitely not let that happen.

“It would have been good for this town. Think of the people that would move to this hole-in-the-wall place. It would help the economy.” Bryce shrugged.

“Are you insane? First of all, you’d be taking away a restaurant that the people you’re talking about would want. Most of those people would end up in St. John’s spending their money.” Isabelle was getting really pissed.

“We’d just bring in more businesses. I’m sure most of the hicks in this town would sell once we offered them money.” Bryce snorted.

“The hicks? Listen here you arrogant son of a bitch, the people in this town are not a bunch of hicks. As a matter of fact, there are people in Hopedale that are considered geniuses.” Isabelle, of course, was referring to Sandy and Keith.

Keith had an eidetic memory and had scored off the charts on most of the exams he’d been given as a kid. Sandy was a computer genius and was sought after by many government agencies for her skills and intelligence.

“Don’t take what I said personally. I wasn’t referring to you, but come on, you know most of the people in Hopedale aren’t the most well-educated.” Bryce scoffed.

“I’m related to most of the people in this town and I can guarantee most of them are very well-educated.” Isabelle was furious.

“Young man, take me advice and leave before ya get hurt.” Nanny Betty’s stern voice caused Isabelle to turn around.

“Who is going to hurt me?” Bryce laughed.

“I think you better listen to Nan,” Bull said in his deep, threatening voice.

He and Trunk stood behind Nanny Betty with their large arms folded over their chests. If Isabelle didn’t know the men so well, she would have felt intimidated, but because she did know them, the only one who should feel threatened was Bryce.

Ben ‘Trunk’ Murphy also worked for Keith and Bull. He’d become like family since he moved to Hopedale with Keith and the rest of the guys. He had a quiet demeanor but was one of the nicest people in the world, that was unless you fucked with people he cared about.

“It looks like Max and Dem have the fake insurance adjusters on their way. I suggest you do the same.” Isabelle nodded toward where Roman’s brothers were escorting Archer and Terry back to their vehicle.

“Landell, those men told me that you sent them.” Her father growled as he stomped next to Bryce.

"I didn't send them. I swear. I was here to warn you about them." Bryce held up his hands and for the first time, his cool, arrogant demeanor was gone.

"I just talked to the real Archer Strang and he's on the way here now. Those two pricks said you gave them the name of the adjuster. How did you get that information?" Her father glared at Bryce.

"I didn't tell them anything. I got a call telling me that two guys were sent here to make an offer on the property to Isabelle." Bryce sighed. "It's why I was here. I didn't want them taking advantage of your situation."

Isabelle actually burst into a fit of laughter. The guy who had been haunting her for months to sell didn't want anyone taking advantage of her. He was just afraid she'd take the new buyer's deal and he'd lose his large condo sale.

"Ya know, I wanted ta believe ya. Until ya said dat last part. We all know yer fadder has been tryin' ta get our Isabelle ta give up her restaurant. I tink yer here now ta bargain shop. Well, young man, I'll not let ya take advantage of anyone in me family. Get outta here." Nanny Betty shook her arthritic finger in Bryce's face.

"I agree with Nan. You need to leave. Now." Trunk growled.

"Ditto," Hulk sneered.

"Fine, but don't come to me and say I didn't warn you. You're not the only one losing here. I'm telling you whoever is doing this is trying to destroy my deal. You guys are going to get caught in the middle." With that, Bryce spun around and stomped away.

Isabelle, her father, Nanny Betty, Hulk, and Trunk watched him get into his car and speed away. Isabelle turned back to the restaurant and sighed. If her insurance didn't come through, she wouldn't be able to rebuild. She just didn't have the savings anymore.

She could get a loan from the bank or if she was desperate, she could ask Tom Roberts, but she'd have to be out of options before she'd ever do that. Maybe she should just sell it to Bryce and get out before she couldn't.

Isabelle looked up at the building where the beautiful writing of the name was charred from the fire. It still stood out as beautiful and she knew she could never give up on her dream.

"I get the feeling Bryce isn't lying," her father said.

"I agree." Bull nodded.

"Maybe we should get Sandy and Smash to do some digging." Trunk pulled out his phone.

Gage 'Smash' Hodder was the other computer analyst on Keith's staff, and except for Sandy, he was probably one of the best in the country. Between him and Sandy, Isabelle was sure they'd find out who was trying to sabotage Bryce's deal. If in fact someone actually was.

Either way, Isabelle needed to think about how she was going to bring back *A Taste of Hopedale*. She didn't want whoever burned down her business to win. They could have killed Roman and she wasn't about to let the bad guys win.

Chapter 24

"Roman, you aren't supposed to be lifting anything," Marcella yelled from behind him.

He'd been out of the hospital for a week and after almost a week stuck in the place, he'd never been so glad to leave. Isabelle didn't give him a choice and made him come to her house to stay, not that he put up much of an argument on that point. He practically lived there anyway, before he got hurt. The problem was his sister had decided to stay for a couple of extra weeks to help Isabelle take care of him. As if he couldn't take care of himself.

That was where the annoyance began. Marcella wouldn't allow him to do a thing. Apparently, picking up a plate with a bologna sandwich was too heavy, according to his sister. He should beat the shit out of his brothers for suggesting Marcella stay to help.

"For fuck sake, it's a damn sandwich," Roman snapped and proceeded to the living room.

"Those are stoneware and are heavier than normal plates." Marcella followed him.

“Cella, I love you, really, I do, but you’re starting to get on my last fucking nerve.” Roman eased into the recliner and prayed Isabelle would return from her meeting with Keith.

Keith had offered to help her rebuild the restaurant. Besides his security company, Keith also owned a construction company that he also ran out of his property. Everyone referred to it as The Compound because it was fenced around the whole area and had a huge security gate.

The insurance had offered Isabelle enough to rebuild the destroyed part of the restaurant, but there wasn’t nearly enough to purchase all the equipment that had been destroyed. It was why his brothers agreed to stay for a couple of more weeks. They’d contacted their boss who agreed to donate some building material to help rebuild. He was also a Newfoundlander and in true Newfie style wanted to lend a helping hand.

With all the free labor Isabelle had for the rebuild, she was able to lower the cost and purchase some of the equipment she needed. Roman was glad his family could pitch in. He just wished he was there too.

“I’m going to continue to get on your last fucking nerve until you go back to see the doctor. When he says you can go back to normal activity, I’ll back off.” Marcella narrowed her eyes at him.

“I’m in hell,” Roman muttered under his breath.

"And I thought living with me was heaven." Isabelle snickered from the doorway.

"You're my heaven, but that woman is going to put me in the mental hospital." Roman reached out for Isabelle's hand.

She walked over and sat on the arm of the chair. Roman wasn't having it and tugged her into his lap. He stopped her words of resistance by pressing his lips against hers and slowly kissing her until she sighed into his mouth.

"God, I missed you," Roman whispered against her lips.

"I was only gone for an hour." Isabelle giggled.

"I know, but you were out of bed before I got up this morning. I wanted to fool around, badly." Roman groaned.

"I don't know if that's a good idea." Isabelle sighed as he nuzzled against her neck.

"I'm fine, Tiger," he whispered against her ear.

"Did you ask the doctor?" She moaned.

"No, but I'll call him right now." Roman had to clench his teeth when she shifted in his lap.

"I think we can wait until tomorrow." Isabelle laughed. "I can help you with that later. Maybe take the pressure off."

When she wiggled her eyebrows up and down, Roman wanted to go to bed right at that very second. Who cared if it wasn't even six in the evening? It seemed like the more pregnant she got the more he wanted her, if that was even possible.

It was at that moment Marcella walked back into the living room. Roman wanted to tell her to get out, but her face was pale and she looked about ready to throw up. His first thought was something had happened to one of his brothers.

"Cella, what's wrong?" Roman stood up when Isabelle got off his lap.

"Roman, the police are here." Marcella's voice quivered. "They said they have a warrant for your arrest."

"What?" Isabelle and Roman shouted together.

Marcella glanced behind her as Aaron and two uniformed officers entered the house. It wasn't what his sister said that had him concerned, it was the look of anger on Aaron's face. He glared as if he could rip Roman apart limb by limb.

"A.J., what's going on?" Isabelle stepped in front of Roman.

"Roman Young, you're under arrest." Aaron's voice was harsh.

"What the hell for?" Isabelle shouted.

"Cuz, stay out of this," Aaron warned.

"I will not. You walk into my house without being invited and want to arrest Roman. I want to know what for." Isabelle was pissed.

"Arson, destruction of property, and attempted murder." Aaron's voice was cold and steady.

"Are you out of your fucking mind?" Isabelle shrieked.

She didn't curse very often, but when she did, she was fuming. Isabelle was normally calm, but Roman didn't miss the way her body trembled in anger and he knew that it couldn't be good for her or the baby.

"Isabelle, stay out of this," Aaron warned again.

"My brother would never do any of those things." Marcella shouted at Aaron.

"If you both interfere with this, you'll be arrested as well." Aaron wasn't joking.

"I'd like to see what happens if you arrest me, asshole." Isabelle took a step toward her cousin.

"Back off, Isabelle. We have evidence that says he not only did this but could possibly be involved with the murder of Cindy Finney." Aaron turned back to Roman.

"You've lost your mind." Isabelle gasped and Roman decided it was time to put an end to the situation before Isabelle did get arrested.

"I didn't do any of that. A.J., you know me." Roman could barely get the words out.

Aaron didn't say a word. He only nodded to one of the other officers and the man walked behind Roman to put him in handcuffs. As Roman was led out of the house, the officer read him his rights, but Roman didn't hear any of what the man said because as they guided him out, Isabelle shouted behind them. The last thing he saw was Isabelle collapsing to the step and Marcella crouched next to her.

Roman's head spun as he was driven to the police station and brought into an interview room. The handcuffs were removed but the door was locked when the officer left him alone. He'd never been arrested in his life and he scanned around the small room as he tried to get his head around what had just happened.

It seemed like he'd been sat in the room for hours. The only person he saw brought in a bottle of water and left without a word. Roman wanted to talk to someone because this all had to be a mistake or a joke. Aaron was a jokester sometimes and maybe it was just a prank on Roman. The memory of Isabelle's tears and Aaron's angry eyes told Roman it was no trick.

The door opened again and Roman looked up. James and Aaron walked into the room silently and sat across from him at the large table in the middle of the room. Neither man looked at him while they opened the folders they carried with them.

"Roman, this doesn't look good." James pushed a paper across the table.

“What?” Roman stared at James.

“This is a receipt from your credit card. This is a list of the items used to rig the propane tank to blow up.” James tapped the receipt.

“Are you fucking kidding me? I don’t have the slightest clue what I would need for that or how to even go about doing it. For Christ’s sake I was almost killed when it exploded.” Roman threw his arms up in the air.

“Then how do you explain this?” James slid a paper across the table.

Roman looked down and his body froze. In front of him were detailed instructions on how to turn a propane tank into an explosive device. He lifted his head and glanced back and forth between James and Aaron.

“I’ve never seen this before,” Roman admitted.

“Really? We found that in the glove compartment of your Jeep. Roman, were you hired to destroy Isabelle’s place?” Aaron snapped.

“What? No. Are you crazy? I never lock my Jeep. Anyone could have shoved that in my vehicle and I’d never do anything to hurt Isabelle.” Roman shot to his feet.

“Then why would you have these things?” James seemed a lot calmer than Aaron, but Roman didn’t miss the detest in his eyes.

He couldn't blame the men for being pissed at him. They seemed to have all this information that pointed directly at him. Roman had to remind himself they were just doing their job. The problem was the proof they had seemed to lead to the wrong person.

"I am going to say this as clear as I can. I've never seen that paper before, and I certainly didn't buy that shit. I'd never hurt Isabelle. She's the love of my life and I'd die before I would do anything to harm her." Roman slammed his hands on the table. "We're having a baby, for fuck sake. Do you get it now?"

"Maybe you aren't as happy about the kid as you want us to believe." James leaned back in the chair and crossed his arms over his chest.

"I'm over the moon about the baby and when you guys figure out you've got the wrong person, you'll see how much I love her and our baby. I'm going to spend the rest of my life with her. She's the reason I get up in the morning, the reason I breathe, and if anyone should be able to spot that, it's you two." Roman shoved the chair out of the way and started to pace the small room.

"Why did you come back to Newfoundland?" Aaron asked.

Roman knew where they were headed, but he'd already told Isabelle why he'd left the mainland. He'd been accused of making sexual advances toward his boss's wife. He didn't do it, of course. His boss's wife was the aggressor. When Roman turned her down and told her he'd go to her husband if she didn't stop, she told her husband Roman had been coming on to her.

"I got fired." Roman turned and stared at Aaron. "But you already knew that, didn't you?"

"Yes, but why did you get fired?" Aaron asked.

"You obviously know that too. Why do I have to relive it?" Roman leaned his back against the wall and shoved his hands into his pockets.

"You tried to kill your boss," James blurted out.

"Wait? What?" Roman moved so fast that he tweaked his side and he buckled over in pain.

He took several breaths to calm himself until the pain passed. When he glanced up at James and Aaron, they seemed concerned for a moment, but Roman slowly stood up and cleared his throat.

"I didn't try to kill him, or anyone." He spoke as confidently as he could.

"That's what he told us," James replied.

Roman shook his head as he eased into the chair. What the fuck was going on and why was this happening to him? It was at that moment the door opened and a man stepped inside who Roman recognized. He was a friend of Mike's and a lawyer.

"That's enough, guys. I need to talk to my client, alone." Jason Brenton walked up next to the table.

"I didn't ask for a lawyer." Roman was confused.

"Nope, Isabelle called me," Jason replied as Aaron and James headed out of the room. "Turn off the recording devices, gentlemen."

James nodded as he exited the room and Aaron pulled the door closed behind them. Jason didn't speak a word as he looked up to the corner of the room. Roman saw the camera mounted there and wondered who else had watched the interrogation. When the red light went off, Jason turned back to Roman.

"I'm going to get you out of here, but you're going to have to stay away from Isabelle." Jason pulled several papers out of his briefcase.

"No fucking way," Roman shouted.

"Sorry, that's non-negotiable, since the attempted murder charge is because she could have been killed in the restaurant." Jason flipped through some papers.

"Are you fucking kidding me?" Roman choked on the words.

"No, but don't worry. I've got a feeling none of this is going to stick." Jason didn't look up as he continued to organize the papers in front of him.

Roman stared at the man as he explained what would happen. Roman would be arraigned and bail set. Apparently, his brothers and sister were ready to post his bail and found a place for him to stay in the city.

“I’m not leaving Isabelle,” Roman snapped.

“It’s either you stay away from her for now, or you stay in jail. It’s up to you.” Jason raised his eyes to look at Roman.

“I hate this.” Roman shoved his hands through his hair.

“You don’t have to like it. All you have to do is follow the conditions of the release,” Jason explained.

“Fine,” Roman grumbled several minutes later, but he only agreed to make sure he could get out and prove his innocence.

Roman was fingerprinted, photographed, and put in a cell until he could have his time in front of the judge. Luckily, they’d kept him in the Hopedale lockup which had two cells and he was the only one in custody.

It took almost forty-eight hours for his arraignment and to have his time in front of the judge. When he was led into the courtroom in handcuffs, he’d never felt so low in his life.

His brothers stood in the courtroom and looked ready to kill when Aaron and James entered. His sister was worse and threw insults at the O’Connor brothers on the way out of the courtroom.

It was Isabelle’s tears that broke his heart. It took every ounce of strength he had not to pull her into his arms and tell her everything would be okay. The only thing that made him feel somewhat better was when Marcella told him Isabelle didn’t believe for a second that Roman was guilty.

Roman didn't know how long he'd have to go without contact with Isabelle. It was as if there was a weight on his chest when he thought about not being able to see her, hold her, kiss her, and talk to her. He prayed that whoever set him up didn't use this opportunity to do something else to hurt her.

Roman and his siblings were on the way to the car when a large hand grabbed his shoulder. When he spun around, he came face to face with Kurt's angry glare. He braced himself to be punched or worse, but instead, Kurt took a step back. His glare was no less lethal.

"I'm trying hard not to believe you had anything to do with this, but the evidence keeps piling up against you. So, here's a promise. If you're responsible for this, I'll personally make sure you spend the rest of your life in jail." Kurt's voice was cold and low.

"My brother didn't do this." Marcella stepped toward Kurt, but Roman pulled her back.

"I hope you're right, young lady. If he did, he's going to be in a huge world of hurt." Kurt growled.

"Are you threatening my client, Mayor O'Connor?" Jason stepped next to Roman.

"It's not a threat, Brenton, it's a promise," Kurt spat as he turned and walked toward Isabelle on the other side of the parking lot.

"He's a fucking dick." Maximus growled.

“No, he’s not, Max. He’s a dad who thinks I tried to hurt his daughter. You’d be the same way if someone tried to hurt one of your kids.” Roman turned to his brother. “It’s why I need to find out who’s setting me up. I’m not going to lose Isabelle.”

“That’s going to be tough when the police think you’re guilty,” Demetrios said as they got into the rental SUV.

“Ethan said he’d help,” Marcella said.

“That’s great, two construction workers, a chef, a teacher, and a former pilot turned bartender working together to figure out who is framing you. That should be easy.” Maximus scoffed.

As the SUV pulled out of the parking space and headed to St. John’s, Roman had time to think. He’d have to stay in the small apartment until he was cleared. It was too far away from Isabelle for his comfort, but he didn’t have a choice

Whoever set him up wanted him out of the way. This was the easiest way to get him away from Isabelle and Hopedale, but for what purpose? The only thing he could do was pray that someone could find out the truth and he would be cleared. Roman wasn’t about to live a life without Isabelle and their baby.

Chapter 25

"I don't care what kind of evidence you have. Roman wouldn't hurt Isabelle or anyone for that matter. I've known him all my life. He's my brother's best friend for heaven's sake," Lora shouted at her husband.

Lora was married to Nick, but it seemed she wasn't about to believe her brother's best friend was capable of hurting anyone. It wasn't hard to see that Roman had more than just Isabelle and his siblings on his side. Apparently, so were most of the women in her family.

"How do you explain the credit card purchases?" Aaron asked.

"Hello, I can charge tons of things on your credit card and you wouldn't know until it's too late. It's easy this day and age, A.J." Sandy scoffed. "I could hack into a government system, change your name to whore-boy, and you'd only find out when you went to get your birth certificate."

"Don't even think about it, Sandy." Aaron glared at his sister-in-law.

"You guys have got to at least consider that he could have done this," Nick said.

"I'm not considering it at all because I know he didn't." Lora poked her husband in the chest.

"Consider or not, everything points to him." Aaron crossed his arms as he sat back on the couch in Isabelle's living room.

She just wanted them all to leave because she didn't care what the courts said. Isabelle wasn't about to abandon the man she loved because someone set him up to take a fall for something he didn't do. Isabelle saw his face when he noticed the fire and the only thing she saw was concern for her.

"Aaron, you of all people know how someone can set someone up to look bad." Bethany raised an eyebrow at her husband.

Bethany and Aaron had dated in high school, but because of a rumor, they ended up being separated for years before finding each other again. Bethany believed for years that Aaron used her to win a bet, but it wasn't true.

"Baby, this is a totally different situation." Aaron smiled at his pregnant wife.

"Is it? From what I see, everything you have is circumstantial. Isn't that kind of like a rumor?" Bethany returned.

"I don't care what any of you say. I don't believe he'd ever hurt my sister." Jess snuggled into her fiancé, Wade.

"At least he has a good lawyer," Mike said.

"You're taking their side?" Nick asked.

"I'm not taking anyone's side. I'm just saying he has a good lawyer and that's it. Jesus Christ, relax." Mike held up his hands.

"Fucking lawyers," Nick grumbled.

"Didn't you graduate law school?" Lora reminded her husband.

Nick did graduate from law school and had worked as a corporate lawyer for a few years. When he realized what he really wanted to do was help people, he joined the police academy.

Isabelle had enough of the crowd in her house. She made her way into the kitchen, so she didn't have to hear the constant bickering. She just wanted them all to leave, but when she turned, her grandmother stood in the doorway.

"I'm wit ya, Lassie." Nanny Betty scurried over and wrapped her arms around Isabelle.

"Thanks, Nan." Isabelle swallowed the lump in her throat.

"Da truth will come out in the long run," Nanny Betty whispered. "Doncha worry."

"She needs to be worried." Her father's voice rumbled through the room.

"Dad, don't start because I'm tired of hearing it." Isabelle sighed as she poured herself a cup of tea.

“Sweet pea, you need to prepare yourself for the worst,” her father reminded her.

“And I hope you all have a good apology prepared for when the truth comes out,” Isabelle grumbled.

Isabelle didn’t like to be prepared for the worst. It would mean Roman had betrayed her and she couldn’t allow that possibility to enter her thoughts. He wasn’t that man. There was no way she could be suckered in like that. Someone was out to hurt him and that was the only fact she wanted to believe.

“Kurt, ya need ta leave her be. I knows da lad didn’t do dis and I don’t care what kinda proof ya got,” Nanny Betty snapped.

“Look, I love you all, but please. I need to be alone. Nan, can you get everyone out of here?” Isabelle choked out the words.

“Dey’ll be gone in a jiffy.” Nanny Betty scurried into the living room and Isabelle heard her order everyone to go home.

Her father didn’t say anything else; he simply wrapped his arms around her and hugged her against him. Even if he didn’t believe Roman was innocent, it felt comforting to have her father’s hugs. When she was little, they always made the bad times seem not so bad. If only she was a naïve little girl again.

“Thanks, Dad. I needed that,” Isabelle whispered.

“You’ve got all of us behind you, no matter what.” Her father kissed the top of her head before he released her and followed everyone out through the door.

The sudden silence was deafening, and for a second, she regretted making everyone leave. Isabelle made her way upstairs to her bedroom, but she stopped at the closed door at the top of the stairs.

She and Roman had planned for that room to be for the baby. At the moment, the only thing that was done was it was painted a soft yellow and her grandmother's rocking chair sat in the corner. They'd planned to get the rest of the things they needed after the reveal party that they never had a chance to plan.

She turned the knob and walked inside. The setting sun cast an orange glow around the room and the only thing she could think about was how they would have to put blinds in the room to block out the sun. She sat in the rocking chair and looked out the window. Like her own bedroom, the baby's nursery was on the front of the house with a perfect view of the beach. Isabelle watched the waves crash up on the rocky shore as the sun set behind the horizon.

"Don't worry, Baby Tiger. Daddy will be back soon. He loves you so much. Almost as much as I do," Isabelle whispered softly as she rested her hand on her slightly swollen belly.

She sat back in the chair and rocked as she softly hummed. It was a song she'd heard more times than she could count. Her father would sing it to Isabelle and her sisters when he'd tuck them it at night. "*Toora Loora Loora*" was an old Irish Lullaby that always brought her back to those days. The days when she had no worries and her parents protected her from all the evil things in the world.

Now, she would get a chance to sing it to her own little one. Not as well as her father did, because she wasn't as talented as her dad, but she could hold a tune. Her cousins could all sing as well and some of them even had a cover band. They usually played for charity events or parties but for the most part, it was a hobby for them.

She remembered the first time she met Roman. They were at the pub and her cousins' band was performing for the family party. It was one of her cousin's birthdays. Lora had invited him so Isabelle could meet him before she decided if she would hire him. He'd smiled and she was a goner. Although, she would never admit it then.

Isabelle woke with a start and almost tipped over in the rocking chair. She hadn't even realized she'd fallen asleep, but the shrill sound of her security alarm had her jumping to her feet and searching for her phone in her pocket.

"Damn it," she whispered when she remembered she'd left it in the kitchen.

Isabelle quietly tiptoed to the door of the room and peeked out to the top of the stairs. The alarm still screamed, and she made her way down the stairs. She didn't remember setting the alarm before she went upstairs, but her father might have done it on his way out.

Isabelle was just surprised Cobalt wasn't barking like a lunatic. She didn't like loud noises and tended to bark even if the television was too loud. Isabelle stepped to the bottom of the stairs and she could hear her phone ring.

She hurried to the kitchen while she shouted for the dog. Isabelle picked up her phone as she ran over to turn off the alarm before it woke half the town. She glanced around for Cobalt while she punched in the code and answered the phone

"Hello," she shouted, and the noise stopped.

"Ms. O'Connor, this is Security One. We got an alert that your alarm was set off," the woman said with a slight accent.

"Yeah, I don't think my door was closed completely and it blew open," Isabelle said when she noticed her front door ajar.

"Are you sure you don't need anyone to come by?" The woman pushed.

"No, I'm fine. Thanks." Isabelle didn't give the woman a chance to say anything else and ended the call.

She stepped outside and looked up and down the street. Now she had to worry about the damn dog because Cobalt probably ran out through the door. Before Isabelle had a chance to move down the steps, she heard the pup growl from the corner of the front deck.

"Cobalt, what's wrong?" Isabelle walked toward the dog.

She was scratching at the deck and seemed desperate to get at something on the other side of the rail. Isabelle tried to calm the pup down as she peered over the rail. Isabelle couldn't see anything that would send the dog into such a frenzy, but Cobalt continued to growl as she moved in front of Isabelle.

"What the hell is wrong with her?" Kristy shouted from her doorway.

"I don't know. Cat, I guess." Isabelle picked up the frantic puppy and tried to soothe her.

"Is that what set off your alarm?" Kristy asked.

"Not sure. The door was open. Dad probably didn't close it completely when he left and when Cobalt got out, she set it off, I suppose." Isabelle shrugged.

"Isabelle, maybe I should get Dean to go over and make sure there's nobody in the house." Kristy didn't give Isabelle a chance to answer and called out to her husband.

"Kristy, it's okay. If anyone is in the house, Cobalt will bark like crazy," Isabelle said.

"Too late, I'm already half-way there." Bull jogged up the steps and winked.

The bald man was the love of Kristy's life. It had taken a while before Kristy finally got her happily ever after. Bull, or as Kristy called him, Dean, finally realized Kristy was his future. Not only were they perfect for each other, but they were also the perfect neighbors.

While she chatted with Kristy and held on to the squirming dog who seemed determined to find whatever had her barking, Bull came out and let Isabelle know everything was okay inside the house. Of course, he did make sure to remind her to lock the door and set the alarm when she went in for the evening.

Isabelle never felt nervous living alone. Especially since Bull and Kristy lived next door on one side and her cousin John lived on the other side with his family, but for some reason, with Roman gone, she found the house way too big and lonely. She missed him so much it hurt.

Isabelle made her way inside and locked up the house. Cobalt calmed when Isabelle set the alarm and called her upstairs. Normally, she slept in her kennel next to the door, but Isabelle felt the need to have the pup close by.

In the four days since Roman was arrested, Isabelle had gotten the dog used to sleeping in her room. She'd even had Nick move the kennel upstairs.

Isabelle pulled on Roman's shirt and climbed into the empty bed. Cobalt still wasn't able to jump up on it and had to be lifted. The pup made herself comfy. While Isabelle snuggled into the pillow where Roman slept, a tear slipped out and ran down her cheek.

"I miss you so much." Isabelle sniffed.

Cobalt must have sensed her sadness and immediately started to whine and lick her tears away. Cobalt rested her head on the pillow next to Isabelle.

"You miss him too, don't you, girl." Isabelle scratched the dog's head. "Fuck this."

Isabelle sat up in the bed and snatched her cell phone off the nightstand. She pulled up his number and after a second of hesitation, she tapped it. Hopefully the police hadn't taken his phone, or she could be getting him in a heap of trouble.

"Isabelle." Roman sounded frantic. "What's wrong?"

"Besides me missing you so much it hurts, nothing," she said.

"Tiger, I miss you too. God, this is such complete bullshit." Roman's voice was strained.

"I know." She sniffed.

"Baby, don't cry. I promise we'll get this figured out. I'll be holding you in my arms before you know it." Roman's voice didn't help her emotional state.

"I just needed to hear your voice and let you know I don't believe any of this." Isabelle wanted him to remember that.

"Thank you, Tiger. That means the world to me and I don't care what anyone else thinks of me as long as you know the truth." Roman's voice cracked.

"Cobalt misses you too." She giggled.

"You have her in bed, don't you?" Roman laughed.

"Yes, it's only until you come home." She smiled knowing that it would be hard to get the puppy out of the bed once she was in it.

"You're my home," Roman whispered.

"I love you, Roman," Isabelle said.

"I love you too, Isabelle." For several minutes neither of them spoke, but it wasn't awkward, it was comforting.

"I should let you go," Isabelle whispered.

"Sleep well, Tiger." Roman said.

Isabelle reluctantly ended the call, but she did feel better hearing his voice. Why would someone want to frame him? It didn't make sense, but she wasn't waiting for the police to figure it out. She was going to pull together the best team in the town and clear the man she loved.

The next morning, Isabelle waited for the arrival of everyone she'd sent a text. They were all warned not to breathe a word to anyone outside of the group. Isabelle knew some members of her family would have an issue with what they were doing, but if they were in her shoes, they'd do the same thing.

"The cavalry's here." Sandy's voice echoed through Isabelle's foyer.

"You're a cavalry?" Isabelle chuckled while she made a pot of coffee.

"Oh, honey, I'm just the beginning." Sandy winked as she pulled out her laptop and opened it.

"I'm here," Lora called out.

"Me too." Kristy waddled into the kitchen.

"I'm here too." Stephanie entered with her sister behind her.

"We're so going to get shit for doing this." Marina laughed. "I told James we were all coming over here to make sure you were okay."

"Technically, we are." Jess laughed as she walked in with Billie, Bethany, and Emily.

"Dear lord, I hope all of you don't go into labor at the same time." Sandy laughed.

"Kristy and Billie are the only ones ready to pop." Marina pointed to the two women.

"Yeah, and me, you, and Sandy are outnumbered here." Jess laughed.

"Hey, I'm not preggo." Pam walked into the kitchen with Nanny Betty.

Then Isabelle's Aunt Kathleen, and Aunt Cora, followed by her mom. The women of the family all believed the same as Isabelle. The men were split down the middle, but she wanted to make sure she had the positive bunch and only called in the females of the family.

“So, where do we start?” Marina asked.

Sandy was the first one to speak. She’d somehow managed to get a copy of the file on Roman and the evidence that had been collected. When asked how she managed to get it, she just said she had her ways and not to ask such silly questions.

Isabelle wasn’t a lawyer, but she knew most of the evidence they had was circumstantial. Sandy said the items were bought online and sent to a post office box. They were picked up by someone wearing a dark hooded sweater, but it was not possible to see the face of the person who picked up the contents.

Then there was the statement they had from Roman’s former boss. He’d told Isabelle about that job a while ago and why he was fired. There was no way Roman tried to kill his old boss.

“I’m going to do some checking into the charges on the credit card. I might be able to locate the IP address where it was ordered from.” Sandy frantically tapped the keys on her laptop.

“I’ve been looking at this video of the guy picking up the stuff from the PO box. It’s not Roman.” Lora placed the tablet in the middle of the table and pointed to the guy's hand.

“What are we looking at?” Stephanie asked.

“The ring,” Lora said.

"He's not wearing a ring." Marina enlarged the still of the man.

"Exactly, Roman wears a ring his father made from a steel nut. His dad made them for all his kids and engraved their initials on them." Lora tapped her phone and pulled up a picture of Roman and Ethan.

She enlarged Roman's hand where it lay on Ethan's shoulder to show the ring. Isabelle had completely forgotten about it. He never took it off, even when he showered.

"That's good that we can prove it isn't Roman, but it still doesn't prove he's not involved," Billie reminded everyone.

"Maybe not, but this certainly does." Sandy turned her laptop around.

"Sandy, what are we looking at?" Isabelle's mother asked.

"Do you see those twelve numbers?" Sandy pointed to the screen.

"Yes," most of the women said together.

"I just traced that IP address and it's not even in Newfoundland," Sandy replied.

"Where is it?" Kathleen asked.

"I'm still tracing," Sandy told them.

"Can't some people make those things look like they're coming from different places?" Bethany asked.

Sandy admitted people could, but started to explain why this wasn't the case. Isabelle tuned her out as she stood next to the kitchen window and stared out. Her back yard still had little mounds of snow here and there and she mentally counted them.

"Isabelle, doncha worry. We'll make sure Roman is cleared." Nanny Betty wrapped her arm around Isabelle's waist.

"I hope so. I mean, I can't believe they arrested him on such little evidence." Isabelle didn't understand why.

The front door of Isabelle's house slammed open and her father stomped inside. The look on his face told her he knew exactly what was going on in her kitchen and didn't like it.

"What the hell are all of you doing?" her dad snapped.

"For heaven's sake, Kurt. We're having a chat." Her mother rolled her eyes.

"Really, Alice?" Her father held up a phone and her mother gasped.

"Kurt, don't start," her mother warned.

"Don't start? Are you kidding me? You women are all congregated here to try and clear Roman. What the hell do you think all of you can do that A.J. and the police department can't do?" her father shouted.

"Keep yer tone down, me son. Just who da ya tink yer talkin' to?" Nanny Betty stepped in front of Isabelle's father and pointed her finger up in his face. "I don't ever want ta here ya talk ta any of dese lassies like dat again."

Isabelle's father took a deep breath and blew it out slowly. It was something he did when he tried to calm himself. Like everyone else in the room, her father knew pissing off Nanny Betty wouldn't be pretty. He could probably pick her up and toss her across the street if he wanted, but he'd never hurt a hair on his mother's head. It was why Nanny Betty had no fear of anyone in the family, they all respected her way too much.

"Look, I'm sorry, but you've got to let A.J. handle this." Her father met Isabelle's eyes. "You're not going to find anything they didn't."

"Really? We already found out that the guy from the post office isn't Roman and that the items were ordered from outside of Newfoundland," Isabelle snapped.

"What?" her father gasped.

"It's true," her mother said.

"Sandy, what are they talking about?" Her dad glared at the smiling woman.

"Well, if A.J. had asked me to do this instead of that idiot at the station, he would have found out that there was no way Roman could have made those charges on his credit card from Ontario. He was here." Sandy crossed her arms and smirked.

Isabelle's father wasn't happy with that bit of information and sat down as they continued to give him the rest of the things they'd learned. Since Sandy was technically part of the Hopedale Division of the Newfoundland Police Department, she wasn't really doing anything illegal, but since they didn't request her help, technically, she could be reprimanded.

Isabelle also learned that they were waiting for forensics to check for DNA or fingerprints on the tank and the wires used. They weren't really sure they'd find any, but until they could say one way or another, Roman was still their number one suspect.

"You need to bring this information to A.J. and stop this little investigation before any of you get hurt. For Christ's sake more than half of you are pregnant," her dad grumbled.

"We're pregnant, Dad. Not handicapped." Kristy returned.

"Women." Her father sighed.

An hour later, Aaron, James, and Nick were in her kitchen, just as annoyed as her father. She didn't care. If they could prove that Roman wasn't involved in any of this, then he could come home to her. Not to mention the women in the family were dying to prove they were right.

"I can't believe you wanted to be involved in this." Nick glared at Lora.

"Why wouldn't I? We're the only ones who believe Roman," Lora snapped.

Isabelle hated to see the rift between the couple and she prayed that they could get through it. They were so perfect together, and Lora's daughter adored Nick.

"Baby, it's not that I don't believe him…" Nick was cut off when Lora put her hand over his mouth.

"Don't you baby me," Lora warned.

"Look, if you guys interfere in this, you can get in a lot of trouble." Aaron tried to pull the legal aspect of what they were doing.

"Oh, so if we don't stop, you're going to press charges against all of us?" Bethany smirked at her husband.

"No. Yes. No… Jesus, of course not. There isn't a judge in this province who wants to deal with all of you, but the department can press charges if you screw with the investigation." Aaron sighed.

"Then let them. At least you'd be pressing charges on people that have actually done what they were accused of. Not like Roman, who is being railroaded." Billie slammed her hand on the counter.

Isabelle was tired of listening to the arguing. She snatched her coat off the hook and walked out of her house. A few minutes on the beach would help calm her frayed nerves and help her focus on the task. She made her way across the road and headed down the steps to the beach. All she wanted to do was block out the sound of everything except the ocean.

The wind was cold and she pulled her jacket tightly around her as she took several deep breaths. The smell of the salty air and the sound of the waves crashing on the rocky shore was like a remedy for stress.

With her family at odds with each other, she felt responsible for the tension. It wasn't something that happened in her family and the fact that it happened because of her situation wasn't something she wanted to think about. The only thing she wanted was to have everything back the way it was. Roman by her side and her business thriving while they awaited the birth of their baby.

Isabelle covered her belly with her hands. They'd been given the envelope with the gender of the baby almost a month earlier and she still didn't know if it was a boy or girl. She didn't want to know until Roman could be there with her.

Isabelle tipped her head back and looked up at the cloudy sky. She didn't pray very often, and she should be ashamed to even say it, but her life was always what she wanted. The only thing she ever did was thank God for that because other people needed so much more.

"Dear God, please help Roman. You know he didn't do this, but you've got to help A.J. and my family prove it," Isabelle whispered.

"Maybe I can help." A strange voice whispered from behind her.

Isabelle spun around but before she could say a word, she was hit in the face, hard. Then something was pulled down over her head. Isabelle was woozy from the blow to her face and she shook her head to clear her thoughts. Before she could clear her head and call for help, something hit her again, and everything went dark.

Chapter 26

Roman sat on the sofa and stared at the television. If someone had asked what he was watching, he wouldn't be able to answer. Maximus sat next to him, on the phone with his wife and kids while Demetrios was in the kitchen on video chat with his wife and kids.

Marcella sat in the corner of the couch reading and Roman was the only one who couldn't concentrate on anything but how much he missed Isabelle.

"All right, baby. I love you and I'll call you tomorrow." Maximus's voice was interrupted by a knock at the door.

Marcella jumped up and made her way to the door of the apartment. Roman followed her only because he was tired of sitting and he wanted to see who was at the door.

"What are you doing here?" Marcella's angry voice had Maximus and Demetrios on either side of Roman.

"I need to talk to Roman." Aaron stepped around a very angry Marcella.

“What’s wrong now? Did you discover he’s the reason the glaciers are melting?” Marcella shouted.

“Cella, shut up,” Maximus snapped.

“A.J., what’s wrong?” Roman knew by the look on Aaron’s face it was something bad.

“Roman, you may want to sit down,” Aaron said.

“No, what’s wrong?” Roman’s heart pounded in his chest.

“It’s Isabelle, she’s missing.” Aaron’s voice cracked.

“What do you mean, missing?” Roman choked on the words.

“It’s a long story, but she went to the beach, I’m assuming to get away from the crowd in her house. When Uncle Kurt went to look for her, she wasn’t there. The only thing he found was her phone and one of her shoes,” Aaron explained.

“Fuck. Fuck.” Roman grabbed Aaron by the shirt. “This is your fucking fault. If you’d believed me, I would’ve been there with her. What the hell is wrong with all of you? Can’t you keep your own family safe?”

“Roman, don’t do anything you’ll regret.” Maximus grabbed Roman’s arms and pulled him back.

“Regret. Are you fucking kidding me? The woman I love is gone and nobody knows where she is. Half her fucking family are cops.” Roman struggled against his brother’s hold.

"I was just doing my job, Roman. According to the women in my family, not well." Aaron glanced at Marcella. "Please don't be pissed at me, but I need to do this."

"What?" Marcella narrowed her eyes.

"Roman, we need to take you into the station," Aaron said as another officer walked in through the door.

"You think he kidnapped Isabelle?" Marcella shouted.

"We need whoever has her to think we're blaming you." Kurt walked in behind the police officer.

"What are you saying?" Maximus released Roman.

"Roman, I know you had nothing to do with this. We've got evidence to support it." Aaron nodded to the uniformed officer.

"But you're still arresting him." Marcella threw her hands up in the air.

"We need to make this look real in case we're being watched," Aaron said as Roman was cuffed and led through the door.

"Meet us back in Hopedale," Roman heard Kurt tell Marcella, Maximus, and Demetrios.

Roman wanted to throw up as he was driven back to the town. The police officer in the front seat didn't speak the whole way and Roman was glad. He was afraid if he spoke, he'd lose every ounce of composure he had.

Who the fuck would take Isabelle? Was she hurt? He couldn't think about what could happen to her. He silently prayed whoever had her didn't hurt her or the baby. Roman couldn't survive if something happened to her, and she'd be devastated if the baby was hurt.

At the station, Roman was ushered into an interview room and the handcuffs removed. It made him feel uneasy because of what happened the first time he was brought in. The only difference was the door was left open and he was not being accused of a crime.

"Roman, I'm sorry you had to be brought in like that again," James said as he entered the room.

"I don't care, I want to find Isabelle." Roman started to pace the room.

"Sandy's checking all video surveillance around the beach," James explained.

"Jesus, where is she?" Roman plowed his hands through his hair.

"Roman, we'll find her." James' voice cracked.

It had to be hard on James, Aaron, Nick, and John. They were police officers and had to remain professional, but knowing someone in their family was in danger had to be difficult. He couldn't imagine what it must be like for them, because he felt as if someone had torn out his heart.

More than three hours later, Roman sat on a chair in John's office. John was the current Chief of Police and had taken over when Kurt retired. John brought Roman into his office to make him more comfortable while they waited for word of Isabelle. The comfort didn't help with the waiting, it only made it easier to sit.

"Roman, would you like a cup of coffee?" Jess walked into John's office with a tray of Tim Horton's cups.

"Thanks." Roman accepted one of the cups and gave Jess a weak smile.

Jess was also a former police officer, but she had left the force to do what she loved more. She had her own flower shop and she also taught Karate at the Hopedale Community Center. She'd taken over after Kurt retired from the Karate school.

"God wouldn't take her away when she just found you." Jess' eyes were filled with tears.

Roman stood up and placed his coffee on John's desk. He pulled Isabelle's sister into his arms and let her cry on his shoulder. It was all he could do at that moment and it gave him something else to do besides thinking the worst. Wade had gone out searching with the rest of the O'Connors, but they still wanted to keep Roman at the station.

"She's my big sister and one of the strongest people I know." Jess pulled back and wiped the tears from her eyes.

Roman was too choked up to respond, but he nodded as Jess sat on the sofa. He picked up his coffee cup and eased down next to her and continued to pray for Isabelle's safe return.

For several hours, people came and went, but Roman was focused on a picture on top of John's bookcase. It showed the whole family of O'Connors, but Isabelle's beautiful smile was the only thing he could see. That was what he had to think about because if he thought about what could be happening to her, he'd go insane.

Chapter 27

Isabelle rolled over on her side and groaned. Her face hurt and her jaw felt as if she'd been hit with a sledgehammer. It was difficult, but she managed to open her eyes and brought her hand up to her aching cheek.

She didn't have to see a mirror to know it was swollen. Isabelle cringed as she pressed her finger against the bone under her eye. It was tender and puffy.

She wasn't in a familiar place. There was a faint smell of burnt wood and stale beer. Isabelle pushed herself up to sit on the dirty couch she'd been lying on. It was stained with God knows what and she shuddered with disgust at the sight of it. Isabelle moved her focus to the rest of her surroundings. None of it looked remotely familiar and that was unsettling.

Isabelle eased off the couch and got to her feet. The room spun for a moment and she grabbed on to the arm of the sofa until the dizziness stopped. The taste of blood in her mouth made her want to vomit, and she spit out as much as she could before she threw up.

Once the vertigo stopped, she scanned the her surroundings for a way out. The room was dimly lit, but she managed to make out the door and quietly moved toward it. She didn't know why she had no shoes, but she didn't care. If she had to walk on broken glass to get out, she'd do it.

Isabelle covered her belly with her hand as she leaned against the door to listen before she tried to open it. It was quiet and she took a deep breath as she reached for the knob. Hopefully, whoever put her in the room wasn't outside waiting.

"I'll get you out of here, Baby Tiger," Isabelle whispered.

She slowly turned the knob and pushed the door. It didn't budge and she cursed under her breath. Isabelle scanned the room for another way out, but all the windows were boarded up and there was no other door. She frantically searched the room for something to either pry the board off the window or open the door.

The only thing she saw was the couch and a small table with several bottles of water on it. She was thirsty but she wasn't about to drink random bottles of water in a room she was locked in. If someone was willing to punch a woman in the face and kidnap her, who knew what they would do.

She spotted her jacket on the arm of the chair and prayed her phone was still in it. She snatched it up and frantically searched the pockets, but to her disappointment, there was nothing there. She eased down on the couch and swallowed the lump forming in her throat. Isabelle refused to lose it.

"Where the hell am I?" Isabelle whispered.

She placed her hands on her belly and gently rubbed in circles to calm the movement of the baby. Isabelle learned quickly that when she was upset, the baby tended to be more active. The last thing she wanted to do was stress out the little one.

"It's okay, Baby Tiger. We're going to be fine," she murmured.

Isabelle licked her lips as she glanced at the bottles of water. She couldn't go too long without fluids, but she was terrified of what could be in the bottles. She made her way to the table and picked up one of the bottles.

Isabelle carefully checked the seal and was relieved to see it wasn't broken. She squeezed it to make sure that nothing was injected into it. When she was as confident as she could be in her situation, she opened the bottle and took a small mouthful. It was warm, but it was water.

She didn't know how long she'd been in the room or what time of day it was. All she knew was she needed to get out of wherever she was. Isabelle wasn't about to sit down and cry over her situation. That wasn't her way, and she had another little life to protect as well.

Isabelle made her way around the room to each of the three boarded-up windows to see if she could pull off the thick wood. She was about to step up on the bed to check the top of one when the door opened. The man who had introduced himself as Archer stepped into the room with what looked like a fast food bag.

"Eat," he snapped as he scrambled back to the door and closed it before she could say a word.

Isabelle wanted to ignore the food, that was until her stomach growled. She quickly realized if she was going to get out of this situation, she needed to keep her strength up and the only way to do that was nourishment.

She opened the bag and pulled out the burger inside. She was still concerned that the food could be drugged, but what choice did she have? She needed to eat, because if she didn't, she'd never have the strength to kick the shit out of that asshole.

Isabelle ate one of the burgers and left the other in case her captor didn't return. He might have brought her food today, but she didn't know how long she'd been there or how long she would be. He might not even return to give her anymore. Isabelle didn't know if she should be happy about that or terrified.

Her current problem was she desperately needed to relieve herself. Part of the perks of pregnancy was the sudden urge to pee without warning. She walked to the door and knocked.

"Hello, I need to visit the ladies' room," Isabelle shouted.

When she didn't get a response, she knocked again and shouted a second time. Still nothing. There was no way she was going to soil herself. Isabelle scanned the room again to find something she could use, but the door swung opened and her arm was grabbed roughly.

"Come with me," the fake Archer grumbled as he dragged her behind him.

By the time she was able to catch up with him, he had shoved her into a small room with a toilet. Isabelle spun around when he slammed the door behind her, leaving her in a dark room with a small stream of light that entered from an opening at the top of the boarded-up window.

For what seemed like days, this continued. He'd bring her food and water then she would practically scream out for him to come back to take her to the bathroom. She didn't sleep much and she had no idea how long she'd been there.

"I need to use the ladies room," Isabelle shouted out through the locked door.

"For fuck sake," the fake Archer grumble from outside the door.

"I'm pregnant, I can't help it." Isabelle snapped when the guy seized her arm and pulled her to the toilet.

"Make it quick," he snapped.

She relieved herself and washed her hands while she took in her surroundings. She needed to get her wits about her. The fake Archer was not a big guy and Isabelle had been trained in self-defense since she was a young child. Her father was a Karate instructor and taught Isabelle, her sisters, and cousins. It had been a while since she trained, but she knew how to protect herself.

"Hurry up," the fake Archer yelled through the closed door.

"Almost done." Isabelle spotted a plunger in the corner of the bathroom.

Isabelle picked it up and pulled the stick from the rubber piece. It took some doing, but she managed to tuck the stick into the back of her jeans. She looked at herself in the cracked mirror and prayed for the strength to do what she had to do.

"I'm…I'm ready," Isabelle shouted.

The fake Archer pushed open the door and grabbed her arm roughly again. Isabelle reached behind her and wrapped her free hand around the stick where it was tucked into her waistband. When she had a strong grip on it, she slipped it out of her pants and with one swift movement, swung it across her. It connected with the fake Archer's face and he roared out in pain, but he didn't release her. It took another hard blow to his face for him to finally drop her arm.

She hadn't hit him hard enough to knock him out, but he rolled around on the floor, screaming like a little girl and clutching his nose. Isabelle rolled her eyes at his dramatics, but she didn't have time to make fun of him. She had to get out of there and fast.

"You fucking bitch. You broke my fucking nose." He sounded like a child as he continued to shout at her.

Isabelle wasn't taking a chance that he would follow her. She hated to do it to the man, but it was him or her. Isabelle lifted her foot and slammed it right into his crotch. The squeal he made hurt her ears, but she turned and ran as fast as she could, still holding the stick in her hand. If he somehow got up, or there was another person there, she wasn't going to go down without a fight.

She found a set of stairs at the end of the hallway and almost tumbled over them as she took them two at a time. When she got to the bottom, she realized where she was. Isabelle was inside the building next to her restaurant. With a sigh of relief, she ran to the front of the large room. There were two exits that led to Harbour Street and she made a bee line for one of the doors.

Isabelle was disappointed to see a huge chain wrapped around the handles and locked with a padlock. She cursed under her breath as she glanced toward the steps to see if she was being followed. She could still hear the whimpers from the fake Archer, but he could recover quickly.

She went to the other exit at the other side of the building, but it was locked too. Isabelle ran to the back where the bar used to run the length of the brick wall. She stepped behind it to see if she could find a place to hide until she came up with a plan to get out of the old club.

Her restaurant was on the other side of the brick wall. When she bought her side of the building, she was informed that the wall had been installed on either side of a fire barrier because her kitchen was attached to the club. Isabelle had thought it was a little overkill but considering the club only seemed to have smoke damage from the fire, it obviously worked.

Isabelle spotted an open area that used to house one of the large speakers for the sound system. She was positive someone in heaven was watching out for her. Isabelle could climb up and hide until she could figure out how to get out of the building.

Isabelle climbed on the bar and pulled herself up into the small opening. She blew out a breath of relief when she managed to get herself inside before the fake Archer started to scream out to her. Isabelle held her breath when she heard the fake Archer stumble down over the stairs, cursing her with every step.

"I don't know where she went. All I know is my nose is broken and I think she drove one of my balls up inside me." Archer complained.

Isabelle assumed he was on the phone, considering she couldn't hear another voice. She was up high enough that she wouldn't be easily seen, but she could still manage to peek out to see where the asshole was standing.

"She's got to be in here somewhere. All the doors are secured and there's no way she'd find the crawl space." There was a pause before she heard the man's voice again. "You don't think I know that? I'll check upstairs again. Maybe she's hiding on the other side." Isabelle heard the fake Archer stomp up the other set of steps and she pressed her body as close to the wall as she could.

"God, please don't let him find me," Isabelle whispered.

The words were barely out of her mouth when the wall behind her moved. She listened as Archer ambled around above her and shouted at whoever blamed him for her escape. Isabelle pushed against the wall again. It popped out and she scooted back into the opening.

Isabelle wasn't sure where she was, but she knew that she could hide in the area if she needed, but when she narrowed her eyes and looked around, she spotted a ladder. It looked like one of the old fire escape ladders people had on the back of buildings, and was attached to the brick. Considering it had been inside a wall for god knows how long, it didn't look very old.

She didn't care if it was a hundred years old or two days old. She had to take a chance and see where it went. She hoped it would lead her to the roof or anywhere as long as she got far away from the fake Archer.

Isabelle carefully put the board back to cover the hole and slowly made her way up the iron ladder. It was a tight squeeze as she climbed higher and higher. It looked as if someone had knocked down boards to make the small space that she squeezed herself into. If she was as pregnant as Kristy, she would never have fit through the opening. With each step, she glanced up to see how far she had to go. She had to see where it led.

The fake Archer's voice disappeared as she climbed up. When Isabelle finally reached the top, she saw a crawl space. It looked filthy, but she maneuvered off the ladder and got on her hands and knees.

"I hope to God this leads me out of this place." Isabelle whispered as she prayed nobody heard her and she didn't fall through the ceiling.

The space was no more than two feet high, but it extended the length of the building. When she looked in the other direction she tried to figure out where it would take her. The intense smell of burned wood was horrible but it made her realize that she was above her restaurant.

She continued to crawl forward a few more feet to a large opening. She eased closer and peeked down and breathed a sigh of relief when she saw she was right. It was her restaurant and she was directly above the dining room.

Excitedly, she scanned the room to see if she could get down to the floor without hurting herself. All the tables were gone from the area and it was about a fourteen-foot drop to the floor.

"You can't stay up here forever," Isabelle whispered as she scooted around and dropped her feet down.

She rolled over on her stomach as best she could and slowly pushed herself down until she could hang into the room. She looked down, and she was still about eight feet from the floor. Isabelle didn't have a choice because it was the only way out. Isabelle let go and dropped to the floor.

Her left ankle twisted, and a pain like she'd never experience before shot through her leg. Isabelle bit down on her lip to keep from screaming in agony. The man who'd taken her was in the next building, and if he heard her, there was no way she could run from him with an injured ankle.

She had to make it to the kitchen and hide out until the construction crew showed up. She wasn't sure when that would be, but at least she was in a safe place. Isabelle scooted on her bottom across the floor and had to stop a few times to deal with the pain. It seemed to take forever to make it out of the dining room. When she finally did, she dragged herself into her office.

It was still in rough shape, but all the burned boards had been removed and replaced. Isabelle grabbed a tarp from the corner and curled up under it in the corner of the room. She closed her eyes and took several deep breaths to help deal with the throbbing pain of her rapidly swelling ankle. She also felt really cold and the cloth tarp didn't help warm her as she wrapped it around her.

“Okay, Baby Tiger. We won’t be here too long. Someone will come save us,” Isabelle whispered as she curled up under the tarp shivering.

Chapter 28

Isabelle had been gone for two days and Roman was ready to snap. Her entire family were now at Isabelle's house and Aaron had brought Roman there after the first night. He wasn't able to sleep, but he crawled into the bed where they slept and hugged her pillow.

The sun was up and Roman just wanted to go back out and look. Nobody had called to say they had her and he had seen enough crime shows to know that the longer someone was missing, the worse it could be.

Everyone in Hopedale searched the town for two days, but it was as if she'd just disappeared. Roman had gotten apologies from all of Isabelle's family who had thought he was responsible for the fire. He appreciated it, but the only thing he wanted to hear was that they found Isabelle safe and sound.

Keith showed up before six with most of his security staff and the men on his construction crew again. They were going to expand the search to other towns. Kurt and Alice had made a plea on television for Isabelle's safe return, but she was still gone. The number of people who were out looking for her was incredible.

Alice and Kurt were beside themselves with worry and Nanny Betty had turned Isabelle's kitchen into a buffet of food that would feed a small army. Apparently, it was her way of coping with the situation.

Everyone was dealing with Isabelle's disappearance in different ways, but Roman didn't want to be around anyone. He stepped out onto the front deck and hooked the leash on Cobalt shortly after everyone had arrived.

"I'm taking the pup for a walk," Roman told Maximus as he made his way down the front steps.

"Are you sure that's a good idea?" Maximus asked as he sipped a cup of coffee.

"I don't care. I need to get away from all this for a few minutes." Roman didn't wait for a response.

He crossed the road and walked down to the beach. He strolled across the rocky shore as Cobalt kept her nose down, sniffing as if she was on the hunt. Roman was sure the abundance of scents was probably exciting the dog.

Cobalt seemed happy to be running next to the beach and Roman let out enough of the extended leash so the pup could feel like she was free. She ran after a seagull and barked when the bird flew off before she could catch it.

When they were across from the restaurant, Cobalt stopped and turned back to Roman. She bolted toward the building, whining and tugging Roman with her.

"Cobalt, stop it." Roman retracted the leash but it only made the dog more frantic.

Roman crossed the road to see if the dog would calm, but instead, she kept jumping against the entrance of the restaurant. Something in the back of Roman's mind told him Cobalt wanted inside the building, but it wasn't like she knew the place. As far as he knew, the dog had never been to the restaurant.

"Hold on, girl." Roman pulled out his phone and called Kurt.

"Hello," Kurt answered.

"This may sound off the wall, but can you grab the keys to the restaurant and come check it?" Roman said as he tried the front door.

"Why? We had the dogs in there the first day she was gone" Kurt told him.

"Cobalt is going nuts to get inside." Roman replied as he walked around the front of the building and tried to look in the windows.

Paper had been placed against the glass to keep people from looking inside. Cobalt was practically pulling Roman's arm out of its socket to get into the building.

"On the way," Kurt said and the call ended.

Roman stepped back and looked up and down the street. It was only seven in the morning and since it was a Sunday, not many people would be around.

He glanced back toward Isabelle's house and saw Kurt jog down the road with Keith, Aaron, and Nick. Kurt opened the door and before Roman could step back, Cobalt pulled from his hand and ran into the building.

Roman ran after the dog through the open kitchen door and back to Isabelle's office. All the air whooshed out of Roman when he stepped into the room and saw Isabelle on the floor with Cobalt licking her face.

"Isabelle," Roman and Kurt shouted together.

She pushed herself up from the floor. She was weak and as disheveled as she appeared, Roman had never seen anything look so great. He fell to his knees in front of her as Aaron tugged Cobalt away.

"Jesus, Isabelle, where have you been?" Kurt pulled the tarp off her.

"To hell," Isabelle choked.

"Come on, let's get you out of here." Roman took her hand.

"I think my ankle is broken." Isabelle pushed the rest of the tarp off her leg.

Her ankle was swollen to twice its size and badly bruised. She also had a large black and blue mark on her cheek and below her left eye. It infuriated Roman because there was no doubt someone had hit her. Without a second thought, Roman picked her up in his arms and followed Kurt out through the building.

While he hurried outside the restaurant with Isabelle in his arms, he heard Kurt make a call to someone to bring a car right away. Roman could tell by the way her ankle was positioned that it was broken, and he couldn't be sure how long she'd been like that.

"It's okay, Tiger. I got you." Roman kissed her temple as he carefully maneuvered her out the door.

"It hurts so bad." Isabelle sobbed against his chest.

"I know. Just hold on so we can get you to the hospital." Roman choked on the words because it killed him to see her in such agony.

"The baby is still moving." Isabelle sniffed.

Bull screeched to a stop in front of the restaurant and Kurt yanked open the back door. Isabelle's father ran around and hopped into the other side in order to slide Isabelle across the seat without causing her more pain. Roman settled her and lifted her injured leg so that he could rest it on his leg.

"I'm going to hold your leg so it doesn't bump around on the drive to the hospital." Roman held the ankle as steady as possible and it killed him that it caused her pain.

Kurt sat on the other side of the seat and positioned Isabelle so she could lean back against him. Bull drove the vehicle and Alice sat in the front as well. Isabelle winced a few times on the way to the city and cried out once when Bull hit a bump in the road. Roman didn't like the way she shook. He was aware she was probably going into shock.

"Isabelle, stay with us now." Kurt must have seen it too because proceeded to ask her what happened.

She seemed to calm more as she answered her father's questions. Roman listened and cringed when she told him about how her abductor hit her with something to knock her out, and how she woke up in a dirty room in the old club next door.

Kurt immediately called John to get a search warrant for the building, but Roman doubted anyone was still there. Isabelle's father had fury in his expression, so it was probably a good thing that he wasn't anywhere near the club when it was raided.

Roman was glad he wasn't close by either because there would be no way to control his anger at someone who'd hurt Isabelle. When he thought about how scared she must have been, it made him physically ill.

Isabelle's Uncle Sean met them at the hospital. He had been in town and made sure there was an orthopedic specialist as well as an obstetrician ready when they arrived. It was one of the perks of having a family member who had connections with some of the top doctors in the province.

Isabelle was loaded carefully onto a gurney and wheeled into the hospital while she clung to Roman's hand. As they started to bring her into the trauma area, she argued that she wasn't going without Roman, but her father managed to calm her down and let her know that as soon as they were done checking her, he'd make sure Roman was by her side.

Roman didn't like seeing the expression on her face as the doors closed behind her. He leaned against the wall and slid down to the floor as he cupped the back of his head and dropped his head against his knees.

"She's going to be fine." Bull crouched in front of him and dropped his hand on Roman's shoulder.

"I want five minutes with the bastard that did that to her," Roman snarled through his teeth.

"You and me both." Bull nodded.

Two hours and twenty-two minutes passed before Roman was permitted to see her. She was asleep when he walked into the room and he couldn't take his eyes off her as he sat down. She looked so fragile, but he knew she wasn't. Isabelle was tough as nails.

Before he went in to see her, the doctor told them that the baby was fine. There was no serious damage to her cheek or eye, but her ankle was broken. They put her in a cast and she was given something for pain. She'd argued about the medication at first, but the doctor assured her it was safe and wouldn't hurt the baby.

Roman quietly pulled a chair next to the bed and took her hand in his. He shuddered at what she must have gone through. She beat up a man with a stick and knocked the bastard on his ass. Then climbed through a crawl space to make her way out of her situation. Isabelle was amazing.

"She's probably going to sleep for a few hours," Alice whispered from behind him.

"Good, she needs the rest." Roman smiled up at Isabelle's mother.

"Kurt said they're searching the building now." Alice sat on the foot of Isabelle's bed.

Roman didn't say anything, but he sent a prayer up that they would find the fucker who took Isabelle. She'd told her father it was one of the men who impersonated the insurance adjuster. Roman had been in the hospital when she met with them, but her father and Roman's brothers had been with her.

It made him wonder if they'd planned to take her then, but when she didn't come alone, their plan was changed. All he knew was someone had to be watching her in order to know when to grab her. Roman didn't know how everything that happened to him and

Isabelle was connected, but Roman had a feeling someone was out to get him, and Isabelle was just a means to an end.

Chapter 29

Isabelle was never so glad to see her house in her life. She'd been kept in the hospital overnight just to make sure everything with the baby was okay. Luckily, Baby Tiger was strong and healthy and made it through the ordeal better than Isabelle.

The clunky cast was annoying and she was in pain, but she refused to take the medication unless she couldn't handle it anymore. No matter what the doctor said, she wanted to be sure not to subject the baby to a lot of the drug.

When she got home, she learned that the fake Archer was found dead in the building with a bullet to the head. Isabelle tried to feel sorry for the man, but she really didn't. Now the police were trying to find out who hired the kidnapper.

The police worked to find out the man's real name but Isabelle didn't care who he was. Keith had also assigned two of his security men to her house to make sure nobody got near her again. For the first time in her life, Isabelle didn't mind the overprotective men in her family.

She was relieved to find out that all the charges against Roman were dropped and all the men in her family who believed he could be involved in the fire apologized to him. Mostly because Nanny Betty demanded they all give him a personal apology.

Isabelle knew Aaron was only doing his job and although she was pissed at him, at the time, she couldn't blame him for being a good cop. She was also glad that the couples of the family who were at odds had made up and were happy with each other again.

"Hey, Tiger." Roman walked into the bedroom, holding a tray. "Thought you might be hungry."

Roman placed the tray across her lap and eased onto the bed next to her. She looked down at the tray and laughed. There was no way all the food on the tray was just for her. When he pulled out a second fork, she laughed.

"I figured you wouldn't mind sharing." Roman winked and shoved a forkful into his mouth.

"I don't mind sharing at all." Isabelle reached up and cupped his face. "I missed you so much."

"I missed you too. I'm not going anywhere ever again." Roman leaned forward and pressed his lips against hers.

The kiss was slow and tender and Isabelle didn't want it to stop, but Roman pulled back and smiled. He looked into her eyes and at that moment, the baby kicked. Isabelle covered her belly and laughed as a tear slipped from her eye.

“Is Baby Tiger making his presence known?” Roman gently moved the tray and placed his hand around her stomach.

“What makes you think Baby Tiger is a he?” Isabelle laughed.

“Just a hunch, but it doesn’t matter to me one way or the other. This little one is already loved so much.” Roman leaned down and kissed her belly.

Isabelle covered the back of his head as he started to speak to her stomach. As Roman told the baby about their families, Isabelle lay back and closed her eyes. His soft soothing voice not only calmed the baby, but it lulled her into a deep sleep.

Isabelle woke to a commotion outside her bedroom. She looked around, but there was no sign of Roman. She needed to use the bathroom desperately and was relieved to see the crutches propped against the nightstand. Isabelle clumsily got out of the bed and grabbed one of the crutches to help her to her feet.

As she reached for the other one, the door to the bedroom opened and Marcella was immediately at her side. Isabelle rolled her eyes as the woman frantically started shouting to Roman.

“What are you doing?” Roman ran into the room with a paint roller in his hand.

“I need to pee, but I could ask you the same question.” Isabelle nodded toward the paint roller.

"I was getting it for your dad. He's going to do the gender reveal by painting the room." Roman grinned.

"That's not fair, you're not supposed to know either until the reveal." Isabelle slowly made her way toward the bathroom.

"Don't worry, your dad isn't letting him in the room." Marcella laughed. "As a matter of fact, none of us are allowed in there."

Isabelle wasn't surprised that her father would go to such lengths to do the reveal. Apparently, he wouldn't even tell her mother what was in the envelope. He'd made her mother buy two sets of baby things, one for a girl and one for a boy. He said the one that wasn't used, he'd give to one of the other pregnant women in the family.

"He's out of control." Kristy stepped into the room as Isabelle made her way out of the bathroom.

"Who?" Isabelle asked.

"Our father." Kristy blew out a breath as she eased into the chair in the corner of the room.

"How much longer do you have?" Marcella asked as she helped Isabelle back into the bed.

"Less than a week. I'm due April first." Kristy grinned. "April Fool's day. What a day to go into labor."

For the next several days, her father hid in the baby's room and had even gone as far as attaching a lock so that nobody could peek inside. Then the following week, her family filled the house for the baby reveal. Her dad was like a kid in a candy store and Roman wasn't much better. They were running around making sure everything was ready and driving everyone crazy.

"This is why you don't let Dad do this shit," Jess whispered to Isabelle.

"Leave him alone. I think it's sweet that he and Roman are so excited." Pam laughed.

"I just want to know." Isabelle chuckled.

"I just want this baby out." Kristy grumbled as she pointed to her belly.

Kristy was annoyed because it was the day after her due date and her baby was still not out. Isabelle couldn't blame her sister because Kristy looked completely uncomfortable.

An hour later, her father made the announcement that everything was ready for the reveal. Roman and Isabelle were the first two permitted up to see the room and then everyone else could check it out.

"If you don't like it, I can fix it." Her dad looked so nervous.

"Dad, open the door." Isabelle laughed as she lifted her crutch to push the door.

Isabelle gasped as the door opened to reveal the room. It was decorated with balloons and painted a pale blue. The dark oak crib was draped with a blue and white blanket and a large banner hung in the corner with the words, *it's a boy*, written on it.

"Are you ready for an O'Connor boy?" Her father smiled.

"It's a boy?" Roman gasped but it was the expression on his face that had Isabelle confused.

"What's wrong?" Isabelle asked.

"I was right. Mom was right," Roman murmured.

"What?" Isabelle watched as Roman eased into the rocking chair and picked up the pale-blue stuffed bunny.

"I dreamed about Mom when I was in the hospital. She told me she'd keep my son safe until we were ready to hold him in our arms and to give you..." Roman looked up at her and a tear slipped from his eye.

"Sounds like she came to you in your sleep." Her father dropped his hand on Roman's shoulder.

Isabelle made her way to the crib and smoothed her hand across the rail. It was surreal that in less than six months, her and Roman's baby would be in that crib.

"I'll leave you two alone for a bit. When you're ready for everyone to come up, let me know." Her father walked out of the room and closed the door.

A few seconds later, Isabelle heard everyone shout with excitement. It seemed her father wasn't going to make anyone wait to find out the gender of her baby. Isabelle turned to Roman and he smiled at her.

"A boy." He laughed.

"A boy." She giggled.

"Marry me," Roman blurted out.

"What?" Isabelle almost toppled over, but Roman caught her.

"I want to marry you. I want to be your husband. I know this wasn't the most romantic way to ask, but I love you, Isabelle. I can't think of a better time to ask, than right here and right now. You and me together in the room for our son. I love you." Roman reached into his jeans pocket and pulled out a chain.

"I love you too." Isabelle sobbed on the words.

Roman held up the chain, and at the end of the chain was a ring. It was beautiful and it looked old. She watched him as he slipped it off the chain and held it between his fingers.

"This was my mother's engagement ring. She gave my older brothers both my grandmother's rings to propose to their wives. She told me when I was ready that I would get hers. When she died, I put it on a chain and have worn it around my neck since. The only time it was removed was when I ended up in the hospital." Roman slowly dropped down to his knee and took Isabelle's hand.

She'd seen the chain and the ring at the end but she was afraid to ask him about it. Isabelle thought it was for a former girlfriend that he might still harbor feelings for.

"Isabelle, I love you and our baby boy. Would you make me the happiest man on earth and do me the honor of marrying me?" Roman held up the ring.

"Are you sure?" She choked out the words.

"I've never been more sure of anything in my life." He stood up and looked deep into her eyes. "You're my life."

"Yes," Isabelle whispered and wrapped her arms around his neck. "Oh, no. I can't."

Isabelle stepped back and pushed the ring back at him. Roman looked confused and she knew she had to explain. She took his hand and tugged him toward the rocking chair. He sat down and she sat in his lap.

"Roman, it's not that I don't want to marry you. I do, but I know my father. He's old-school and if you propose without asking for his blessing, it'll hurt him." Isabelle cupped his cheek. "But for the record, I will marry you, but until you talk to Dad, I can't take the ring."

"I understand." Roman smiled. "I would never disrespect Kurt like that. The minute I talk to him, you'll know."

Roman cupped the back of her head and she lowered her head to meet his lips. Their kiss was slow and passionate with all their promises sealed.

"Come on, we want to see the room." Shouts of her's and Roman's families echoed from outside the room.

Isabelle pulled away reluctantly and laughed as Roman groaned and rolled his eyes. She could feel his excitement under her and she would have loved nothing more than to drag him to the bedroom and make love to him all night.

For a few hours, they relaxed and enjoyed the togetherness of their families. They laughed, and talked to everyone, and for a few hours, they forgot someone out there wanted to hurt them.

Isabelle lay in the bed after everyone had left for the night. Trunk was posted outside her house and Roman was double-checking the locks and alarm. Isabelle moved her leg and cursed the heavy cast.

"Tiger, are you okay?" Roman walked into the room and closed the door.

"Yeah, I'm just tired of this stupid thing." She lifted her foot.

"In another week, you can get the walking cast on. I think they're fiberglass and it's lighter." Roman yanked his shirt over his head and started to unbutton his jeans.

Isabelle's eyes dropped to his zipper and she watched him as he pulled off the jeans. When she raised her eyes to meet his, he had a sexy grin on his face.

"Is there something you want, Tiger?" He slid into the bed next to her.

Roman pulled her closer and slipped his hand under her t-shirt. His hand gently massaged her lower back as he placed soft kisses across her mouth and down the side of her neck.

Isabelle moaned as he cupped her ass and pulled her against his growing erection. It was awkward with the cast, but she wasn't about to stop. It had been so long since they'd been intimate, she was starting to think they never would be again.

"It seems like forever since I've made love to you," Roman whispered against her cheek.

"I want you so bad." Isabelle moaned when he sucked her earlobe between his lips and gently nipped it.

Isabelle reached under the blankets and cupped his balls through his boxers, making Roman curse and thrust his groin into her hand. Isabelle reached inside his waistband and she didn't have to wonder if he was turned on.

Roman's hard erection throbbed in her hand as she lightly stroked him while she gently squeezed his balls through his boxers. He thrust into her hand over and over as he covered her lips with his and plunged his tongue into her mouth.

He glided his hand under her shirt again and gently cupped her breasts. Isabelle had mentioned that they were a little tender and she could tell he was taking it easy. He gently pinched her nipple as he pulled his mouth from hers and tugged down the neck of her shirt.

"Take it off, Tiger." He growled into her neck.

Isabelle released his cock and quickly made her shirt vanish. Before she had a chance to lay back down, Roman had her nipple in his mouth while he tugged and teased the other. Isabelle leaned back on her hands. Her core throbbed as he sucked and nibbled at her breasts.

"Roman, I need you to touch me." She moaned.

"Lay down, baby," he whispered.

When she was on her back, Roman crawled over her and slowly kissed his way down her body. She giggled as he kissed around her swollen belly and then moved lower. He licked around her aching clitoris as he separated her folds with his fingers.

Isabelle shuddered when he licked from her opening up to her throbbing bud. Over and over, he teased her to the brink of ecstasy. She fisted the back of his head to try to guide him to where she wanted him most, but it was no use. Roman wanted to take his time and drive her insane.

"Roman, please," Isabelle begged.

"Please what, Tiger?" Roman blew against her wet pussy.

"Make me come." She growled.

Roman didn't make her beg anymore. He clamped down on her clit and sucked it hard into his mouth while he plunged his finger inside her.

Isabelle gasped with the sudden movement, but seconds later she was moaning in pleasure as he brought her to the edge and then pulled her over.

"Oh, God." Isabelle moaned as he made her come hard and intensely.

Before she could come down from the fog, Roman was over her and pushing his hard cock inside her. He slammed into her and then held himself there for a few seconds before pulling almost all the way out and slamming in again.

"Fuck, Isabelle. You're so fucking wet." Roman groaned as he thrust into her again and again.

Roman lowered his head and covered her mouth with his. She kissed him back with every ounce of love and passion she felt for the man while he plunged into her. She could feel another orgasm building as he pounded his cock inside her.

"Baby, I'm going to…" Before he finished Roman pushed hard inside her, making her body react to the pressure and she trembled under him.

Roman's body shook as he pulled out a little then pushed in again. He groaned and Isabelle could feel his cock jerk inside her.

"Fuck, I didn't think it was going to stop." Roman chuckled as he dropped his head into the crook of her neck and rolled them over on their sides.

He managed to stay inside of her, but she could feel him soften and knew he'd slip from her body long before she wanted him to.

"I love you," Roman sighed against her lips.

"I love you too," she breathed.

"I'm never going that long without making love again." Roman growled.

"Good." She giggled making him slip from her body.

"That's the part I hate." He moaned.

"What?" Isabelle lifted her head to look at him.

"When I'm not inside you." He wiggled his eyebrows up and down.

She didn't say it but she wouldn't mind having him inside her longer. It wasn't that he didn't satisfy her because he did, several times. Isabelle loved being that close to him.

Now if only they could get back to their normal lives and not worry about some crazy person who seemed set on ruining both of them.

Chapter 30

Roman woke to someone shouting out his name. He glanced over on the other side of the bed, but Isabelle was still sound asleep. He looked to the other side and almost leaped out of the bed.

Maximus was crouched next to him with a smirk on his face. Apparently, he hadn't yelled, he was just really close to Roman's ear. He couldn't understand why his brother would be in his room and it took him a minute to clear the cobwebs from his brain.

"I didn't want to wake Isabelle. You need to come downstairs. Now," Maximus whispered and quickly left the room.

Roman slipped out of the bed and threw on his jeans and shirt from the day before. He quietly closed the bedroom door behind him to make sure he didn't disturb Isabelle. He still wasn't fully awake and practically stumbled down the stairs.

Aaron, Sandy, Kurt, Maximus, and Demetrios were in the kitchen crowded around the table. They stopped their conversation when he walked in and Kurt pointed to the chair across from him. Roman wasn't sure he liked the expressions they had.

“What’s wrong?” Roman asked as he sat in the chair and wrapped his hands around the cup of coffee Demetrios slid in front of him.

“We still haven’t been able to identify the guy who took Isabelle. He’s not in the system and nobody has come forward with a name,” Aaron began.

“That means you don’t have a lead.” Roman sighed.

“Not really. There was another guy with this idiot. He said his name was Terry Howe, but since the other guy’s name was fake, we’re assuming this guy is as well,” Aaron explained.

“Still sounds like a dead end.” Roman shrugged.

“Well, your brother is a smart cookie.” Aaron smirked.

“I am.” Maximus laughed.

“I was talking about the other brother.” Aaron shook his head.

“What did he do?” Roman glanced at his older brother.

“I didn’t get a good feeling from those idiots that day and I managed to snap a picture of them in case we needed it.” Demetrios pulled up something on his phone and slid it across the table.

“Do you know that guy?” Aaron asked and Roman looked at the picture, but he didn’t recognize him.

“I don’t know him.” Roman shook his head.

"That's the guy we found dead in the club. The guy who took Isabelle." Aaron tapped the table next to the phone.

"Look at the next picture and see if you recognize that guy." Demetrios nodded toward the phone.

Roman swiped the screen and another picture of a man popped up. He picked up the phone and stared at the sly-looking man. This guy did look familiar, but Roman was having trouble remembering where he knew the man.

"You recognize him?" Aaron asked.

"I think so, but I can't for the life of me remember where I know him from." Roman enlarged the picture a little to see if he could get a better look.

"Well, thank God you have me around." Sandy smirked as she pulled out a tablet and started to tap on the screen.

"Yes, we're blessed." Aaron rolled his eyes.

"Don't mess with me, whore-boy." Sandy pointed at Aaron.

"Hey, I'm a happily married man now. Stop calling me that," Aaron grumbled.

"You will always be my little whore-boy." Sandy winked.

"Why do we even try with her?" Aaron shook his head.

"Because I'm the genius that you all love." Sandy tapped the screen of her tablet once more then placed it on the table.

“What’s this?” Kurt asked.

“I sent these pictures to that guy we worked with before in British Columbia, Lyon Tu. He sent the pictures to a friend of his. His friend did a facial recognition and found something on this Terry guy,” Sandy explained.

Kurt picked up the tablet and Aaron glanced over his shoulder to see as well. They both read for a few minutes before they looked up and turned the tablet to him.

“This guy’s name is Terry, but his last name is not Howe.” Aaron pointed to the picture.

“His name is Terry Masters,” Kurt said.

Roman stared at the picture and his mouth fell open. On the screen was a picture of Terry with three other people. The first one was the dead guy and the other two were Barry Masters and his wife Crystal.

“Wait, are you telling me all this is happening because of me?” Roman snatched the tablet from Kurt.

“It looks like it.” Sandy was now working on a laptop.

“They were setting me up from the beginning.” Roman stared at the phone.

“You need to arrest them,” Maximus snapped.

“We would, but we can’t find them.” Aaron blew out a breath.

Roman listened while Aaron explained what they'd been doing over the last couple of days. They didn't want to say anything to Roman until they could prove it. They'd contacted Barry's wife and she'd called them back.

"It looks like she left him after he fired you. She's out west, but she said Barry went crazy when she left. He was convinced she was coming to Newfoundland to be with you. Truth was, she ran away with one of the waiters." Aaron snorted.

"She was a piece of work, that's for sure. I'm pretty sure she screwed every male employee in the place and probably some of the female." Roman rolled his eyes.

"So, you think he's here?" Demetrios asked.

"We don't think, we know." Sandy turned her laptop around and showed a still screen shot of inside Isabelle's restaurant before the fire.

"He was in the restaurant," Roman whispered.

"On this video, he's ripping into Cindy." Sandy hit *play* on the security video.

Roman remembered the day that Cindy had come into the kitchen upset because some asshole had upset her. She said the guy was awful and remembering Barry, it was something he would do. He wasn't the nicest person in the world and Roman had seen him rip into a lot of people.

"But Cindy left before we did. Didn't she come back the night she died?" Roman asked.

"Pretty sure he was waiting in the restaurant." Aaron pulled out a rolled-up paper.

"When Isabelle told me she got out through a crawl space in the ceiling, it got me thinking." Kurt unrolled the paper.

It was the blueprint of the club and Isabelle's restaurant. Kurt slid his finger along an opening just below the roof and Roman stood up to get a better look.

"When they divided the building, they didn't go right to the roof. We think someone got into the place through that space," Aaron said.

It started to make sense. How things happened but nobody ever saw it. Things broke for no reason, the rat, Cindy's murder, and the fire. It was just hard to believe that Barry would exert that much energy to do anything himself.

"I think he's the one trying to purchase the building. I also think he tried to make it look like Roman was the one fucking with the restaurant." Kurt sat back in the chair.

Roman dropped his head in his hands and tried to get his head around everything he heard. Barry could have killed Isabelle and the baby. Roman didn't care what happened to him, but the thought of what could have happened, if Isabelle hadn't escaped, made his blood boil.

The fact that Barry would be so vindictive for something Roman didn't do, showed how insane the man really was. If Isabelle hadn't escaped, he probably would have tortured her until he could get his revenge. Roman wanted five minutes alone with the asshole to show him he'd fucked with the wrong people.

"I'll call Bryce." Isabelle's voice startled him and all heads turned to the doorway of the kitchen.

Isabelle stood in the entrance with her crutches tucked under her arms. She had pure fury on her face and determination in her eyes, which immediately concerned Roman. He jumped to his feet as she hobbled toward the chair and supported her while she eased down to the seat.

"No way," Roman finally said.

"If I call Bryce and tell him I want to sell, he'll contact the buyer. It's that simple." Isabelle shrugged.

"How does that help?" Maximus asked.

"I'll tell him I want to meet the buyer before I sign. I'll give him some bullshit about wanting to know who the new owner is." Isabelle seemed to get way too excited about her plan.

"No," Roman and Kurt said together.

"Do you really think you're going to win this argument?" Sandy snorted. "For Christ's Sake, she's an O'Connor, and a pregnant one at that."

Kurt clenched his teeth together and Roman glanced around the table. Aaron seemed resigned to the fact there was no arguing with his cousin. Maximus seemed unsure of the situation and Demetrios looked as excited as Isabelle did.

"I'm so fucking glad that kid is a boy." Kurt stood up and started to pace the floor. "There's enough stubborn-ass women in this family now."

"I love you too, Dad." Isabelle giggled and turned to Sandy.

"Because the men in this family are so easy-going." Sandy didn't even try to hide her sarcasm.

"So how do we do this?" Isabelle pushed.

"Here's what we do." Sandy leaned in close to Isabelle.

That was that. The decision was made but there was no way in hell Roman would let her meet Barry alone. The man was obviously out of his mind. There were plenty of places he could keep out of sight in the place and be there if Isabelle got into trouble.

"Can we include everyone in this little plan of yours, Sandy?" Kurt grumbled.

The group was quiet as Sandy, Kurt, and Isabelle laid out the plan. It wasn't going to be just her in the building, and for a few minutes, there was resistance to Roman being present. Kurt backed him up and agreed the more people who were there, the better chances they had to keep Isabelle safe.

The evening closed in quickly and Roman had to make his way to Isabelle's parents' house. She wanted to spend some time with her sisters and Pam, which worked out well for him. Isabelle refused to let Roman go alone and enlisted Bull as his bodyguard.

"You're a smart guy, you know that?" Bull asked as they strolled up the street.

"Why would you think that?" Roman snorted.

"You were smart enough to know it's pointless to argue with Isabelle. Those women are all as stubborn as their grandmother. You see my bald head? I had a ton of hair when I met this family." Bull chuckled.

"Seriously?" Roman stared at Bull's shiny head.

"No, just kidding, but I'm sure if I let it grow out, it would be grey." Bull laughed.

"Can't control Kristy either, huh?" Roman nudged Bull with his elbow.

"There are some times she likes to be controlled." Bull smirked.

Roman burst out laughing as they arrived at Isabelle's parents' house to see Kurt sat on the front step. Bull looked almost ready to run as he locked eyes with his father-in-law.

"I hope he didn't hear that." Roman laughed.

"He hasn't pulled out a gun, so I'm guessing not." Bull chuckled.

"What are you two doing here?" Kurt asked as he put a glass to his lips.

"I'm here to steal some blueberry pie." Bull ran up the steps.

"Get the fuck away from my pie, asshole." Kurt slapped the back of Bull's leg.

"Too late, your wife already promised me some." With that, Bull walked inside and closed the door.

"I'm sure she has some for you too." Kurt glanced at Roman then scanned up and down the road.

"I'm actually here to talk to you." Roman sat next to Kurt on the step and took in the full trees on the other side of the street.

"I knew this was coming sooner rather than later," Kurt grumbled and tossed back the rest of his drink.

"I love her, Kurt." Roman wouldn't ever beat around the bush when it came to Isabelle.

"I know that." Kurt didn't look at him.

"She's the best thing that ever happened to me." Roman went on as he pulled the chain out of his pocket.

Kurt turned and tilted his head when Roman held up the chain with his mother's ring at the bottom of it. Kurt raised his gaze and looked directly into Roman's eyes.

“I’m already married.” Kurt smirked.

“I’m not. I’d like to ask your daughter and give her my mother’s engagement ring. That’s if I have your blessing.” Roman held the ring in his fist.

“Why should I give you my blessing?” Kurt opened Roman’s hand and picked up the ring.

While Kurt scrutinized small gold band, Roman tried to put together the words that would explain how he felt about Isabelle. He could say he loved her, but somehow, that just didn’t seem like enough to explain how much Isabelle meant to him.

Roman knew what would happen, but he hoped there would be some hint to tell him that Kurt would be happy about Isabelle becoming Roman’s wife. Still, he swallowed hard as Kurt lifted his head.

“I love Isabelle, but even saying that out loud, it doesn’t seem like a strong enough word to tell you how much she means to me. She’s my reason for waking in the morning and…” Roman was interrupted when Kurt held up his hand to answer his ringing phone.

Roman waited nervously for Kurt to finish on his phon and swallowed hard when Isabelle’s father ended the call. Kurt stood up slowly and narrowed his blue eyes. Roman was startled and jumped off the step because Kurt looked about ready to kill him.

"Do you honestly think I'd give you my blessing to marry my daughter after what you did? You, sneaky little bastard," Kurt roared at the top of his lungs.

"Kurt, I didn't do anything. What are you talking about?" Roman replied.

"Because of you, my daughter almost died and there might not be enough evidence to throw you in jail yet, but I'll never allow you to marry my daughter. You better find a good lawyer because I won't rest until I see you behind bars." Kurt slapped the chain in Roman's chest. "Stay away from her or I'll put you in a world of hurt."

"Kurt, what's going on?" Alice yanked open the door and stepped out looking completely confused.

"I'm throwing out the trash." Kurt growled.

"I don't understand, Kurt. Why are you so mad with him?" Alice held on to Kurt's arm and Roman was glad because he looked like the man was ready to leap off the steps.

"Don't worry, babe. It's going to be fine." Kurt turned back to Roman. "Get the hell away from my house."

Roman backed away from Kurt's house, but he wanted to keep his eye on anyone that might follow him. Roman hurried back to Isabelle's place with the chain and the ring still tightly held in his hand. The closer he got to her house, the faster he moved.

He was almost at the top of the steps when her front door opened. Isabelle stood in her doorway, tears rolling down her cheeks and her hands fisted at her sides. Her sisters stood behind her and when he tried to step closer, Isabelle held up her hand.

"No, don't you dare come inside here. I never want to see you again. How could you do this to me? I loved you and you betrayed me. You've ruined everything," Isabelle shouted and Roman could see her hands tremble as she gripped onto the door knob. "Don't ever come back here again."

The door slammed before he had a chance to respond and he turned to face the ocean. The ocean wasn't the only thing about to get rough.

Chapter 31

Isabelle stood inside her restaurant with Jess the only one visible. She'd received a phone call that morning and held Bryce off until closer to the lunch hour. It gave everyone time to get settled in their hidden areas.

Once this was all over, she could get her life back together. She wasn't letting anyone destroy what she loved. Her stomach was in knots, but she wouldn't let anyone know. If they did, Aaron or her father would call the whole thing off.

The man she was about to meet with tried to destroy what was important to her. Isabelle was about to get payback for everything he'd put her through. For the hundredth time she asked Jess the time, but before her sister could respond, Bryce stepped into the building with an elegantly dressed man.

Isabelle recognized him from the picture Aaron had shown her and she reached for Jess' hand for support. She refused to stand with the crutches, which was why she stood next to the bar.

"Hello, Isabelle." Bryce's smile was wide and completely fake.

"Bryce, this is my sister, Jess." Isabelle glanced at Barry.

"It's nice to meet you, Jess." Bryce nodded.

Jess simply smiled as she squeezed Isabelle's hand. Her sister didn't like any of the Landell family any more than Isabelle did. Jess considered them a bunch of snobs who thought the world owed them a favor.

"Isabelle, this is Mr. Masters. He's the one purchasing this building." Bryce waved his hand around above his head.

Isabelle clenched her teeth together to prevent from saying something that would end the plan before it got started. Barry didn't acknowledge her at first as he glanced around the room.

Barry was tall with thinning black hair. He wasn't thin, looked in decent shape under his suit. His eyes were narrow and looked too close together, but it was his smile that gave Isabelle the creeps. It appeared sinister, but she wasn't sure if she just saw that because of what he'd done, or he really did look like an evil man.

"It's nice to meet you, Mr. Masters." Isabelle knew her tone wasn't as friendly as she wanted, but in her mood, it was the best she could do.

"You can call me Barry," he said as if he were talking to a dog.

"Okay, Barry." Isabelle smiled.

"What happened to your leg?" Barry asked, but she didn't miss the smirk he tried to hide.

"My ex had me abducted so he could go behind my back and purchase the building next door. I escaped and ended up breaking my ankle." Isabelle sniffed and dropped her head.

It was heart-breaking to think about Roman doing something so horrible. The thought made her tears real and she wiped her finger under her eyes to wipe them away.

"What a horrible man. Has he been arrested?" Barry asked.

"No, there isn't enough evidence because the man he paid was killed. Anyway, I'd rather not talk about this. It's too upsetting for me." Isabelle turned around and Jess handed her a tissue.

"Look, my sister wants to unload this building. There are too many painful memories here for her now," Jess interjected.

"I can imagine, but it's not what I expected. I mean, it looks completely gutted." Barry walked around the dining room with his arms behind his back.

Isabelle held her breath as he got way too close to where Nick crouched behind some boards propped against the wall. He turned back and made his way toward the kitchen. It didn't make her feel less uneasy because there were officers hidden there as well.

Bryce watched him as he tapped his fingers against his legs. It was the first time since she'd known him that the man looked nervous. It put Isabelle on edge. If Bryce didn't seem comfortable with Barry, it was obvious he didn't trust the man either.

"So, has your boyfriend hung around?" Barry said, but he didn't turn around.

"I don't know, and I really don't care." Isabelle swallowed the lump in her throat.

"So, you're telling me if he knew you were in danger, he wouldn't come save you." Barry still had his back to her.

"He was the reason I was in danger in the first place. Since he's out of my life, I don't have to worry about that," Isabelle insisted.

"That's where you'd be wrong, my dear." Barry turned around with a gun pointed directly at her.

"Barry, what the hell…" Before Bryce could finish the statement, Barry turned the weapon and pulled the trigger.

Bryce gasped for air as he held his hand to his chest. The front of his shirt started to soak with blood and Bryce dropped to his knees. Jess pushed Isabelle behind her and started to reach for the weapon that she'd hidden behind the bar.

"I wouldn't do that, sweetheart. I would suggest all of the people hidden around here come out or I'll put a bullet in one of these pretty ladies." Barry slowly walked toward Isabelle and Jess.

"Why did you shoot him?" Isabelle crouched next to Bryce, but it was too late, he was dead.

"He was only a pawn in my plan for revenge against the man who destroyed my marriage. Where is he?" Barry lifted the gun so that it was pointed directly at Isabelle.

"I'm here, Barry." Roman stepped out from behind one of the coolers where he'd been hidden.

"Roman, I didn't think you'd have the guts to show your face once your lady here knew the truth." Barry stepped closer to Isabelle.

"She has nothing to do with what happened and she knows the truth. She knows that I'd never hurt her. It's me you have issues with, Barry." Roman took a step toward Barry, and Isabelle swallowed hard.

"Issues? You stole my wife and broke up my marriage," Barry shouted.

"I didn't do that. Your wife was fooling around long before I started to work for you," Roman replied.

Barry stalked toward Roman, the gun down by his side. Isabelle felt an arm grab her around the waist and she was pulled back behind a divider. She looked up to see Trunk glaring out into the main dining room as if he was ready to pounce on Barry the minute the guy made a wrong move.

Isabelle could still hear them and she could peek around the corner to see part of the area. She held on to Trunk as she listened to the intense conversation.

"Dear God, keep him safe," Isabelle whispered.

"My wife never thought about another man until you made a move on her. I'm just glad I was able to put in motion the destruction of your life," Barry screamed. "You'll never be happy thanks to the things I've done."

Her father had been right, the minute Barry saw Roman, he started to fall apart. If it was one thing her family learned over the last few years, it was how unstable someone could be when they were obsessed with something.

"What are you going to do, Barry? Follow me around for the rest of your life and screw up everything good that happens to me?" Roman was pushing him and Isabelle knew it.

"Don't be silly. I'm going to take away everyone you love. Starting with this pretty woman." Barry kept his gun trained on Roman as he pulled open the door and motioned to someone in the car.

Isabelle tried to look around the corner to see who was coming in through the door, but Trunk kept her back too far. Isabelle held her breath as she waited to see who the woman was that Roman loved.

He'd told her once that he'd never been in love before and even Marcella had said it. Isabelle could only think of one other woman that Barry could hurt and Isabelle froze.

Chapter 32

Roman stood stock still as two men dragged his sister into the building. She looked terrified and he didn't like the way her shirt had been torn open. Roman saw Maximus and Demetrios stiffen where they stood in the kitchen doorway and he knew that things were about to get bad. When Marcella met Roman's eyes, he realized she wasn't afraid, she was pissed.

"She's a pretty little thing. It's too bad I can't have some fun with her before you watch her die." Barry ran his gun down the side of Marcella's cheek and down between her breasts.

"You wouldn't be able to get it up, you dickless piece of shit," Marcella screamed at Barry.

He didn't seem pissed at her reaction. He actually seemed amused because he laughed when she spit at him. Roman knew his sister wasn't about to break down in tears because of this asshole. The problem was he could see Barry was on the edge.

Roman took a step toward Barry but stopped when the asshole pressed the barrell of the gun hard against Marcella's temple.

After everything that he'd been through, there was no way he would let the bastard hurt anyone else.

"Let her go, Barry. You've got a problem with me, why don't you put down the gun and come work this out like men. Let's put an end to this by seeing who's still standing at the end. You're a man, aren't you?" Roman shrugged out of his jacket and dropped it to the floor.

"I'm more of a man than you are," Barry snarled.

"Then prove it. Put down the gun and come at me." Roman didn't think Barry would take the bait, but it was the only way to distract the man from Marcella.

Several minutes passed while Barry glanced from Marcella to Roman. The two men holding her appeared confused, but as far as Roman could see, they weren't holding weapons. It meant if he could get Barry to drop the gun, then Aaron and Nick could make their move without anyone else getting hurt.

"You want to take me on in a fist fight? How trailer park is that?" Barry laughed, but he did lower the gun.

"Are you man enough to take me on? Or is that the reason Crystal needed to fuck other men?" Roman pulled off his shirt and stood there in just jeans and sneakers.

Barry's face turned scarlet red and he stalked toward the bar. For a moment he glared at Roman then slowly lowered his gun and placed it on top of the counter. He ripped off his jacket and carefully placed it on top of the gun.

“You know, I was provincial boxing champion in Ontario two years in a row during high school.” Barry loosened his tie, and in his obsessive-compulsive manner, folded it.

“When was that, fifty years ago?” Roman chided.

“You’re not that much younger than me, Roman. I’ll prove to you who’s the bigger man.” Barry placed his folded shirt on top of his jacket and motioned for the two men to move Marcella to the other side of the room.

“Let’s go, old man. Crystal told me you couldn’t get it up without that little pill,” Roman hoped he could get one good punch in before Barry got taken down.

“I’ll gut you just like I gutted that stupid waitress.” Barry growled and lunged toward Roman.

That was what they needed. They wanted Barry to confess to every crime he’d committed since he arrived in Hopedale. It was why Roman didn’t give the signal to Aaron.

They’d agreed that when everyone was safe, Roman would kiss his ring and Barry would be taken down. With Barry’s confession of Cindy’s murder, Roman wanted to get the asshole to confess to more of his crimes

Roman turned away from Barry’s first attempt at a punch and slammed his fist into Barry’s soft belly. The man buckled over and

Roman glanced toward Aaron. When Isabelle's cousin gave Roman a nod, he knew he had the okay to continue.

"You're no man, Barry. You're a fucking cowardly piece of shit. You stabbed a young defenceless girl, for what?" With those words, Roman slammed his fist into the side of Barry's head and the man fell to his knees.

"She was going to call the police and I had to stop her, and I'm man enough to frame you for all of it. The broken equipment, the fire, the tank exploding. Your little girlfriend escaped before I could get a chance to fuck her and I would have fucked her good. Imagine the last guy she would have seen before she died was me and not you." Barry spit out blood and got back to his feet. "If I go to jail, you bastard, I won't be going alone."

Rage took over and Roman slammed his fist into Barry's face. Blood sprayed out of Barry's nose as his head snapped back from the impact. Roman didn't give the man a chance to come back from it and punched his other fist into Barry's stomach.

"You're finished, you sadistic bastard." Roman roared as he continued to punch Barry.

"I'll see you dead first." Barry screamed as he fell to his knees.

Before Barry could get up, Aaron had him on the floor with his hands in cuffs. Nick wrapped his arms around Roman's chest and pulled him away from Barry. The two men holding Marcella were also on the ground being cuffed, and Jess was removing the zip ties from Marcella's hands.

"Roman," Isabelle yelled and before he had a chance to say anything she threw herself into his arms.

Nick released him and he pulled Isabelle into his arms as he buried his face into her neck. She was safe and Barry couldn't hurt her, or anyone else ever again.

"I'm okay, Tiger." He held her tightly against him.

"It's over." She sobbed into his neck.

"Yeah, Tiger. It's over." Roman glanced over her shoulder to see Kurt stood on the other side of the room.

Kurt smiled and nodded at him. Roman knew what it meant. Kurt hadn't been able to tell him the previous evening because they needed to make the fight look real in case someone was watching them. The nod told Roman that Kurt gave his blessing and Roman wasn't waiting another second.

Roman pushed Isabelle back and reached into his pocket. The confusion on her face made him smile, but there in front of the police arresting Barry and his goons, two of her cousins, her father, his brothers and both their sisters, Roman dropped down on one knee.

"I'm not waiting anymore. Isabelle. Right here, right now. I'm asking you the one thing that will make me the happiest man in the world. Isabelle, will you marry me?" Roman held up the ring again.

Isabelle glanced over her shoulder to where her father stood, and Kurt nodded. She turned back to Roman and dropped down to the floor with him as tears streamed down her cheeks.

She wasn't the only one with tears. Roman had waited so long for this day that the relief of finally making her his, and knowing that she was no longer in danger opened the flood gates.

"Yes, I'll marry you. I love you." Isabelle held out her hand and Roman finally slipped his mother's ring onto her finger.

Chapter 33

Isabelle stood in front of the altar and watched her sister walk up the center of the church with their father grinning ear to ear. Jess wanted to wait until all the women had their babies, but Isabelle said she didn't mind being pregnant when Jess got married.

It was late July, and she was the only one still pregnant. Isabelle and Roman decided to wait until after the baby was born before they said their I do's. He stood next to his brothers and sister in the pew behind her cousins and winked when their eyes met.

Jess looked beautiful in her strapless fitted dress. She glowed as she stepped next to Wade at the altar and he looked at her as if she was the only woman in the world.

While they exchanged vows, Isabelle glanced around the church at her huge wonderful family. Not only the ones she was related to by blood, but also the ones who had become like family. With each marriage, their family got bigger and bigger.

Roman's brothers had come back with their wives and kids for the re-opening of her restaurant and the grand-opening of the dance club Roman and Ethan had taken over next to her building.

Marcella had also moved back to Newfoundland to help run the club so Roman could continue to be a chef at *A Taste of Hopedale*. They worked side by side in the kitchen and she loved it.

Like her mother's place, they decided to set it up so that the patrons could leave the restaurant and go to the club to party. It was doing well for the first two weeks open and Isabelle couldn't be prouder. They decided to keep the previous name and called the club *The Rock*. It was a tribute to Newfoundland and the music.

After the ceremony, Isabelle found Roman next to Stephanie and Kristy, mooning over their babies. Kristy's little girl was born a week past her due date and was adorable with her full head of dark hair. Everyone joked that she had more hair than her father, but Bull was smitten with his little doll.

Kristy named the baby, Peyton Elizabeth, in honor Nanny Betty and Bull's late niece. At a little over three months old, she had her mother and father wrapped around her little finger. As well as the rest of the family.

Billie and Mike had a baby girl four days later and called her Aria Mariah. She had Billie's dark hair and olive skin and Isabelle was pretty sure the little girl could hypnotize someone with her large dark eyes.

Stephanie's little girl was almost two months old and was as pretty as her mother. They named her Alexis Maria and she was the first of two O'Connor babies born on that first day of May. Lora went into labor the same evening, and she gave birth to a little boy that she and Nick named, Samuel Sean, after both Nick and Lora's fathers.

Emily's little girl was born on her due date and had the sweetest tuft of red hair. Her name was a bit of an argument between Keith and Emily, but they finally settled on Scarlett Rose.

The last of the O'Connor babies born was Aaron and Bethany's little boy. Everyone was kind of hoping that Aaron would have a girl, but Bethany gave birth to a bouncing baby boy at the end of May, and they called him Jacob Lewis. Jacob was Aaron's middle name and Lewis was Bethany's dad.

Roman was mesmerized by the babies and he didn't hesitate to help out at the family suppers when the mothers needed an extra hand. It made Isabelle long to see him with their own baby boy.

"I swear these babies are like magnets to you." Isabelle chuckled as she sat down next to Stephanie.

"Got to get all the practice I can before Baby Tiger comes." Roman wrapped his arm around her shoulder and kissed her cheek.

"You know we could just drop all the kids off to you for a couple of hours." Kristy teased.

"It probably wouldn't bother him." Isabelle laughed.

They'd come so far in the last few months. She didn't know if she'd ever get over the shock of seeing Bryce killed in front of her or finding Cindy's dead body, but with the help of Roman and a therapist, she could sleep most nights.

The nights she did wake up with nightmares, Roman was always there to hold her until the bad memories disappeared. Then there was Cobalt. She was like this warm comforting blanket that would hop up on the bed and lay across Isabelle's legs until she calmed.

Her father told Isabelle that Cobalt was a natural service dog and Isabelle could see that, but to her and Roman she was their big loving Husky that wanted to protect them.

"Would you like to dance, Tiger?" Roman whispered into her ear as a slow song began.

They walked to the dancefloor and he pulled her into his arms. Well, as much as he could with her six-month pregnant belly. She rested her head against his chest, and they swayed slowly to the music.

Isabelle couldn't be happier if she tried. Her life had changed so much in a year and it got better each day. She never thought she'd ever find a love like she had with Roman.

"I love you," Roman whispered into her ear.

"I love you too." She tipped her head back and looked up into his eyes.

"This will be us next year. Are you sure you still want to do it?" Roman smiled.

"There's nothing I want more," Isabelle replied, and Roman kissed her as if they were the only ones in the room.

Epilogue

Pam smiled as she danced with her date. It wasn't a real smile because the guy was annoying and the only reason she asked him was to get her mother to stop trying to get her to call Damon.

He'd left town over a year earlier and hadn't looked back, but who could blame him? She didn't exactly make him feel welcome, but it was the hardest thing she ever did. She had to keep her life in Hopedale and the life she had in Ontario separate.

Her family didn't know where she'd worked while she lived in the big city. It wasn't terrible and she'd met Damon. It had been the best time of her life when they were together, but she knew it wouldn't last.

Damon was a loner who had been glad she didn't have a family. Of course, he didn't know her real name at the time. Damon never found out the truth until he showed up in Newfoundland to help with the rescue of a couple of teenagers.

Imagine his surprise when he found out that Trixie Knight was really Pam Nightingale, and she had the biggest, best family in the world. Damon just didn't like nosey, in-your-face families. Those were his words, not hers.

He'd told her the best thing about being with her was that he didn't have to worry about a stupid controlling family. That was the night she'd left his bed while he slept and never contacted him again.

Of course, her mother, Cora the Cupid, fell in love with Damon the second she met him. Her mom also told Pam that Damon was her one and only, and she needed to realize it before he lost patience and found someone that would make him miserable.

The fact that her mother was never wrong didn't help the situation, but how was she supposed to start a relationship or, in their case, restart a relationship that started with lies. She couldn't. Besides, it didn't matter since he wouldn't be returning to Newfoundland.

Pam thanked her date and excused herself. She needed to get some fresh air and get far away from the wedding. She loved her cousins and was so happy they were all finding love. Pam just needed to get back to her shop and put together the order that had been placed that morning.

"Hey, I need to run to the shop and box up an order. It should only take me an hour or so." Pam told her mom.

"Can't you do it tomorrow?" Her mother complained.

"Sorry, Mom. It's a last-minute order and the guy is picking it up in the morning." Pam kissed her mother's cheek and hurried out of the hall to her car.

She felt like a coward leaving her date at the wedding with her family, but she didn't care. Pam needed to get away.

****

Damon Blackwood sat at the bar in the same exotic bar where he met the one and only woman to ever steal his heart. Of course, at the time, he didn't realize that Trixie Knight wasn't a real person. She was a fake.

Pam was so ashamed of her life in Toronto that she hid it from her family, and that life included him. When he arrived in Newfoundland a few years earlier, he was shocked to find out that his Trixie was actually Pam Nightingale from Hopedale.

A sweet woman from an amazing family who treated him better than his own. The only thing he was to his family was a disappointment because he'd taken a different path and decided to fight for his country.

His family didn't know what he'd done in the army. They didn't know how many lives he saved, or how many he took to save others. No, to his family, he'd taken the wrong route in life and was a failure.

"You want another, handsome?" The pretty barmaid with the huge tits asked as she leaned over the bar.

"Yep." Damon could have her on her back and slamming into her in less time than it would take him to pull the trigger of a sniper rifle.

He just wasn't interested. Whenever he thought about taking another woman home, he felt guilty. Like he was being unfaithful to his heart. It was stupid, but it was a feeling he couldn't shake. It was why he spent his evenings drinking himself into a stupor and heading home to pass out in his huge empty apartment.

"I'm off at two, if you're interested." The barmaid slid the drink in front of Damon and ran her long fingernail down his bicep.

"Thanks, maybe another night. Long day." Damon smiled and slammed back the drink.

He tossed a couple of twenties on the bar and headed out into the night air. He lived about a block from the club and he made his way there while he fumbled in his jeans' pocket for his keys.

Damon was almost at his building and thankful because the humid July night in Toronto was stifling. As he unlocked the main door in the building, his phone buzzed in his pocket.

He thought about ignoring it, but the only people who called him were his boss, or his friends Adrian and Elijah. If they were calling him at midnight, then there was a problem. Damon glanced at the screen to see a blocked number. It had to be his boss.

“Hello.” Damon put the phone to his ear as he stepped on the elevator.

“Damon, it’s Keith O’Connor.” The deep gruff voice rumbled in his ear.

“Hey, Keith.” Damon stepped off the elevator and headed down the hall toward his condo.

“Pam’s missing,” Keith choked out.

“I’ll be on the next plane.”

About the Author

What does someone say to describe themselves? You could start with giving what others say about you. Scratch that. It doesn't really matter what others think about you. It matters what you think of yourself. So here we go.

First of all, I'm a wife and mother. I'm also a grandmother. That alone would fulfill any woman's life and to be honest it does. But.....

I'm also a writer. Someone who loves to tell stories of love, suspense, heartache and of course happily ever after. For most of my life, I've written those stories for myself. A type of therapy, I suppose. I love the characters I create. They become part of who I am because there's part of me in them.

So.... Now that you know this about me. I hope when you read my books, you fall in love with them.

You should also know that I'm a Newfoundlander. What is that you ask? Well we're a proud people who live on an island, off the east coast of Canada. Some people believe Canada ends with Nova Scotia. It doesn't. If you keep going east, there is a beautiful island full of amazing people and magnificent scenery. That is where my stories are set because let’s face it. The best stories always come from the places you know and love.

If there is anything else you would like to know about me. Ask me!

Coming in October

O'CONNOR GIRLS

Book 4 - Hidden Target

O'Connor Brothers Series

Read about the sexy O'Connor Brothers

In Books 1, 2, 3, 4, 5 & 6

Available on

Amazon and

Kindle Unlimited.

Also Available

Dangerous Therapy

Book 1

Officer John O'Connor is giving up on life after a terrible accident. His family are at their wit's end when he refuses any kind of therapy. The only thing keeping him sane is his dreams of a beautiful woman he pulled in for a traffic violation months before.

Physical Therapist Stephanie Kelly is healing from a broken heart. When she is hired by Nightingale's personal care and physical therapy, she's ecstatic, but she's shocked when her boss asks her to take on a new patient. Shocked because the patient is her boss's nephew and he's not exactly keen on therapy. He's also the cop who's been heating up her dreams.

As Stephanie helps John get back on his feet, they grow closer, but someone is out to hurt Stephanie, or worse. After multiple attempts on her life, John's family tries to figure out who's after the woman he loves and stop them before it's too late.

Dangerous Abduction

Book 2

Widower James O'Connor has been fighting his growing attraction to his brother's sister-in-law for four long years, but when someone breaks into her home, destroying everything she owns, James takes her and her young son into his home. The break-in wasn't random. Marina and her son are in danger, and James swears to protect them, but can he keep them safe?

Marina Kelly dedicates her life to caring for her sweet little boy, Danny. Since she broke free from her abusive husband, she's sworn off men, but when James O'Connor keeps entering her thoughts and her dreams, it takes everything she has to keep her feelings hidden. Now, her sister and parents are out of the province, and she's in danger, Marina has no choice but to accept James's help and try to hide her attraction and growing feelings.

The attraction between them impossible to resist. Only her ex's family secret may tear it all apart. Can Marina and James unravel the family's hidden mystery without losing each other?

Dangerous Secrets

Book 3

Ian O'Connor has everything going for him. He's got the O'Connor drop-dead good looks, an incredible body and to top it off he's a doctor. Why wouldn't anyone want the man but none of that was the reason Sandy Churchill was head over heels in love with the man. After he had stood her up for their first official date, she was wary of taking another chance. When she ends up in the hospital because she turned her back on a criminal determined to get away from her, Ian admits that he loves her and wants another chance. A secret from his past throws Sandy into a tailspin, but she has a secret that she's hiding from everyone.

Ian's on cloud nine when he finally takes a leap of faith and tells the woman he's loved for four years how he feels and wants a chance to make up for his screw up. They have two weeks of bliss, but a murder and secrets come back to haunt him. Sandy's reaction tells him there's another reason why she's avoiding him. She's hiding something, but he has no idea what and to make matters worse there's danger coming from her past that could hurt the people he loves the most.

Dangerous Beauty

Book 4

When you come from a privileged family, you're expected to follow a particular path in life. Unless you're Emily Bradshaw. Defying her father, Emily turned down a full scholarship to Dalhousie University. Instead, she followed her dream and opened her own salon in the small town of Hopedale with her friend. She's happy. Then her mother vanishes. Her father receives threatening messages and hires Newfoundland Security Services to protect his children. Emily doesn't like the idea, especially when the man that walks into her salon dressed in a black leather jacket makes her weak in the knees. Emily knows she's in danger but not the kind her father is worried about.

Keith O'Connor isn't expecting his newest security job to be anything out of the ordinary. Then he walks into Snippy Gals, a beauty salon in Hopedale. Keith gets the shock of his life when an auburn-haired beauty turns to face him. Emily is defiant, sassy, and her sexy curves have him in a complete spin. Fighting his feelings for her becomes almost impossible, but when Emily's mother is found, a family secret is revealed turning Emily's life upside down. Can Keith help her cope and keep her out of the clutches of a vengeful stranger?

Dangerous Silence

Book 5

Mike O'Connor's reputation earned him the name Mr. Homerun, but after two hours with Billie, he's ready to change all that. There's one problem. She disappears before he can find out her last name.

Billie Carter had little choice but to leave when she received a desperate text from her friend. Peggy and her daughter have no family, both are deaf, and Billie wants to protect them from an abusive man.

When Peggy is brutally murdered, Billie is determined to protect Chloe. Like a dream come true, Mike walks through her door to help. They soon learn that the little girl is not the only one in danger, and it may take more than Mike to keep them safe.

Dangerous Delusion

Book 6

Lora Norris quit a great job and moved to Hopedale to escape an unknown stalker. Little did she know that finding employment at Jack's Place would lead her to some of the best friends she would ever have. Of course, there is also one man she wanted to be a lot more than a friend, but can't take a chance and put him in danger.

Nick O'Connor never thought the pretty waitress working at his Aunt's diner would give him a second glance. Especially with his playboy reputation. She's friendly toward him but doesn't seem the least bit interested.

When women show up dead and bearing a striking resemblance to Lora, Nick and his family do everything to protect her and her little girl. As they admit their feelings for each other, the danger moves closer than they even realize.

Dangerous Witness

Book 7

Aaron (A.J.) O'Connor is the youngest of seven brothers. His reputation for being a love 'em and leave 'em kind of guy is only a mask to cover the heartbreak he suffered at the hands of his high school sweetheart at the tender age of eighteen. Thirteen years later, she's still the one he dreams of.

Bethany Donnelly left Hopedale on the last day of high school and hasn't looked back since. Finding out the love of her life played her for a fool and only used her to win a bet broke her heart. Now her boss wants her to return to Newfoundland to investigate an employee he suspected of illegal activity. That means facing the one man who can destroy her. The one she's never been able to forget.

Now Bethany's back, and Aaron's determined to find out why she left. First, he's got to keep her safe from a killer intent on taking her away from him forever.

O'Connor Girls

Book 1

Available on

Amazon and

Kindle Unlimited

Hidden Betrayal

Book 1

Kristy O'Connor never hid the fact that she wanted Dean 'Bull' Nash. He's kept her at arm's length since they met but he's pushed her away for the last time.

Dean loves Kristy more than he could ever tell her. He wants her desperately, but his family secrets could destroy them both.

When he can't stay away from her any longer, murder and a shocking betrayal shake them to their core. Can their new relationship survive?

Hidden Enemy

Book 2

Jess O'Connor has watched her seven cousins and younger sister find love and start families. She's happy for them, but she's ready to find her own happily ever after. She sees that with the sexy mechanic that makes her heart thump and her body ache.

Wade Rivers not only owns one of the best repair shops in the city but he's also a single father. When he decides to expand his business, someone doesn't want him to succeed. Even with concerns someone is out to hurt him, he loses his heart to the first woman to turn his head in years. Jess makes him feel whole again.

Will strange incidents at the garage bring them closer together or will things blow up around them??

Rhonda Brewer

Keep up to date on all things new.

Follow me on

Facebook

Twitter

Instagram

Sign up for my newsletter and never miss another release!

http://www.rhondabrewerauthor.com/talk-to-me

www.ingramcontent.com/pod-product-compliance
Lightning Source LLC
Chambersburg PA
CBHW060149260626
47160CB00001B/195
* 9 7 8 1 7 7 5 2 6 8 3 9 0 *